Joan

Joan

A novel of Joan of Arc

Cover design by Peter O'Conner

www.BespokeBookCovers.com

Title graphic based on Joan's actual signature

First Edition: July, 2014

ISBN-13: 978-1497435933

ISBN-10: 1497435935

Also by Freeman Ng

Who Am I? - a personalizable picture book

The Wineskin Project - gospel plays for church use

Haiku Diem - a daily haiku feed begun in July, 2010

Three Daughters Press

www.AuthorFreeman.com

To Fran

first and best of the Voices
that called me to this path

To...

- Watch a video of the songs that appear in the story
- Hear the exact pronunciations of the French names and phrases used in the story
- Download a study guide suitable for use by reading groups and classes
- Download a summary of historical alterations made by this novelization of Joan's story

Go to...

www.JoanNovel.com

The Butterflies of Domrémy

The girl dances in the meadow, her only companion a breeze that wafts her this way and that. She lifts her face to the sky and stretches her arms wide. One step and a turn, two steps and a turn. Her feet swish through the tall grass of the field flecked with color from the ragged wildflowers that thrive in its dense mane. As she dances, she sings a song whose cadences match the stately sweep of her dance:

Orléans, Beaugency,
Notre Dame de Cléry,
Vendôme, Vendôme!

Butterflies gather around her, fluttering just outside the sweep of her arms or tumbling crazily inward to cling to her swaying shoulders.

At intervals, she breaks off her singing and whirling to gaze at some far sight, or to pick up a fallen leaf or living beetle for a close examination. Then the energy of her dancing is so thoroughly transformed into utter attentiveness that you also hold yourself perfectly still for fear she will detect your presence by your slightest movement, forgetting that, on this occasion at least, she will only be allowed to hear your voice.

Her dark hair gleams reddish in the sun like yours used to, and her eyes are a startlingly solid green, also like yours. Her face, turned now upon a blade of swordgrass she holds between her fingers, exhibits a concentration so intense as to resemble ferocity.

For a moment, you wonder, *Is she me? Am I not dead, after all?*

No. Your memories of the Fire are still vivid: the flames you strained to see but could only hear crackling, the numbing cold they spread through your body when you had expected an unendurable burning. No dream but your final experience of earthly life.

You are Margaret of Antioch, slain most cruelly and unjustly four hundred years after the death of your Lord for your faith in him, but a thousand years have passed since then as if they were a single day, and this girl you watch dancing in a meadow is Joan of Domrémy.

Remembering your task, you approach her, but at first, can't think how to get close enough to her in her dance. However, like the brave butterflies that found their way onto her shoulder, you eventually catch the rhythm of her movements, and are soon matching her every step and pause and twirl, an invisible partner in a dance without rules. You draw even closer until your lips are almost touching her left ear and whisper, "Joan!"

She gasps and stops at once: her eyes, her mouth, her whole being wide open. However, her gaze is set on the nearby hills. You look yourself, but see nothing except a small plume of dust, raised, perhaps, by a caravan of travelers descending into the valley.

"I am a messenger from God," you begin, and she breathes, with no surprise in her voice and her eyes still on the hills, "Yes."

You continue, "So commands the King of Heaven: Be a good girl, and go to church."

She laughs!

She turns with a smile in your general direction and says, "Yes, Lord!" But then, after a quick look back at the hills, adds in a low voice, "Is that all?"

You try to maintain the oracular tone you began with.

"Yes - for the present. I am Margaret of Antioch, and I will speak to you often from now on."

"I know you!" she cries, and you freeze again, afraid that she can somehow see you after all, but she continues, "My mother taught me about you; there is a statue of you in the church! You are one of our patron saints."

You didn't know that! Already in your own time, certain great believers of old had come to be considered the special helps and guides for certain groups of people. The martyred healers Cosmas and Damias of Syria, for example, were the patron saints of doctors and surgeons, while St. Joseph, that good man who journeyed with his pregnant wife to Bethlehem and an unknown future, walked with all travelers on their long roads.

You are now counted among their number.

"Whom in this world do I stand for?" you ask.

She laughs again before she answers, "Women with child!"

The air is filled with the unmistakable sounds of a City: the babble of anonymous conversations in the street punctuated by momentarily clear outbursts of laughter or exclamation, the rattle of cart wheels over stone pavement, the dull boom of construction work. The smells of roasting meat and baking sweetcakes contend with one another, first one then the other prevailing with the shifts of the wind. Above all, a brighter sun than that of Domrémy spills upon the ground a river of flowing, crisscrossing shadows.

"'Ware, missy! Move!" comes a shout from directly behind you, but you know it can't be meant for you. An enormous cart passes by you – through you! – while a young girl several paces in front of you screeches in delighted alarm and scrambles to get out of its way.

You are, and are not, in the marketplace of Antioch. Catherine will be appearing soon; this is where she regularly meets you. You haven't yet been able to decide whether she really transports you one thousand years and many more miles back into the past, or if this is just a vision, conjured to make you feel more at home when she calls you into her presence. Once, you sought out a particular house that was dear to you and found some other family living there, but that might only mean that this is Antioch from just before or after your time.

It really doesn't matter, though, for whether the people around you are real or not, there's an impassable gulf between you. They can't see or hear you. (Or run you over with their carts!) They serve only as the backdrop to your talks with your teacher and guide.

"Well done, my child!"

The familiar voice fills you with warmth that blossoms into a broad smile on your face. Turning, you drop to one knee and intone, "My lady Catherine." She laughs and replies as always, "See thou do it not!" and you spring to your feet to embrace her, rising onto the tips of your toes to bury your face in her neck. You breath in the fragrance of her perfume – a thing unheard of in Antioch, though you lived hundreds of years later than she did – and feel the few loose strands of her elaborately arranged hair tickle your cheek. When you step back, she says, "Tell me!"

"I delivered the message, but she had bigger news for me than anything I had to tell her. Did you know that I'm a patron saint?"

"I did."

"Of pregnant women."

"That is what I understand."

"But I never had a baby. I was never married. I was just a girl."

Catherine smiles and begins to walk down the street. It's the great avenue that runs the length of your beloved city, flanked by columns and paved with stones fitted together so expertly, not a crack can be seen big enough to lose a coin in. You leave the marketplace and pass through the temple area, entering a small park that offers a view of the river.

"I bore three children in my time," she says. "And I can see how women since your day might have embraced your story: a

Freeman Ng

young girl who also suffered and endured, and who, by her courage and faith, passed through her travails to embrace life new-born!"

Your cheeks flush. Thankfully, Catherine doesn't look over at you, but continues striding serenely across the grassy square.

"Is Joan going to have a baby?" you ask her. "She can't be more than thirteen years old!"

"She is twelve, but in her time and place, girls can be married off as early as age fourteen. We may well be with her at least that long."

You come to a fountain and stop to watch the play of its waters, light and sparkling, over the Roman war hero cast in stone at its center.

"I liked talking to her. I liked just watching her sing and dance in the meadow. But why are we instructing her to be a good girl? She doesn't seem to need it."

"The ways of God are a darkness and a delight. There is always a reason behind them, even if we cannot see it. We may be preparing her for a future in which it will be much harder for her to be good, or for some subtle test of her virtue. Perhaps if we did not start visiting her now, her youthful enthusiasm for God would fade naturally over time, but now it will not. Or the reason could simply be your enjoyment of her company.

"We are not merely messengers, but friends and fellow travelers with those to whom we are sent. It is important that we come to like them, to love them even, for in this way, the love of God is made manifest."

You return to Domrémy the next day with another message for Joan: "Work hard and diligently." You're told that at some point during the day, she will sneak off to pray in the church, and that's when you should deliver the message.

Is that it? you think to yourself. *Does she shirk her responsibilities?*

Her day begins before dawn, when she goes out into the fields with her three brothers and her father. Though the two older boys are assigned most of the hard labor of the plowing, she more than fulfills her share of the work, carrying water out to them and clearing the field before them of the larger rocks and other obstructions. The youngest of the boys is given the same jobs to do, but though he appears older and stronger than Joan, he takes two breaks before she joins him on his third.

She carries the water jug over to where he sits beneath a tree.

"Thank you!" he says, taking a long drink. "I thought about stopping by the jug on my way here, but it would have made a longer walk."

"But the refreshment of the water would have more than made up for it!" she says with a giggle.

"Maybe. I could not take the chance!"

She laughs again and kisses him on the head.

"My poor brother!"

"Pierre!" comes their father's shout from the field.

He sighs and pulls himself back onto his feet.

"No!" he tells Joan when she rises to join him. "You just got here. Stay and rest, and I will carry on for us both for a while."

Their father calls a halt to the hard labor an hour or two past midday, and they return to the house for a meal. The children plunge their dirt caked arms and faces into a trough of water next to the front door. Their mother greets them from the door.

"How did the plowing go?" she asks their father.

"Good!" he says. "We finished fully half the field. We should be able to cover the rest before nightfall."

"Jacques!" she whispers, drawing him in past the door. "Do you realize you were out there for eight hours?"

When the family is seated around the table and grace has been said, he tells the children, "You did good work today. We will finish the plowing tomorrow. Jacquemin and Jean and I will survey the fencing around the pastures this afternoon and make any repairs that might be needed. Pierre, Joan, you will plant the first quarter of the south field."

Isabella puts her arm around the youngest daughter, who

stands shyly by her side.

"And Katie and I will prepare supper, won't we?"

Out in the south field, Joan takes up her work at the same pace she left it off, hauling baskets of cut potatoes out to the freshly plowed rows and pushing them carefully but swiftly into the churned up soil.

"Slow down!" Pierre calls out to her. "We have all the rest of the day for this!"

"The sooner done, the sooner free!" she shouts back at him.

"Okay," he says, "but stop at that bush!"

When she finishes her half of the field, Joan sets off back to the village, but just as she comes within sight of her home, turns aside and follows a path the leads back out toward the woods. About halfway between the village and the wood, it climbs a gentle hill, at the top of which stands a small building with narrow windows and a cross set upon its roof. As she approaches the doors, an old man who must be the priest is just exiting them. When he sees her, he smiles and holds open the door, gesturing for her to enter and bowing as she passes in. You glance quickly around to see if anyone's watching, a habit from your days of secret and dangerous belief, then realize such caution is no longer necessary and follow Joan into the close, cool darkness of the chapel.

Within, candles flutter briefly at the intake of dusty air. Joan walks straight down an aisle flanked by rows of wooden benches, but you pause just inside the door.

This is a real church.

Like the catacombs of Antioch, it's dark and silent, weighty with the presence of the Holy. The air is rich with the smell, not of earth, but of aged wood and plaster.

You walk up the aisle to a stone font decorated with carved images of flowers and birds. When Joan passed it on her way to the altar, she dipped a finger into the water and then traced the shape of a cross on her forehead with it. You try to do the same, but your hand passes through both water and stone.

Hung on the walls are paintings depicting scenes from the scriptures, or so you assume. You don't recognize most of them, but are able to identify the Noah's Ark and the Parting of the Red Sea on one wall, and the Stoning of Stephen on the other.

You come to an alcove in the front left corner of the church, where a number of small statues are set on shelves with burnt down candles before them, and you remember that one of them must be of you. You survey their ranks, and at first, have no idea which one it might be, for the statues are unlabeled, and of course would not resemble the people they represent. Then you come to the figure of a girl holding a shepherd's crook.

This is me.

You recall the scent of olive trees, and the dry, pale heat of the Antioch summer. You picture the face of your best friend, Sennie, and then other faces less kind.

How can I be a saint when I did nothing for God in my short life except die for no good reason?

Just before Joan exits the church, you remember your charge and whisper to her, "Work hard, and diligently."

Though you feel odd giving her such a command after watching her do more work in one day than you ever did in a week, she receives it happily, smiling and saying, "Thank you, Margaret! I will do my best."

When she gets back to the field, the corner she was assigned to plant with Pierre looks finished, and he sits under a tree stripping the leaves off a fallen branch.

"You are just in time!" he tells her, and tosses her the branch. He stands and you see that he has another one in his hands.

"En guard!" he cries, striking a fencer's pose.

"For France and the King of Heaven!" she replies, and throws herself into an attack on her brother that surprises you with its abandon.

"Ha!" he cries, and "Ho!" as he dodges or deflects the sweeping blows that she rains down upon him. He strikes back infrequently, and then only gently.

"I am the Duke of Burgundy," he intones ominously. "And I would rule this land on behalf of my friends, the English!"

"Never!" cries Joan. "This is the kingdom of France! The English will not prevail!"

She continues to press him, windmilling the branch tirelessly, until it catches him on the hand and he drops his "sword", gasping in pain.

"Oh!" cries Joan. "I'm sorry! Are you all right?"

"Protest not!"

Pierre stands at attention, straight-backed and tragic with his arms by his side.

"You have won the day," he tells her in measured tones. "And I will go now in defeat and disgrace."

"Nay," says Joan. "Let us be friends rather, and think no more of our past battles, for we are kin."

They shake hands as solemnly as if they were the kings of two great kingdoms indeed. Then Pierre looks up in the direction of the pasture.

"Behold!" he cries. "It is the king of England, come to continue the war!"

Their older brother Jean walks toward them across the field.

"Let us join forces," says Joan, "and win back this land for our own people!"

Shouting and brandishing their branches, they rush upon Jean, who crouches to receive them. He easily flings Pierre to one side and captures Joan in a bear hug that she struggles to free herself from.

"Save me!" she cries.

When Pierre comes running at him again, he lets go of Joan and charges right back at his astonished brother, knocking him to the ground.

"Save *me*!" shouts Pierre, and Joan jumps onto Jean's back to be spun around and around.

The three of them play like this for another hour, wrestling and sword fighting and racing each other across the unsown fields until their mother's voice floats through the settling dusk, calling them in to supper.

That night after everyone else has gone to bed, Joan sits with her mother spinning thread. They work in silence for a long time while the spindle fills the room with its soft whirr and click, and then Joan speaks.

"Tell me again about running away."

Her mother nods, smiling.

"Once upon a time, there was a girl named Isabella who lived in the great city of Paris, which at that time was still the capital of France. Because her family was very well off, she had all the culture and camaraderie of the city at her beck and call. Yet, her heart was never at ease, for she was a proud girl who thought herself above all pastimes and pieties.

"So it was that when the time came for her to be married, she refused every match her parents tried to make, and they fell into constant, bitter fighting. Finally, her parents threatened to marry her to the next suitor who came along, with or without her consent, and she declared that she would run away rather than suffer that fate. But where in this world could a young woman go all by herself in safety and propriety? She thought and thought, and finally found the answer. She decided to go to…"

"Rome!" whispers Joan.

"Yes. In those days, groups of nuns or students or retired priests often made pilgrimage to that holy city. She found such a group and convinced them to let her join them, and so the way was made. After a journey filled itself with marvels, she came to that place which was the center of the Faith on this earth. She stayed there six months, and though she had arrived with no interest in religion, there was really nothing else to do in that city except attend the masses and listen to the lectures of renowned teachers and holy men and converse with the other pilgrims about their journeys, and in the course of those six months…"

Freeman Ng

"God spoke to her."

"Yes, and it was a changed woman who returned to her home. She reconciled with her parents, but told them she could no longer live in Paris. She left them again, but this time with their blessing, fleeing the wealth of the great cities, and came to the farmlands of Lorraine, where she met the man who would become her husband and the father of her children."

The spindle continues its whirring. Mother and daughter work away in silence for a while longer. Then Isabella says, "Well, I think it is time we both went to bed."

She takes Joan's hand and leads her into the children's room. They step carefully past her snoring brothers to the corner she shares with Katie.

"Sleep well, Joan. I will see you again in the day God brings."

"Mama?"

Isabella turns at the door.

"Did God speak to you in any other way when you were in Rome? Besides the masses and the words of the great teachers?"

"Most certainly. Through the shrines and the churches, the fountains and the wide sky itself. I will spend the rest of my days deciphering all that He told me."

The next morning, you go out the door of the house intending to follow Joan into the fields, but find yourself instead walking onto a familiar stone pavement. Around you lies a neighborhood of small houses packed tightly together, some of them fronted by narrow flower gardens. Catherine stands waiting for you in the street.

"My lady!" you say again, dropping to one knee.

"See thou do it not!" she replies with a smile, lifting you to your feet.

You walk through the residential district of Antioch.

"How did you like your first full day in Domrémy?" she asks.

"I liked it a lot. Joan has such a good life! I could almost envy it, except for the farm work."

"You were a shepherd. Was that not hard work?"

"I wasn't a real shepherd, just a watcher. Sometimes if a sheep got sick or injured, but mostly, I just stood there."

Catherine laughs lightly and stops to lean against a garden fence. A lone butterfly battles the summer breeze above a bed of flowers.

"Tomorrow," she says, "Joan's father will take the boys to do some work on an old monastery near the village. I do not know if he will ask Joan to go along, but if he does not, speak to her and tell her she must go, too."

"I will, my lady. But if he won't change his mind, what can she do? Wouldn't it be better for me to tell *him* that he should take her?"

"It has not been granted to us to speak with any other mortal, and most of them would not be able to hear us, anyway. Only have faith that as Joan was meant to go to the monastery, so the way will be opened to her."

She raises a hand in a gesture of farewell and dismissal.

"Wait, Catherine! Who are the Duke of Burgundy and the King of England?"

"Ah. I see you have heard the news of these times. England is a neighboring country that is at war with Joan's people. They have been seeking to conquer France for many years now. The Burgundians are a party of the French who are on the side of the English. Between the invader from without and the civil war within, this land has known little peace for many generations."

"But Joan and her family live in peace right now! They plow their fields, and play in the meadows. They spin thread! Is Joan in danger?"

"War or not, the rivers still flow. But it has also been easier for the people of this region to carry on as if there were no threat, for they live the farthest from the English invasion. They will be the last to fall, should England conquer all, but no English soldier has yet set foot in this valley."

You recall Joan's alarm at the far off sight of travelers entering the valley the day you first met her.

Freeman Ng

"Will they? Is that why we're here?"

Catherine shifts a little on her feet, but continues to smile down upon you.

"You will know in good time," she says.

When you return to the house the following morning, Joan, Pierre, and Jean are up, but their father nowhere to be found.

"Did he go out to the fields already?"

"I don't see him."

"And where is Jacquemin?"

"Mama?"

Isabella comes out of her bedroom.

"Softly. Katie is still asleep. Your father has gone to speak with the elders. A messenger came in the night with news of import. He sent Jacquemin to Greaux to pass it on."

"What is it? What was the news?"

"I do not know," she says. "We will have to wait for your father's return."

She sets out food and they eat in silence. As they are finishing, the door opens and a tired looking Jacques enters.

"Good," he says. "You have eaten. There is a change of plans for today. Instead of the planting, we are going to make a short trip."

Joan and her brothers look at one another with expectant smiles, but Isabella's face darkens.

"Where?" she asks.

He answers her matter-of-factly.

"The Isle."

"The Isle!" shout Jean and Pierre in delight, but Joan remains silent, and her mother brings one hand swiftly to her chest.

"To do some work," Jacques tells her. "No other reason. You can stay home with Kate and Joan. It will be perfectly safe. Only a few of the men are going. The rest will remain in the village."

Isabella nods mutely.

"We will need to pack food," he says. "Enough for the whole

day. We won't return until late. Jean, harness the oxen. Pierre, load the wagon with all the tools."

"Joan!" you whisper, and she cocks her head slightly. "You must go, too!"

"Papa!" she blurts as her brothers go out the door. "I wish to go, too."

"We're going to work. It will be hard labor," he says curtly.

"I work hard!" she cries.

He looks down at her for the first time.

"Yes. Yes, you do. Very well. Go help Pierre with the wagon."

"Thank you!" she gushes, and dashes out the door.

Jacques goes over to the pantry and loads a few things into a basket while Isabella stares silently at his back. Then he turns and says, "The English have taken Beaugency."

They drive the wagon five miles through the woods alongside the river.

"What will we be doing?" ask the boys. "Is the refuge almost ready?"

"Nearly," says Jacques. "We will deepen the well, and repair the last few holes in the walls."

"Will we be moving there once it's done?"

"No, no. The Isle is a place of last resort. If we are fortunate, we will never need to go there."

They ride in silence for a while.

"Are the English coming?" asks Joan in a low voice.

"If they're coming, I want to join the watch!" declares Jean.

"Jacquemin isn't even old enough yet," says Pierre. "Do you think you can get special treatment just because of Papa?"

Jacques doesn't answer, and they lapse into silence again, turning their attention to the landscape passing them by on both sides. He eventually replies, but so softly that none of the children hear him.

"Soon enough," he whispers. "Soon enough."

Freeman Ng

The wagon emerges from the woods at a point where the river widens or branches to flow around a large island in its midst. On the island stands an old stone structure, almost perfectly square in shape and completely unadorned, surrounded closely by smaller wooden buildings. They cross over to it on a rickety bridge just wide enough for the wagon to pass.

On the other side, they find men already at work, and Jacques quickly dispatches the children to various work parties. Pierre is assigned to a group perched on the roof of one of the wooden structures. Jean follows his father to the monastery itself. Joan's job is to help with the well, which is located inside one of the wooden buildings abutting the monastery.

For the next six hours, Joan carries buckets of soil out of the well house and empties them in a big pile near the monastery entrance. A man shares this job with her, but a couple of hours into the morning, he takes a long look at her as she stoically trudges back and forth with her arms wrapped around the heavy buckets, and tells the men doing the digging, "You are fine here. I will go help with the stonework."

Everyone takes a break in the late afternoon. They sit in the shade of the stables, passing around loaves of bread and a jug of water.

"I think a few hours more will do it," says Jacques.

"It will be a relief to my mind to have it ready and waiting," says one of the other men.

"Papa," says Joan. "Does the monastery have a chapel?"

"Of course."

"I wish to go pray. I will be back in time to resume the work."

He nods and she trots off. You follow her in through the low entrance and down a short, dark hall. Light shines from a doorway on the left, and when you reach it, you see that it opens into a small chamber lit by candles set at intervals around the walls. They aren't the only form of illumination, however. Standing before the altar is Catherine, shimmering in a fall of light from some unseen source.

"Catherine!" you cry, and then clap a hand over your mouth,

but Joan doesn't hear you or see her. She walks up to the altar and kneels before it.

"Father in Heaven," she begins, and goes on to pray the Lord's Prayer.

When she finishes, she gets up and turns to leave, but Catherine says, "Joan!"

"I am here," she replies, peering up at the cross behind the altar. "Margaret?"

"I am Catherine of Alexandria, and I come, with Margaret, at the command of the archangel Michael. Have you been a good girl? Have you worked hard? Have you done always that which was right in the sight of God?"

"I hope that I have, and if I haven't, I hope I may do better."

"Well answered. Now tell me, what do you know about the war your people are fighting against the English?"

"Only that they wish to conquer us, but that God will never let it happen."

"True enough. Nevertheless, the war is not going well at present. The English occupy nearly the entire country now, and they have also claimed, since your king died, that the true heir to the throne of France is their own young prince Henry. So they seek to conquer France by both arms and the laws of royal succession."

Joan's face begins to take on that look of concentrated fury that you saw on it the first day you met her.

"Do you know who your true king is?" asks Catherine.

"The Dauphin!"

"Yes. Charles the Seventh, whom your people call the Dauphin, is a true son of the departed king and the rightful heir to the throne of France. He dwells now in the city of Chinon, waiting for better days, but if the armies of the English reach him, that time may never come."

"Why can't he go to Rheims right now?" asks Joan. "Have all the bishops gone over to the English?"

"Why should Charles go to Rheims?" you say aloud. "And what does the Church have to do with it?"

Catherine doesn't answer you directly, but smiles at you before she replies to Joan.

"It is true that the kings of France have always been crowned at the cathedral of Rheims, and the Dauphin would still find enough loyal bishops to conduct the ceremony. However, it would be dangerous for him to make the trip, and even if he made it safely to Rheims and was welcomed by the people of the city, there would still be many who might not accept his coronation with so much of France now in English hands."

"Then he must march against them and take back what was his!" cries Joan.

"Perhaps so. Perhaps he will. Pray for him. Pray for France, that her deliverance might come swiftly."

You spend the rest of that day expecting an English army to come marching out of the woods at any moment, but the work proceeds undisturbed and the workers return to Domrémy late that night. The next day, and the day after, and the day after that, they go out into the fields as usual, and Joan and her brothers have their carefree play, and night deepens once more around the whirr of the spindle and the voice of Isabella Romée telling some tale of her past journeys. Weeks go by with no more trips to the Isle and no talk of the English, except in the fanciful personal combats staged by Joan and her brothers. *The River flows*, you think to yourself, as spring moves into summer in the valley of the Meuse.

As the hard work of the planting begins to abate, the pace of life slows, while losing nothing of its rhythm. Joan continues to rise early and go out into the fields, though the work of maintaining the crops is less backbreaking than the plowing and the planting were. She sneaks off to pray as before, but is able to spend much more time at it, sometimes even drowsing into an unexpected nap as she kneels in the darkness of the chapel. She plays just as energetically with her brothers, but also finds time to dance and sing in the meadows, alone or with other girls her age.

Except when you're spirited away to Antioch by Catherine, you stay by Joan at all times, following her out to the fields and around the house as she does her chores, watching her tirelessly spin thread at her mother's side, or looking down upon her face softened by sleep.

The messages you're given to repeat to her are always as bland and unnecessary as the first. *Learn your prayers*, and *Do good to others*, and *Trust in God*. You continue to wonder what their purpose can be, even as you faithfully deliver them. Joan continues to receive them in all earnestness.

Early one evening, she's alone in a meadow whiling away the time, having completed her chores for the day and snuck off twice already to pray in the church. She lies on her stomach with her head in her hands, watching the faint trembling of a dandelion plant directly in front of her face. Just then, you whisper a message you have for her, "Pray unceasingly!"

She cocks her head to hear you, then nods slowly to herself as if she's just received a profound insight and is vowing to better her ways. You guess that she will slip off to the church one more time to pray, but instead, she settles back down before the pretty weed and remains there for another hour until she's called in to supper!

When autumn rolls around, the people of the village explode into a renewed vigor of labor that exceeds even the hard work of the spring. Every man, woman, and child issues forth into the fields for the harvest, with every person having a job to do.

It's a season of shouting. Overseers call out instructions to groups of men scything the fields or stacking bales of hay. Women converse loudly over the noise of the threshing. Children shout greetings to one another from the tops of adjacent fruit trees, while their older siblings yell up at them to be careful and to get on with the picking.

Watching the entire village engaged in this way, you realize that Joan's involvement with the work on her family's farm and on the Isle was unusual. You assumed that other children her age worked as hard for their families, but Joan is the only young child

Freeman Ng

and the only girl of any age who joins the adults in the heaviest labor of the harvest. You watch her toting baskets of fruit in from the orchards, or taking her place in a line of men stacking hay, and notice that everyone treats her like a fellow adult: one who may not be as strong as they are, but who is just as hard-working.

"Joan, help! Lift it here. Good. This end first."

"Joan, if you're unoccupied elsewhere, we need more hands with the hay."

"Joan, you are good these things. Do you think all those bushels will fit into that loft?"

At the end of each day, the whole village sits down together to piles of freshly baked bread and enormous pots of stew made from vegetables harvested that very day. Joan most often takes her meals up in a tree, sitting side by side on a heavy branch with her best friend among the other children of the village.

"Did you see Lily today?" says the girl one evening. "She all but followed Jacquemin into the fields! I think your family will be planning a wedding soon."

"I like Lily," says Joan. "She and Jacquemin will be happy together."

"You like everybody. I couldn't believe you were working right next to the smith today! He gives me the creeps."

"He's a good man!" protests Joan.

"Then why don't you marry him?"

"He already has a wife!" says Joan with a laugh. "And he likes her just fine. But how about you? Who do you want to marry?"

"No boy in *this* village," sniffs her friend, and then her eyes light up. "God! I will marry only God!"

As the work of the harvest winds down, a shift occurs in the weather: Winter arrives. Though it doesn't rain many more days than in any other month, the air grows colder and the rainfall harder. The skies become permanently overcast, and the days go dark earlier and earlier.

The people of Domrémy come in from the fields and spend

most of their time indoors in this season. Joan and her siblings sprawl among heaps of blankets strewing the floor around the fireplace to hear their parents recite the tales of their heritage. Isabella tells stories from the Bible, while Jacques recites the history of the family, which includes many valiant warriors. Above the fireplace hangs the family crest, a banner depicting the fields of Arkon, the region where he was born, with two real swords mounted beneath it.

Sometimes, they end these sessions by singing the song Joan sang the day you first met her, which you now know is a round that tolls the names of the great cathedral cities of France:

> *Orléans, Beaugency,*
> *Notre Dame de Cléry,*
> *Vendôme, Vendôme!*

Isabella usually begins the song, accompanied by Katie, and then Jacques and Jacquemin begin it anew as Isabella sings the second measure. Jean and Pierre jump in next, and finally Joan. They sing it several times through, their voices weaving the simple tune into a complex rise and fall of music, and then reach the end, first Isabella and Katie dropping out of the song, and then Jacques and Jacquemin, and then Jean and Pierre, until finally, Joan's solitary voice sounds the final notes a final time.

Two more years go by, just like the first, in the light-suffused meadows of Domrémy. You begin to feel like you've always lived here, a second sister to Joan not much less visible than shy Katie. Or rather, the days begin to mirror that time in your life when you were Joan's age and every day was the same in the small world that was the city of Antioch. Sometimes, lying with Joan in the rustling grass of a meadow looking up at the stars, with your sight filled entirely by their distant brilliance, you imagine yourself that child again, lying on the roof of your house, dreaming of the future.

In a thousand years, the stars have not changed.

One day, you enter the church with Joan and follow her as she stands briefly before each of the paintings on the walls. Because this is Easter week, the usual set has been replaced by a series depicting various moments in the crucifixion of Christ: Jesus carrying his cross up Calvary Hill, Jesus accepting the kind but futile gesture of the woman Veronica, Jesus nailed to the cross beneath a darkening sky.

When she kneels before the altar to pray, you join her, adding your own prayer to hers.

O God of all times and places, I thank you for bringing me here, though I don't understand yet what your purpose for me can be. I don't seem to be urging Joan to any virtue she doesn't already possess in full measure, and I know nothing of the history that Catherine is teaching her. Nevertheless, I am content to watch and wait and do the work I've been given. Let me worship you and serve you as I was not able to do in my life. Let me be a good friend and guide to Joan.

Only two things disturb your perfect happiness during these years.

First, the news that Catherine brings of the war grows darker. Demoralized French forces capitulate to the English again and again, and the major cities of France fall one after another. Some regions go over to the English of their own choice, without a fight. Soon, only one stronghold remains: the city of Orléans, which sits in a key position along the Loire river. When it falls, all will be lost, for there will be no more shield between the Dauphin (or Domrémy!) and the armies of the English.

Second, Joan gradually stops dancing and singing in the meadows. This upsets you even more than the military news, because you fear it could be your fault: that she might be reacting to your visits by trying to become more serious in life. Neither you nor Catherine ever told her to stop dancing, and you can't think of any other reason for her change in behavior.

Often, on her way to the church, she comes within sight of the other children as they chase one another through the tall grasses.

"Joan! Come and play!"

"She is going to the church again."

"She's too good and godly to play with us."

"Maybe she is planning to become a nun!"

"Maybe she will go on crusade and become a famous hero."

"All hail Saint Joan! Stay and bless us!" they tease, but she only smiles and waves, and passes on.

The Regions of Light

One spring night (your fourth in Domrémy!) after Joan and the other children have gone to bed, a lone traveler knocks on the door begging for food and a place to sleep.

"Of course," says Isabella. "Come in."

"Thank you! Thank you!" cries the visitor. "I cannot tell you how many doors have been shut against me!"

"I am Jacques," says Joan's father, stepping forward to stand between his wife and the stranger. "I am doyen of this village."

"I understand, sir. You and yours have nothing to fear from me. Indeed, only three weeks ago, I slept under a roof just like you, in my own bed! I was an apothecary in the city of Orléans, but now I fear I will never see my home again."

"Come, sit and tell us what happened," says Isabella, and taking him by the arm, guides him to a seat at the kitchen table. He tells his story between mouthfuls of food.

"It is the English. They came in great force four weeks ago. By the time we knew of their presence, they had the city half surrounded. Some of us risked flight. I made it to Chécy and have been traveling east ever since. I am leaving France." He shakes his head sadly with that final confession. "There is no hope, nothing left to stay for."

Jacques sits across from the refugee.

"The English have taken Orléans?"

"Not yet. They did not attack the city itself, except to overrun the towers that guard the gates, so that no one can get in or out any more. They are going to starve the people into submission!"

"Then they will march on the Dauphin," says Jacques frowning. "They may even try it now, if their siege is strong enough that they count Orléans safe in their hands."

"I think it is possible. All through my flight, I heard rumors of an English advance. They followed me all the way into this valley. I fear I will not escape this house in time, much less the country!"

"Jacques!" exclaims Isabella.

"Hold off!" he grumbles, getting up from the table and pacing back and forth. "We've received no warnings from the towns to the west. Still . . . Jacquemin!"

The eldest son shuffles bleary-eyed from the children's room.

"Go to the homes of the elders. Wake them if they are sleeping. Tell them I have heard a report that the English have Orléans under siege and may be pressing on into the valley. I will speak with them in the morning, but we ought to warn everybody in the village to be ready to go to the Isle. Assist them in this as they wish."

"Yes, father," says Jacquemin, and he is soon out the door. The three adults look after him for a long while, until Isabella breaks the silence.

"We thank you for this warning. You had best get some sleep. We were about to go to bed ourselves, and it seems we will all wish to get up earlier than usual tomorrow. We don't have an extra bed, but the end of the hall there is the most comfortable place to lay down some blankets."

"No!"

Joan stands at the door to the children's room.

"Let him take my bed. I will sleep in the hall."

Isabella's face is transformed from surprise into a tender smile.

"I might have known you would speak up! We cannot take in so much as a lost puppy but you insist it sleep in your bed."

"It is only what God commands," replies Joan.

"It is only that you obey," corrects her mother.

That night, you sit as always by Joan's side. Moonlight from the kitchen window illuminates her face with a cold, unearthly light. Though you don't sleep any more yourself, you've discovered that you can enter to some extent into Joan's, sharing her repose and drifting through the vast, bright worlds of her dreams. The night deepens, releasing by slow degrees the heat of the day, replacing it with the chirping of crickets and the snoring of the others within the house. You breathe in and out in time with Joan, with every exhalation expanding into realms beyond the shell of your self, with every inhalation drawing closer to her thoughts and sensations. You feel the hard floor beneath her, the increasingly cold air prickling her face.

When you try turning over to relieve a dull pain forming in one side, there's a clanking of metal. Shackles weigh down your wrists, and the wooden floor of the house is now rough stone, cold and damp. Stone surrounds you on every side as well, and in this dream, there is the certain knowledge that beyond these walls are others, and beyond them more yet. So many that not even God Himself can see through to where you're imprisoned, nor Justice, nor Light. You are alone, forsaken, in the hands of an enemy with no capacity for mercy.

"Margaret!"

You start awake, confused about where you are and then alarmed about who in the house could possibly be addressing you. Then you see it's Catherine.

"Margaret," she says, "there is a message we must deliver to Joan tonight, and you must come with me to receive it."

"Tonight? She's already asleep."

"She will wake soon, and we must be ready. Come."

You follow her out of the house.

This is the first time you'll be going with Catherine to receive a message for Joan. Always before, she's passed them on to you. You put this new development together with the bad news brought by the exiled traveler and the horrible nightmare you dreamed with Joan.

"Catherine? I'm afraid."

"Do not fear, my child. I will confess, it is no easy thing to appear before Michael, for he is of the highest order of all the angels. However, this also means that he is closest to the throne of God, and nothing he says or does can turn to evil for us or for Joan.

"Now close your eyes and do not open them until I tell you, and then slowly."

You do as she says. The moonlit blue of the night goes to black. Catherine's hand around yours is warm, and that warmth spreads slowly through your body. Your eyelids flush red, and the red grows brighter and brighter as the sounds of the night fade.

"Now, very slowly, open your eyes."

You open them to see that you're surrounded by flames!

"No!" you cry. You try to run, but Catherine's arms encircle you. You thrash and kick against her.

"Look at me!" she commands. "Look into my eyes!"

You lock your gaze on her gently smiling face, and begin to calm a little.

"See? I am here with you. Can you see the sky above my head? Is it not the strangest colored sky you have ever seen? Perhaps it is like some sunsets you have known, only deeper and filling all of the sky. And the ground beneath my feet, it is like the finest marble in the temples of Antioch, is it not? Of course, you must imagine marble shot through with veins of orange and bronze. We had such stone in Alexandria.

"Come, stand upon it all by yourself."

She slowly releases you. Looking around, you begin to perceive a landscape in what had first struck you as fiery chaos.

"Are those mountains?"

"Perhaps. I have never been able to decide."

Above the masses that might be mountains, blazing lights that could be stars spread themselves across a red and purple sky. Between you and the mountains stretches a wide plain of light.

"Is this Heaven?"

"It is the place Michael meets us," replies Catherine. "Just as I meet you in Antioch. Though he cannot consider this comforting!"

You look more fully around you. The whole world seems alive, like the flames of a fire indeed. All your life – until its very end – you reveled in the sight of fire. The hearth of your home, the blacksmith's furnace, the bonfires of the winter solstice: you could spend hours staring into the endless lapping of flames. Now it's as if the very earth burst forth with that aliveness, and you recall a scripture you once heard recited, about the mountains dancing for joy.

"Not comforting, but exhilarating!" you cry, and attempt a couple of dance steps yourself, light and leaping.

"Margaret!" exclaims Catherine. "You are adapting to this place much better than I! The best I can do, even after many visits here, is to not be afraid."

You stop, for you catch sight of a distant figure approaching over the plain. It's like a statue of a robed man, wielding a torch or burning branch in one hand. And it's clearly traveling swiftly. It grows larger by the moment, and the flames of what you now see is a sword stream backward behind it. You look up questioningly at Catherine, who nods in reply.

Michael continues to approach until he appears about the size of a normal man standing ten paces away, though whether that's indeed the case, or he's actually a thousand feet tall and a mile away, you can't easily tell in this world of immaterial light. His face is pale and impassive, like the faces on some ancient statues you've seen, and his long flowing hair snow white, so that, except for the fire running up his sword, he looks like a statue cast from the finest white marble indeed.

Then you are given the message you must deliver to Joan.

Just as you return to the hallway where she's sleeping, she

rouses with a stifled cry. She looks around fearfully, clutching one wrist in the other hand, and then sighs and begins to breathe more steadily.

"She was having a bad dream," you explain, and shudder a little yourself at the memory of it.

"Let us wait, then," replies Catherine. "Our news is grave, and it will be better if she is calmer first."

However, Joan looks up at you.

"Catherine? Margaret? I can see your faces!"

Catherine nods at you to speak. You wonder at this, but she smiles and gestures for you to proceed. So it is that after all the simple platitudes you've passed on to Joan, it is your voice that will deliver this most momentous message of all.

You look into Joan's eyes. For the first time, they look directly back into yours.

"Joan, daughter of Jacques of Arkon and Isabella Romée, daughter of France, daughter of God: By your sword will the English be driven from Orléans. Your hands will set the crown of France upon the head of the Dauphin. Your voice will pronounce your people's liberation. So declares the King of Heaven and Lord of all the nations."

She doesn't respond. The seconds tick by, and she remains unspeaking and unmoving. Her silence fills the house, quieting the snorers and even reaching beyond the walls to subdue the chirping crickets. The only sound is her breathing, still shaky from her fearful waking. You count her trembling exhalations – eight, nine, ten – and wonder if she will ever speak.

"No. No! Joan!"

You jump at the voice of Joan's father sounding from his room. He appears at the door, looking frantically around in the dark. Then he sees Joan's face, as still as a stone in the moonlight.

"Joan! What are you doing up?"

"I had a bad dream."

Her voice is very small, very young again.

"It's all right." He laughs shakily. "I think I just had one myself! Are you all right now?"

"Yes, father."

"Go back to sleep," he says. "It was just a dream."

"That is a good idea," says Catherine when he has gone. "We will speak more of this tomorrow, Joan, and for many days to come. There is much still to say and to plan, so do not let your heart be troubled. We will tell you more about what you must do, and you will find that you will be able to accomplish all that God calls you to, and all will be well."

"Yes, Catherine," she says, and lowers herself tentatively back onto her bedding.

Twice more before the morning, Jacques wakes with a cry and comes out of his room to check on Joan. Once, you hear Isabella whispering to him in concerned, questioning tones. The stranger from Orléans tosses and turns all night, unable, perhaps, to stop running, and just before dawn, Pierre has a coughing fit that rouses his complaining brothers and causes Kate to slip into her parents' room to beg a place in their bed. You remain awake through all this, afraid to reenter Joan's dream of the stone cell, which you can sense just beneath the blanket of her sleep.

No one in the house passes that night untroubled.

The next morning, the women and children of the village pile into wagons that carry them through the pathless wood to the refuge in midst of the river. The wagons teeter across the narrow bridge to the island, where their passengers quickly set up house-keeping.

Because they've come here only as a precaution, they try not to fall behind on any of their daily work. A line of spinning wheels stands at attention in the shade beneath the west wall of the monastery, while a phalanx of butter churns guards the entrance. The handful of men who came along while the rest remained behind to carry on with the farming busies itself stabling the horses, while a pack of the youngest children roam the grounds, exploring this new place.

Joan helps her mother with the cooking as well as she can, but drops a whole platter of bread, and must be continually prodded to resume chopping the vegetables. She looks anxiously around at the smallest sound or the least sign of movement.

"Do not worry," Isabella tells her. "No enemy will be able to sneak up on us here," but you guess that she's really seeking a glimpse of you and Catherine.

That night, she volunteers to stand watch.

"In truth, it would be a help," the men tell Isabella. "We would like to have three shifts of four, but there are only eleven of us. She won't be alone at any time, and it will save one of us having to watch twice."

Joan is assigned the south side of the island for the first watch of the night. You stand with her at dusk, watching the waters of the river flow past you into the deepening dark. She seems distracted no longer, but calm, thoughtful. With one hand, she holds the spear that she insisted she be issued. (For the other guards also bear them.) Her other hand hangs loose by her side.

Half way through the watch, the voice of Catherine adds itself to the murmur of the river.

"So, my dear child. You have had time to think about what God is calling you to. Does it still distress you?"

"No."

"And will you accept the charge that has been laid upon you?"

For a moment, brief and yet packed with whole histories of the world that might come to be, you hear only the sighing of the river and the buzz of insects in the night. Then Joan says simply, "Yes."

No English attack materializes and the villagers return to Domrémy the very next day. Your regular routine of life resumes for a time, but under the cloud of knowledge that it can't last. You're reminded of this almost every day when Catherine appears with more information for Joan about the road she must some day travel. The litany of cities and military strongholds bewilders you: the twelve towers of Orléans and the walls of Beaugency; the way from Chinon to Rheims, and the encampment at Margny.

Joan does her farm work and housework and diligently absorbs Catherine's instruction. All her time outside of those activities she spends in the church, no longer even idling alone in the meadows like she used to, much less playing with her brothers or the other children. You feel a strange unease watching her life narrow with purpose in this way.

One morning, Isabella asks her to stay behind after the rest of the family has gone out to the fields. They sit at the table, where Isabella looks smiling upon her daughter's curious face.

"Once upon a time," she finally begins, "there lived a girl in the valley of the Meuse who was the kindest, bravest, most loving and most devout child the region had known in many generations. She was obedient and hard working at home, and a joy to the local priest. She gave all that she had to the poor, and visited the sick, and gave her help gladly to anyone who needed it. Often (though she didn't realize her mother saw this) she would sneak off to the church to pray, finding it impossible to be away from that sacred place for the whole week between one Sunday and the next.

"While this girl was growing up in her small village, a boy only two years older walked the streets of Toul, not far away. Even as a young child, he was the most valuable helper his father had in his work as a carpenter, even though he often went off on his own to visit the sick or to help some friend or neighbor in need, or to pray by himself in the church.

"As the boy continued to grow in strength and grace, his elders began speaking with him about becoming a priest. Everyone believed that he could do great good in this way. However, he finally decided to serve God through the common life of the world, by marrying and raising children and following his father's footsteps as a builder of strong places to house the lives of the people.

"Now, as it happened, the mothers of these two children had almost as much in common with each other as their children did. They had both made pilgrimage to Rome, for example. In fact, that is how they met, years ago, before either of them had any children.

"In those days, they would never have guessed that they would come to live so close to each other, and that they would raise children so perfectly suited to one another, and that they would meet again by accident one day while accompanying their husbands on business in Greaux.

"On that day, they rejoiced in each other's happiness, and in God's provision, and in the future happiness of their children, whose names were Joan of Domrémy – and Etienne of Toul."

She exhales a sigh of satisfaction and looks expectantly at Joan, who has lowered her gaze.

"Mama," begins Joan haltingly, "I do not wish – I cannot marry – this boy."

"But you have not even met him! I have arranged for the two of us to visit Toul in a few weeks, and –"

"Mama," begins Joan again, "I cannot marry him."

"Joan, I know what you are thinking, but you must trust me. I had long thought that it would be difficult to find a husband that would be your match. In fact, I have had to put a stop to two or three ventures by your father already. I have often feared it might be impossible to find the right person for you, but Joan, I believe God may have provided him!

"Nevertheless, I am not asking you to marry him, but merely to meet him. Your father has agreed that you should not be forced to marry anyone against your wishes, so there will be no harm in taking a pleasant trip to Toul."

"Mama, I *cannot* marry!"

Isabella looks more closely at her daughter, whose face is now divided by two lines of tears.

"Joan, what do you mean? Are you thinking about becoming a nun?"

"There is a call I must answer. Perhaps it will involve holy orders, perhaps not. All I know is that I won't be able to marry until it is fulfilled. I cannot tell you what it is. *You* must trust *me!*"

Isabella Romée sits back in her chair, her face a study in wonder.

Freeman Ng

"I thought the days were over when God could surprise me like this! Very well, I will trust you. How can I not? I will find a way to explain things to your father, and I will send word to my friend that we will not be visiting. But I hope you will not mind if I ask her to check back with me first, should she find another possible match for her Etienne in the future."

Joan darts around the table to lay her head on her mother's lap.

"I hope, truly I hope, that I will be able to please you better then."

That afternoon after finishing her farm work, Joan goes out by herself to the meadow where you first met her. She doesn't dance, but walks straight to a great oak tree that stands alone in the center of the clearing and begins to climb it. The butterflies gather around her, but she soon leaves them behind. She quickly reaches the main branching of the trunk and chooses a path that leads almost straight up, moving with assurance toward the very top of the tree. The branches she clings to grow thinner and thinner until you're sure she must come crashing down to earth at any moment, but she rests upon them as securely as if she were herself a butterfly, and soon pokes her head out from the tree's crown.

From there, you can see all of Domrémy. The homes and the village church in one direction, the fields in another, and beyond the fields, the river. She stays up there for the rest of the afternoon, watching her fellow villagers at work in the fields or moving about the village. When some of her friends come running into the meadow, she doesn't reveal her presence, but only watches them at their play. At one point, her friend Marie is being chased by the others and cries out, "Fairy dance!" apparently changing the game in mid pursuit. The others tumble into one another trying to decel-erate into the graceful sweeping steps that she then leads them in.

"Ha!" laughs Joan, but they don't hear her below.

Soon, the meadow is deserted again and the view begins to be swallowed up by dusk. Then you hear the voice of her mother call-ing her in to supper, and she climbs back down the tree and returns to the house.

"Quickly, we must go! Leave it! LEAVE IT!"

The blackness of night is broken by the crazily swinging light of a lantern and cries from the darkness beyond.

"The oxen! We must take them!"

"Where is Kate? Katie!"

Moments earlier, you were strolling with Catherine down a shady side street in the residential area of Antioch on a bright summer morning, when she jerked her head up as if at a trumpet blast, told you, "Comfort her!" and with a raised hand sent you instantly to this place, which you realize now is Joan's house, in an uproar of panic in the middle of the night.

"Katie! Katie!" her mother cries.

"I have her," replies a calm voice. "I sent Jacquemin to harness the oxen; I will go and help him now. Jean and Pierre are loading the wagon and will meet us by the gate."

The lantern is swung around and its light falls upon the face of Joan.

"We should take the crest, too," she declares. "It is our heritage, and we may need the swords."

Her father looks at her open-mouthed, then blurts out, "Quickly!"

Joan and her sister carefully roll the swords of Arkon into the banner and bring them out to the waiting wagon. The night is filled with the shouts of the villagers and the light of lanterns and torches flying this way and that. A man on horseback thunders past the gate, followed by a group of families hastening along on foot.

"The English!" cries Kate, and the passing group pauses to look in the direction she points. A line of tiny lights snakes down from the hills.

Now you understand. The village must have received warning of an attack by the English, and are fleeing to their island refuge. The group on the road cries out in dismay and, dropping some of their things, begins to break into a wild run.

34   Freeman Ng

"Fear not!" cries Joan, and they stop in their tracks.

"If the English are only just now coming down from the hills, it will take them another two hours to reach us, for they will find themselves descending into the marshes. In less time than that, we will be safe on the Isle. The only danger now is that you will harm yourselves in mad flight. Go swiftly, but calmly. Make sure all your family and friends are accounted for. Go!"

Even in their fear, many murmur in astonishment at the commanding presence of this girl who grew up in their midst. They resume their flight, but in a calmer and more orderly way.

"Papa and Mama will be out soon," she tells her sister and her brothers. "Wait for them here while I go help Jacquemin with the oxen."

She finds her eldest brother almost done harnessing the last ox and sends them out to join the others. Then she's finally alone, and you take the opportunity to deliver your latest message for her, though it's clearly as unneeded as your first.

"Joan, take comfort," you say.

To your surprise, her body is wracked by a single great sob! All the strength seems to melt from it as she nearly collapses against one of the pens.

"I can't do it!" she cries. "I can't!"

"Don't cry!" you beg, but don't know what else to say. All Catherine told you was, "Comfort her," giving you no additional information to relay. You can't assure her that all will be well. You can only say, "Be comforted, Joan, by the love of God that holds you."

She takes one deep breath, and then another. She takes another, standing up straighter each time and blinking the tears out of her eyes. The voice of her father, still edged by panic, sounds from the direction of the gate. She looks up at you and replies, "And the voice of God that guides me."

We are not merely messengers, but friends and fellow travelers with those to whom we are sent.

"Yes," you assent, and then add, though you don't know if it will be permitted, "I will go with you to the refuge, and will not leave you until you have returned safe to your home."

On the road, you finally hear her sing again, only it's no child's ditty, but a song you've occasionally heard harvesters sing in the fields. She leads the other children through the verses, distracting them from their fears. Eventually, many of the adults join in. As the caravan stretches out among the trees, it comes to resemble a band of picnickers or jolly travelers more than a ragtag of frightened refugees fleeing for their lives. Light from their torches and lanterns illuminates the forest canopy above them. Their singing fills the night, clearing the way before them of all danger.

> *Let every good fellow now join in a song,*
>   *Vive la compagnie!*
> *Success to each other and pass it along,*
>   *Vive la compagnie!*
>
> *Vive la vive la vive l'amour!*
> *Vive la vive la vive l'amour!*
> *Vive l'amour, vive l'amour,*
> *Vive la compagnie!*
>
> *Come all you good fellows and join in with me,*
>   *Vive la compagnie!*
> *And raise up your voices in close harmony,*
>   *Vive la compagnie!*
>
> *Vive la vive la vive l'amour!*
> *Vive la vive la vive l'amour!*
> *Vive l'amour, vive l'amour,*
> *Vive la compagnie!*
>
> *With friends all around us we'll sing our glad song,*
>   *Vive la compagnie!*
> *We'll banish our troubles, it won't take us long,*
>   *Vive la compagnie!*

Freeman Ng

Vive la vive la vive l'amour!
Vive la vive la vive l'amour!
Vive l'amour, vive l'amour,
Vive la compagnie!

As the villagers emerge from the wood and catch sight of their island refuge, they break into cheers and begin jogging down to the bridge. Joan continues marching at a steady pace, allowing the others to pass her by until she forms the rearguard of the procession, still singing the song, but all by herself now:

Should time or occasion compel us to part,
      Vive la compagnie!
These days shall forever enliven our heart,
      Vive la compagnie!

Vive la vive la vive l'amour!
Vive la vive la vive l'amour!
Vive l'amour, vive l'amour,
Vive la compagnie!

The refuge at the Isle is much more crowded this time. Every inch of the old monastery – the rooms, the chapel, and even the passageways – is occupied by sleeping families. The stables are packed to overflowing with horses, so that some of them have to be left outdoors with the oxen. No one, on two legs or four, has much room to move around, except for the children, who clamber freely among, around, and sometimes over the piles of bundled flesh or food. Joan navigates through the press with a purpose, seeking out each of her young friends, as well as the elderly priest.

"Father, I want to thank you for your service to us in the church. You have been a good shepherd to me."

"Why, Joan!" cries the frail old man. "You have been such a joy that *I* should thank *you*! Many years ago, when I decided to join the order, my own priest told me that once in a lifetime, if we are fortunate, a parishioner comes along that fulfills the promise of all that we try to do in the faith. For many years, I did not believe him. Then, as I grew older, I began to hope that he was right. In recent years, as I saw my own retirement approaching, I have longed to be granted that justification of every priest's life. And now, I will depart in peace."

In a corner of the kitchen, she tracks down her friend Marie.

"Joan! I'm so glad to see you! Some mess, huh? Do you think the English are really attacking this time?"

"I do. We saw them coming down from the hills."

"Perdition take them! What do you think they will do to the village?"

"I don't know. I only hope everybody got away safely."

"I hope life will return to normal before spring. It will be my last spring in Domrémy, you know. You must dance with us around the maypole this year! I miss seeing you dance."

A tear runs down one of Joan's cheeks, unnoticed by her friend.

"I miss it, too. I promise that I will dance with you indeed, if I am here in the spring."

"If?"

She turns to look at Joan.

"What's wrong? What do you mean by *if*? Are you going away?"

"I think so. I am not sure when, but I think it must be soon."

"Joan! Are you marrying Etienne after all? That would be wonderful! You will beat me. He wanted to marry you in the fall, didn't he?"

"Yes."

"Well, then you are excused from the maypole dance! I will miss you, but then I'll be married myself not too long after. Imagine! By this time next year, we will both be married. Maybe we'll even be pregnant!"

"You will be a good mother," says Joan.

Her friend straightens a little, takes a deep breath, and says thoughtfully, "I believe I will."

They stand together in silence for several minutes, gazing, it

Freeman Ng

seems, at sights beyond the walls of the crowded room. Then Marie speaks again.

"Are you frightened?"

"Yes."

"My cousin was married last year. She told me she was terrified at first, thinking that her life was coming to an end, but it turned out that the old life only ended for a new life to begin. She went from life as a child to life as a wife. Then she went from life as a farmer in Domrémy to life as a weaver in Greaux. Then from life with just her and her husband to life with child, then life as a mother.

"'*Life* is full of *lives!*' she told me. We will never come to the end of them!"

The activity within the refuge has been slowly abating. Lanterns and candles are beginning to be put out. Joan says her goodbyes to her friend and returns to where her family is sleeping. She curls herself into the niche between her father and her mother and falls instantly into a sleep without dreams.

The next morning, the villagers receive word that the English have moved past Domrémy in the direction of the large city of Vaucouleurs, and venture forth from their refuge. As they come within sight of the village, cries of dismay ripple through their ranks. Domrémy lies in ruins. Thin columns of smoke spiral up everywhere from burned homes, the fields are ashen desolations, and the unmoving forms of the animals that were left behind dot the terrain.

When you reach the village, you discover that it was not only animals that failed to escape. The blacksmith's wife shrieks; her husband lies dead in the street, a sword in his hand and his body pierced with arrows. A crowd gathers around the doors of the church, where one of the assistants to the priest, a young man who was planning to enter the priesthood himself, was run to ground. A woman staggers from an old storehouse, her clothing tattered and bloodied.

Despair thickens the air, slowing your movements until you feel like you're wading neck deep through dark waters. Then a wave of horror coming from the direction of the burned fields washes over you so powerfully you almost lose your footing. It's accompanied by an inarticulate, almost animal cry, "Agh! Agh!" The villagers pay no heed, submerged in their own fathoms of grief. You make your slow way toward the source.

It's Joan.

She kneels in the ash of the barley field with her head bowed over something she holds in her hands, a blackened branch or rag of clothing. What could it have been, that it should provoke such darkness of heart? Then you get closer and see it for what it is: the charred limb of a child! You come softly up behind the bent, trembling figure of the girl in your charge, wishing you could speak to her, not knowing what you would say.

A shimmer in the air catches your eye, and Catherine stands before you. You stumble over to her and bury your face in her chest. She holds you firmly, but when you look up into her eyes, you see they are fixed on Joan.

"Catherine!" cries the child of Domrémy. "When will my time come? When will France be freed?"

"Now," says Catherine. "The time is now."

Freeman Ng

The Gates of Vaucouleurs

"No! Absolutely not!"

Joan's father stands at the kitchen table, his arms crossed. Her mother sits across from him with Joan beside her.

"But Papa," says Joan, "Auntie's time is coming soon, and Uncle Durand has already said that I can stay with them and help."

"No, it – it is too dangerous."

"No more dangerous than Domrémy," counters Isabella. "Less so, if anything. The garrison is right there."

"We need her *here*! We have an entire village to rebuild. Durand and Jeannette will be fine. They will have plenty of help from their neighbors."

"It won't be the same. Jeannette came here to help me through the birth of all our children. At such a time, a woman wants *family* to be near."

Jacques sighs and turns away. You don't understand why he's so set against this, but then, Joan's desire to visit her aunt in Vaucouleurs also puzzles you. Two weeks have passed since the day the villagers returned to their burned homes and Joan received, and supposedly accepted, her call to go to aid of the Dauphin, but she has done nothing about it so far, and now she wants to go off and care for her pregnant aunt for who knows how much longer. You find yourself agreeing with Jacques when he says tightly, "This is not a good time."

"Joan," says Isabella, "Go do your chores now."

Joan goes to the door, then turns.

"Father, forgive me. I will do as you say."

When she's gone, he sits with a huff of impatience and glares at his wife, but she reaches across the table to lay a hand on his.

"Jacques," she says in a softer voice, "I think we should find a reason for *all* the younger children to go to Vaucouleurs for a time. Not only because they will be safer there, but because it is not good that they should see their village in ruins like it is now. Let them go for a month, until we can make it look more like their home again."

He bows his head, and then nods.

"You are right, as always. I'll speak to the elders today and we will make arrangements."

She squeezes his hand.

"You are a good doyen to the village, and a good father to Joan."

"God grant it may be so," he says, looking earnestly into her eyes.

Isabella goes to tell Joan the good news and you make to follow her, but just as you reach the door, Jacques pounds his fist decisively on the kitchen table behind you and calls out, "Jacquemin!"

There's no answer for several seconds and he calls again, "Jacquemin!"

Pierre and Jean poke their heads out of the children's room.

"He has already gone out to the fields, Papa. We were on the way ourselves, but did not want to disturb your – discussion."

Jacques smiles grimly.

"Sit. You are good sons. I should tell you this as well."

The two younger boys sit at the table across from their father.

"Joan wishes to go to Vaucouleurs, she says to be with your Aunt Jeannette. I fear there may be more to it. Listen…" He lowers his voice and his sons lean in closer. "Do you remember the refugee from Orléans? The night he slept here, I had a fearful dream. A band of French soldiers retreated before an English army many times its size. They came to a bridge that led to the gates of a walled city and began crossing over it to safety, but their leader remained behind to serve as the rearguard. She wore a golden doublet over her armor, and held aloft a great standard embroidered with angels and fleurs-de-lis. Almost she escaped! But before they could all pass into the city, the bridge was raised and the gates shut. She was trapped outside the walls with only a few of her men by her side."

His sons give one another puzzled looks, and Pierre asks, "*She?*"

Their father only looks back at them, a pointed expression on his face. Then their eyes widen in understanding.

"She ordered her remaining men to flee, but once again, rode at the rear to defend their retreat. An English foot soldier caught hold of her robe and pulled her down, and before she could remount, their horsemen reached her and cut off her escape. They thundered around her, shouting in triumph and threatening her with…the horrible things they were going to do to her. I caught glimpses of her between the circling riders – her face was calm and she held her sword raised high into the air – and then she was lost to my sight."

The three of them sit in silence. You are amazed. What could have prompted such a nightmare, on the very night you told Joan about her martial destiny? Did Jacques somehow *overhear* your communications that night? You'll have to ask Catherine about this – and be more careful when you speak to Joan in the future.

"Maybe it was only a dream, but it was all so clear. I believe it was a warning from God. Joan is planning to run off to fight the English! I have dreamed it twice more since then. And now she seeks to go to Vaucouleurs."

"The garrison!" exclaims Jean.

You didn't think of that. What, after all, were you expecting Joan to do? Politely ask her parents for permission to join the

French army? Now you see that she has in fact spent the past two weeks formulating a plan. You admire her ingenuity, though it seems her father has seen through it.

He snaps his fingers. "I have it! Jean, Pierre, you will go to Vaucouleurs as well. Do not be ashamed to be sent away with the younger children. I am putting you in charge of them; it will be an honor. But I want to you watch Joan especially. Make sure she does not try to sneak off to the garrison. Make sure she has no contact with the soldiers there."

"We will, Papa. We will."

They get up from the table. The boys prepare to go out to their farm work. Jacques lays his hands on their shoulders, something you've never seen him do before.

"You are good sons. If I knew for sure that your sister was going to suffer the fate I dreamed, I would rather kill her myself with my own hands. Do you understand?"

They nod gravely and go on out the door.

Within a week, the arrangements are made. All the younger children with kin in Vaucouleurs will go to stay with them for a month, and those without are placed with other families who agree to help. Three wagons full of children line up on the road one bright morning. Jean and Pierre ride at the head of the group, with a couple of men taking up the rear. Jacques stands by his sons, with a hand on the neck of one of their horses.

"Stay on the main road," he tells them, "and stop at least once to water the horses. Keep a sharp eye out, not just for the English, but for robbers."

He glances back at the lead wagon, where Joan stands at the front of the wagon bed, peering down the road ahead. He comes around to the side of Jean's horse so that only the boys can see his face.

"I dreamed about her again last night, in a dark prison cell, with shackles on her wrists! I felt their weight. When I woke, I was chilled through and my body ached, as if I had been lying upon cold stone indeed, though it was not far into the night and the room was still warm.

"Watch her! Do not let her so much as come within sight of the garrison or any of its people."

The journey to Vaucouleurs is uneventful except for one incident. As Jean and Pierre steer the caravan to one side of a branching in the path, Joan calls out for them to stop.

"We must go to the right in order to cross the river," she tells them.

"The ford is to the left," says Pierre.

"And how would you know, anyway?" adds Jean. "You have never been this way. We came last year with Papa."

She shrugs.

"I don't know about any ford. I only know that if we go that way, we won't cross the river."

"How do you know?" asks Pierre with genuine curiosity, but Joan doesn't answer.

"Let's go," says Jean. "The men will start wondering what we're about."

"Joan," says Pierre. "We'll just go the usual way, and then we'll see, okay?"

She smiles and bows assent.

"It's all right," Jean shouts to the others. "We are proceeding!"

They take the left path to the ford, but when they get there, find the river risen above the roots of the trees by the bank, and the water rough with turbulence.

"Did we come the wrong way after all?"

"No," says Jean. "This is the right place, but the water is higher and swifter than before."

The men join them at the river's edge.

"This will be the runoff from the winter rains. Some years, it comes more heavily than others."

"Can we still cross?" asks Pierre.

"I have taken wagons across when it has been worse," says one man, "but not wagons full of children."

"I think we could try without too much risk, but it is up to you," says another to the boys. "You are the bosses."

"We will cross," declares Jean.

With Jean and Pierre leading the way on horseback, the first wagon descends into the current, which churns briskly around its wheels. Further in, the water gutters along the wagon bottom, sending out alarmingly loud, gurgling rasps. By the time the second wagon enters the water, the first is as deep as it will get, with its wheels almost entirely in the water and its left side buffeted by the swift flow that crashes up against it, sending up a perpetual spray that soon soaks its passengers.

The children in the creaking wagon bed begin to cry out in distress.

"Jean, I think we should turn back!" shouts Pierre.

"We can't! What would we do? Go back to Domrémy?"

"The children are too frightened, and the wagon doesn't look like it's holding up very well. Imagine when all three are fully in the water!"

Jean frowns, then raises a hand to halt the convoy. He goes back to discuss the situation with the other men. Finally, they decide to abandon the effort.

The second wagon is not too far in yet, so it's easy enough to turn it around and drive it directly back onto the bank. When they try turning the first, however, it rocks and tips from the force of the current, and the children scream in terror despite Joan's efforts to calm them. They finally have to pull it out backward with ropes, with two men wading chest deep on either side of the horses to calm them.

"We will have to wait it out," says one of the men.

"We'd wait long," says another. "It will probably get worse before it gets better."

"We could take the children across on individual horses," suggests Jean.

"That would mean many trips, many chances for an accident."

"What if we went back to the fork and took the rightward path up river?" asks Pierre.

There's a pause. Jean scowls at his brother, who keeps his attention fixed on the other men. They mostly shrug and give each other puzzled looks, but one of the wagon drivers, the oldest man in the group, slowly nods his head.

"That could work!" he says. "The rest of you will not remember, but we used to ford the river there. It is farther away and a much longer crossing and that is why we gave it up, but being wider, the water might be calmer there just now."

So it's decided. Jean returns to his horse muttering to himself. Pierre stands alone for a moment looking with a little half-smile at the lead wagon where Joan sits playing some game with the other children.

The party reaches Vaucouleurs late because of the detour, but all the host families are still waiting for them by the road and swiftly carry off the children to their appointed homes. Joan and her brothers arrive last of all at the home of their uncle.

"A quick supper for you all, and then bed," says Jeannette. Joan jumps up to help.

"Tell me more about the ford," says Durand to the boys, and you catch Jean discreetly shaking his head *No* to Pierre. Sure enough, they say nothing about Joan's foreknowledge of the way, but only detail the conditions of the river and the prospects for safely crossing it at each of the two possible places.

You worry more about other crossings that must be made.

While they eat, you slip out of the house and into the dark streets of the city. Sweeping your gaze across the horizon of house-tops, you spot the very top of a castle tower to the north and begin making your way toward it. As you zigzag through the unfamiliar ways, the tower grows taller, and battlements appear beneath it. Soon, the entire castle fills your sight, rising black against the night. It's a mountain of stone eclipsing the stars, the most imposing structure you've seen yet in this land of thatched homes and flowery meadows. For the first time, you understand that what you're sending Joan into is no small skirmish or village raid like the one that struck Domrémy, but War, perhaps even on the scale of wars in your own time, involving thousands of men and terrible engines of destruction.

What difference can one girl make in such a titanic conflict?

You come to the castle gates and find the guards stationed there alert and well disciplined, and the grounds kept up impeccably. This gives you hope that the lord of this place is a right thinking man who will receive Joan in good faith when she eventually comes to him.

"It does not matter whether you are observing a family or a company of laborers, a troupe of actors or an army," Catherine once told you. "You will see reflected in how they carry themselves as a body, the mind and character of their leader. How could it be otherwise?"

Just within the walls, in the first hall you enter, you find several of the officers of the place sitting to a late supper.

"Good victuals tonight," says one of them breezily. "I fear that when we all become English, the food will sorely disappoint!"

This shocks you beyond all measure, but it only seems to disturb one other man in the room.

"What is that?" he demands.

The others keep their attention fixed firmly on their plates.

"I do not say it is a certainty," explains the first. "For all I know, their cooks will prove our betters as well, and we will wonder why we clung so long to our poor land and its fruits. Come, I apologize if my pessimism offended you. I will say now that I am sure the English food will be like the sweet manna of Heaven!"

The second man rises to his feet. He's older and stouter than the first, and carries himself with a stiff authority. His uniform, well worn with the marks of battle, is nevertheless spotlessly clean, and bears elaborate purple insignia that none of the other uniforms display. He looms above his antagonist, who continues to lean back in his chair regarding him coolly.

"This is treasonous talk! What kind of officer –"

"Ease off, Bertrand!" says one of the other men. "You are new here, and do not know Captain de Metz and his history. He has fought for France from the time he was a boy. He is the most decorated officer serving here! It is better to laugh than to despair."

Here he turns and gives a grudging nod to the captain, who bows subtly and solemnly in return from his seated position.

"Why do either?" presses the older man. "The war is not yet lost. Can not God our Father grant us victory over the mightiest foe?"

The captain's reply is gentle, but still tinged with a faint tone of mockery.

"Is not God the father of all?"

"Of course!"

"That is the great difficulty," sighs de Metz. "If he is father of all, he is father to the English as well. They look to him as fervently as we do; only it is their prayers that are answered. Perhaps it would go better for us if God were not so involved, after all."

Unsettled by that exchange, you press on further into the castle, through the loud clanging of pots and rushing water in the kitchens, into the silence of the armory where a couple of men stand lugubriously rearranging the crossbows hanging on one wall, and out to an open courtyard, where you come across an officer handing some papers to a page and saying, "For the Commander, at once."

You follow the boy to a door where you both pause for a moment, unsure whether to enter, for angry shouting emanates from within.

"You think me a coward? Is that it? I say you are fools!"

Other voices murmur for a while, and then the first voice bursts out in anger again.

"Do not speak of the English 'attackers'! They were a dozen drunken rogues who had just burned down an undefended village. *We* were a *hundred* drunken rogues! Of course we beat them! You think it was our courage? You think it was our honor? Our favored place in the eyes of God? It was our numbers!"

There is silence then, and the page takes the opportunity to knock on the door.

"Come!" growls the voice.

When the door opens, it reveals an enormous, powerfully built man, dressed in simple fatigues but wearing the unmistakable aura of Command. He sits at a round table with several other men whom you guess must be his advisors. They watch in silence as he reads the message delivered by the page.

"Numbers!" he declares, brandishing the paper before them. "Paris, Beaugency, Orléans. On and on. There is now no place we can strike where we will not face thousands of defenders. Mark: not dozens, not hundreds, but thousands!"

He looks from man to man. None of them meet his gaze.

"But sir Robert..."

It's the voice of the page!

"Sir, you have never lost a battle to the English. They cannot defeat you!"

The commander glares at the lad, then sighs and answers in a gentle voice.

"That is very true, my boy. Very true. Baudricourt the Victorious, some call me, and I have earned it! But now I will tell you the secret of *how* I earned that name: By arranging to always have the greater numbers. *That* is how you win. And it is possible even when you are much weaker than your enemy: through good intelligence or clever maneuvers or sometimes by simple good fortune. For what matters is who can bring the most force to bear on a single battle, then and there. However, beyond a certain point, this is no longer possible at all. Maneuver all you like, you will still be outnumbered wherever you go. That is where we stand today."

The advisors sit in silence. The page bows his head. You cannot imagine how Joan will persuade such a man to send her to the rescue of France.

"Go to bed," says Baudricourt to the boy. "All of you! My head aches. Boy, first bring me a bottle of wine, then go."

All through your long walk back through the dark streets of the city, you're haunted by the vision of Sir Robert's scowl and Captain de Metz's smirk. You compare them with the face of the nobleman Bertrand livid in righteous indignation, or even with the placid but shrewd simplicity of Durand Laxart's. France is a nation that teeters between these possibilities: despair and hope, malaise and action, skepticism and belief.

When you reenter the house, Jean and Pierre sit whispering at the kitchen table.

"Well then, how do you explain it?"

"I don't. I don't have to! I don't have to explain every coincidence."

"I am only saying that maybe God wants her to join the army. Maybe that's what the dream was really about."

Jean brushes the thought away with a wave of his hand.

"Maybe God wants this and maybe God wants that! If He wished for me to personally escort Joan to the Dauphin himself, He would only have to command it, and I would obey. But He has not – unless you have heard Him speak and have not told me? Then this is all I know: there is no doubt what *Papa* wishes: to keep her from it."

Pierre relents and they retire to their beds. You go to sit by Joan, who will dream that night of the gates of the castle of Vaucouleurs, which she has not yet seen.

In the morning, Durand speaks with Joan and her brothers at the breakfast table.

"I am glad the three of you are here. It is not just Jeannette who needs help, but the business, since she has been unable to do her share of the work for quite a while now. So, you boys will help me in the storehouse today, and Joan, you will take the horse to the blacksmith to be shod."

The boys look at each other in alarm. You are amazed. Will it really be this easy?

"Uncle!" says Pierre. "Maybe Jean or I should take the horse."

"No," replies Durand. "We will be moving heavy loads around, no work for a girl."

"But, but Joan is a poor rider," offers Jean.

"I'm better than you!" she retorts.

"It might not be safe for her to ride into town all by herself," says Pierre. "Maybe one of us could go with her."

"Nonsense!" says Durand. "We don't live in the sticks like you. Vaucouleurs is perfectly safe. The garrison is right here!"

At that, the boys are fairly squirming.

"Uncle," says Joan. "I noticed during our journey that both of their horses also needed shoeing. Perhaps they could ride with me, and we could have all three done at once."

"Ah," says Durand. "Well, in that case, go ahead. Tell the smith to put it all on my account."

"Thank you, uncle! Thank you!"

The boys' sudden gush of gratitude surprises their uncle, who doesn't realize they're really thanking Joan, or God, or simple Good Fortune. You don't understand yourself why Joan would rescue them like this when the path to the garrison lay so open to her.

"Don't mention it," he finally replies. "It is but a trifle, and you are family."

Riding slowly down the street, Joan looks fondly at her brothers.

"I am so glad you're coming with me."

"Not as glad as we are!" says Pierre.

"I did not want to go alone, and I wanted to be able to say farewell to at least part of my family."

The boys halt their horses.

"What? What are you talking about?"

"You will have to bear a message to Mama and Papa and the others. Even if I were allowed to return home first to say goodbye,

Freeman Ng

it would be foolish. They would never let me out of the house again!"

"Joan, what are you saying?"

"You know why I came to Vaucouleurs! And I know that Papa has told you to stop me. I am sorry for the worry I will cause him and Mama, and I hope they won't blame you too much, but I have no choice. God has called me to fight the English."

"Well, you can't!" cries Jean. "We won't allow it!"

"How will you stop me? In two seconds, I am going to put my horse into a full gallop. You can pursue me if you like. You might risk pulling me off in mid gallop – *if* you can catch me! Or maybe you can persuade the soldiers at the garrison that they should not accept my service. I will not fight you, but will leave the outcome in God's hands."

"This is madness," pleads Pierre. "You can't just go like that!"

Jean makes a grab for the bridle of Joan's horse, but she is not caught off guard. She spurs her horse into motion and it flies out of a side gate in the city wall and then down a road that curves around the outside of the town to the castle at its north end.

"Joan! Stop! Come back at once!" cry her brothers, as they set out in pursuit.

It's a glorious morning. The sun glistens off Joan's hair as it streams behind her. She raises a fist into the air as if brandishing a sword. Her laughter floats back to her pursuers, and then her voice in song:

> *Vive la vive la vive l'amour!*
> *Vive la vive la vive l'amour!*
> *Vive l'amour, vive l'amour,*
> *Vive la compagnie!*

She reaches the gates of the castle just ahead of her pursuers. The man who comes out to meet her is the officer, Bertrand, whom you saw defending Hope and Faith the other night. He descends the two steps leading down from the entryway and sits on the middle step, so that his face comes level with hers.

"Good day, young lady. The guards tell me you wish to speak with Sir Robert."

"If he is the commander here, then yes."

"May I ask what it is you wish to say to him?"

"I am sorry," she replies after a pause, "but I must speak only with Sir Robert."

He raises an eyebrow and looks with greater interest at her face, grave with purpose.

"I'm afraid he cannot be disturbed right now. May I take a message to him?"

She glances behind her. Her brothers have gained the road leading up to the gates.

"Very well. But you must promise that you will not send me away, or allow me to be taken away, until he has received the message and answered it."

The nobleman lifts his gaze to take in the approach of the boys.

"Your . . . brothers?"

"Yes, sir."

She keeps her gaze fixed on his. He looks back into her eyes a moment, then nods to himself.

"Very well. I give you my promise, if you will promise to do as your brothers say afterward."

Her serious expression gives way to a wide smile.

"Yes, sir! After Sir Robert replies to my message, I will obey all those in authority over me, in accordance with their rank."

"Very good. Now, tell me your message."

She draws herself up. For the first time in your long involvement in her life, you realize that you're witnessing History, as if you could have been present when Romulus and Remus came to the seven hills of Rome that would be, or stood by Zacharias in the temple when Mary arrived to have her newborn Child blessed.

"I am Joan of Domrémy. I come in obedience to the command of God, who has told me that I must fight the English and promised that I will drive them from Orléans and see the Dauphin crowned our rightful king. I ask Sir Robert to send me to the Dauphin in Chinon so that I might begin my work."

Her listener gapes in astonishment.

"Joan! Joan! Come away from there!"

Jean and Pierre have reached the gates.

"Come away this instant!"

"Your lordship, we apologize. This is our sister. We forbade her to come, but –"

Standing, he raises a hand to silence them.

"Welcome to the castle of Vaucouleurs. I am Bertrand de Poulengy. If you will wait just a moment."

He turns and whispers to one of the guards. The man breaks into a laugh, then falters in the face of his superior's earnest expression. The two men whisper back and forth, with the guard sneaking frequent glances at Joan, and then the guard bows and retreats into the castle. Poulengy turns back to the children.

"We will not have long to wait. Come, let us sit in the shade."

Joan bows and places her hand in the crook of the arm he extends to her. He leads her to where some benches are arranged beneath a trellised cover, to one side of the castle gate. Jean and Pierre follow along behind, still breathing heavily from their mad pursuit and casting perplexed looks at one another.

"I like sitting here in the evenings especially," says Poulengy. "I can watch the sun set behind those hills. But it is probably not as pretty a sight as you can enjoy in every direction in Domrémy. What brings you to Vaucouleurs?"

"We're staying with our uncle Durand Laxart," says Pierre. "We came with other children of the village."

"Ah yes, I heard about that. I am sorry for your loss, but do not be discouraged. They will rebuild more swiftly than you can imagine. I have heard nothing but good about the men of your village."

"Our father is doyen," says Jean proudly.

"That is excellent! I am sure he is a good man. We need many more in these times. We must all do our part."

At that, all three glance at Joan, and the thread of the conversation is lost.

"Well," resumes Poulengy in a lower voice, "you have certainly come here on important business. Tell me, child, how is it that you are so sure God wishes you to fight the English?"

"The same way you are sure we are from Domrémy."

"Yes . . . but – I know that only because you told me. You might have lied. Now, God does not lie, but our imaginations might. How can you be so sure it is God who spoke to you?"

"I think you could tell if we were lying to you, for you are an honest man."

The nobleman sits back in astonishment.

"Pardon me, your lordship," interjects Jean, "but does it really matter why she thinks God spoke to her? It is simply impossible! How could a girl fight the English?"

Poulengy nods thoughtfully at that, but replies, "With God, all things are possible. If He chooses to deliver France by the sword of a girl, I will not oppose it, though I will never understand it. I am not God's counselor, but merely a soldier in His service. And if one truly came who could bring my king to his crown, man or woman, child or frail old man, how I would serve such a one! I would fight, I would die by his side!"

The face of Bertrand de Poulengy seems to shine with its own light in the shaded haven at the foot of the castle wall.

"These are dark times. Men have become discouraged. They have lost hope; they have lost faith. And yet, how big a miracle would it really be for them to regain their fervor?

"In the battle for Beaugency, my company became trapped in a crumbling tower outside the city. We were surrounded by the English, and no one thought we would survive the day. Then we saw, in the dying light that fell upon the nearby hills, the image of a cross! And we knew that God was showing us the way of escape.

"We stormed out of that tower, convinced utterly that our deliverance had come but must be seized with both hands. The startled English fell before us like wheat at the harvest. Indeed, had we thought to turn upon them in earnest battle, we might have retaken Beaugency then and there!"

Jean's face is now aglow as well.

"Have you fought in many battles?" he asks.

"I have indeed," replies Poulengy, and begins telling them more stories of his experiences in the war, with Jean frequently interrupting to ask more questions.

In the midst of a woeful account of the battle Agincourt ("more men perished on both sides that day than in any other battle of the war to this day") a page arrives with a reply from Sir Robert. Poulengy cuts short his narrative and unseals the letter.

Joan rises to her feet, her face solemn with expectation. Pierre darts over to her side and blurts out, "Good luck!" Jean does not reprimand him, but only looks in apprehension from him to her to their host.

Poulengy reads the note silently, frowning, then says, "I am sorry, Joan. Sir Robert will not see you."

She doesn't answer, doesn't move.

"Joan, do you hear me?"

She totters a little on her feet and reaches out for Pierre's support.

"That cannot be. There is some misunderstanding. Take him another message!"

"Joan!" says Poulengy firmly. He reads from the note: "Send her away, and tell her father to give her a sound beating."

Joan's face crumples. "Margaret! Catherine!" she whispers, and you shout back, "Joan! I'm here!" but she doesn't hear your voice.

"Joan," says Poulengy gently. "If God had intended for you to fight, he would also have informed the Commander, don't you think? Perhaps, then, it was not meant to be."

At that, she bursts into tears, collapsing fully into Pierre's arms.

"I am sorry, boys, but the Commander . . . he is a hard man. Listen, I am an esquire of the Dauphin, a noble of the royal court. Here in Vaucouleurs, I must bow to the authority of Sir Robert, but *outside* of Vaucouleurs, I perhaps outrank him. Therefore, when you return to your home in Domrémy, I overturn his command. Do not tell your father to beat her."

"We would not have, anyway," declares Pierre.

"Good. You are fine young men, men of honor. If *you* should ever – with your father's permission – wish to join the army . . ."

"Thank you, sir!"

"We should go now, sir."

They set Joan, still weeping inconsolably, on one of the horses and lead them back down the road, beating a slow retreat from the gates of the castle of Vaucouleurs.

The Maid at the Gates

Joan makes no further attempts to go to the garrison for the rest of her stay. She helps with the business. She takes over management of the household. She cooks and cleans and works diligently to ease the pregnancy of her aunt. Her brothers don't even bother watching her closely. Three weeks later, a healthy baby girl is born.

"Joan Laxart she will be christened! How do you like that?" asks Durand.

"I am honored," replies Joan, bowing her head.

In all her time in Vaucouleurs, she doesn't seem to receive any visits from Catherine or Michael, and you are given no messages for her yourself. Only once are you able to speak with her, a cold morning in the garden when she looks up from the weeding and cries out, "Margaret!" To your surprise, she dashes over to you, reaching out her arms. To your utter amazement, you feel her embrace when it comes! She holds you so tightly you can barely speak; you feel the wetness of her tears on your shoulder.

"I tried! I tried and they turned me away! I don't understand why, and I don't know what to do, and you never came, or Catherine!"

"I've been with you," you tell her, "only I couldn't speak."

"If I cannot reach the Dauphin, what will become of France?"

You don't know how to answer that, so you simply hold her, until your contact is broken and she is alone once more.

After the christening, the wagons return to collect the children of Domrémy.

"You three have been a godsend," says Jeannette to Joan and her brothers. "You are welcome here any time. You must visit often now so you can become good friends with your new cousin. We will be happy to have you."

Later that day, the caravan pulls into Domrémy. Parents converge on the wagons, lifting out their children to happy reunions. Jacques goes straight to Jean and Pierre.

"Well?" he asks.

Pierre swallows hard and begins to speak, but Jean cuts him off.

"Nothing happened. She made no move to run off, even when she would have thought the way was clear. We watched her the whole time, and she never even looked in the direction of the castle."

Jacques breathes a sigh of relief.

"It was just a dream, then, a nightmare because of the news from Orléans."

"Anyway," says Jean, "Even if she went to some garrison and offered to join, why would they take her?"

"You are right!" laughs his father. "I don't know why I was so worried. Come, let us get the girls home."

He moves off toward the wagons. Pierre looks gratefully at his brother.

"I thought about begging you not to tell Papa anything, but I didn't think you would agree."

"Why wouldn't I? She is my sister, too. I don't want to see Papa angry at her. And besides, she will never, ever try it again. That much is clear."

Freeman Ng

Back in the meadows of Domrémy, Catherine finally appears to Joan, in the place by a brook where most of their past history lessons took place. You sit next to Joan on a log, while Catherine stands before you with the rippling water behind her.

"I am truly sorry, Joan. I was given no foreknowledge that you would be turned away so rudely. But be of good cheer. It only means the way will be a little harder than we thought."

"The way seems impossible," says Joan. "That commander, Sir Robert, I do not think he will ever believe me. Perhaps I should go straight to Chinon."

"No. You made a good decision to begin in Vaucouleurs. It is the path ordained for you. And it will be easier the next time around. You have a friend now in the garrison, and you will gain others. Also –" Here she comes over and sits on the ground in front of you, and continues in a lower voice. "Also, an idea has begun to spread through the whole town that, as France was betrayed by the actions of a mother – the mother of Charles, who opened the door for the English by declaring that her son might be illegitimate, which she herself must know is not true! – so it shall be saved by a maid."

"A maid?" you ask.

"A girl who is pure," explains Joan.

"A virgin - like Joan," says Catherine.

"Therefore," she continues to Joan, "when you return to Vaucouleurs, you must announce your mission not just to those in the castle, but to the townsfolk, for they will be much more ready to believe you."

"How did such a story get started?" you ask.

Catherine smiles mischievously, so that you almost expect her to claim the credit herself, but instead, she says, "One of the guards from the castle gates! He heard all that was said between Joan and the nobleman who met you, and when he returned to his home between shifts of duty, he told his wife. She told a neighbor, who told another, and so on. And somewhere in the spreading of the story, someone put the idea of the girl together with the history of the woman, and it made a pattern that was pleasing and, to desperate people, compelling. So the pattern turned into a hope, and hope turned into prophecy!"

"Catherine!"

Joan rises shakily to stand before her.

"I cannot trick people into believing me," she says with great effort, "even for the sake of France. Even – even at the command of God. This rumor of the townsfolk, though it began with my appearance, really has nothing to do with me. It would be a lie."

She's right, of course. You wonder how you didn't see it yourself. But can Catherine really be proposing such a deceitful course of action? Could this really be the direction she received from Michael?

If Heaven were divided against itself, which side would you choose?

Catherine laughs and you're spared the dilemma. She reaches out her hands to take Joan's.

"Joan, my dear: this 'rumor' is also true prophecy! Do you think they come only from the mouths of oracles in smoky temples? And it is very much about you. It is yours to claim, and to fulfill!"

Harvest time comes and goes. You continue to speak to Joan in her rare breaks from the hard labor of the season. The messages, whether delivered by you or by Catherine, are always the same: Time is short.

As the family settles in for the winter, a tremendous restlessness grows in her. Her dreams are blurs of frantic physical activity: rumbling gallops across a bright green field, encased in armor and with a sword in hand; dashes across stark, muddy fields; leaps into the empty sky from dizzying heights. She seems to wake every morning more tired than when she went to bed the night before.

At the beginning of December, a lawsuit is filed against her by the boy in Toul who wanted to marry her, for breach of contract. She and Isabella tell the cleric investigating the case that it was only a possibility explored by the parents and that Joan herself never promised to abide by it. Joan confirms that she still doesn't wish to, and that satisfies the man.

"I am sorry you had to come all the way out here in such bad weather," says Isabella.

"Think nothing of it! It is my job. These cases are very common, and we only visit to make sure the girls are certain about their decisions. And your daughter certainly seems to know her own mind very well! However, if I may be so bold…"

He turns to Joan.

"My advice would be to think very carefully before rejecting the next marriage your parents propose. After all, you are 17 years old now. Time is running short!"

A few weeks later, you and Catherine are called into the presence of Michael again. You are given essentially the same message you've been delivering to Joan for months now, only this time with specific dates attached to it. You and Catherine walk through the streets of Antioch discussing it.

"Mid Lent!" you exclaim. "It's hard to believe."

"Well," replies Catherine. "Orléans has been under siege for almost five months now. Is it so unbelievable that it could fall within the next three? And if it does, all hope is lost indeed."

"But if time is so short, if time's been so short all along, why hasn't Michael told us how Joan is to get to Vaucouleurs? If she doesn't start soon, the worst of the winter will set in, and I don't see how she'll be able to travel to Vaucouleurs, much less to Chinon, under those conditions."

"Perhaps she will not be sent until the beginning of spring."

"Time will be almost out by then!"

"Have faith," says Catherine. "All lies in a passion of patience. When the time is right, Michael will show us the way, and we will reveal it to Joan."

You emerge in the barren wheat field of Domrémy at dusk. In

the distance, the voice of Isabella calls frantically, "Joan! Joan!"

"Something has happened!" cries Catherine.

You find Isabella at the door of the house, her face reddened by tears. Jacquemin and Jean run through the nearby meadows calling Joan's name as well. Jacques confers with the village elders about organizing search parties.

And Pierre?

"I know where he is!" you exclaim. "*He* knows where *she* is!"

"What?" says Catherine. "Where?"

You set off straightway toward the river, and catch up with Pierre a mile from the house, on the road to Vaucouleurs!

"Of course!" exclaims Catherine.

The two of you speed ahead of him, searching for the girl he pursues. When you get to the branching of the path that leads to the two possible fords, you take the right while Catherine goes to the left.

You find her – chest deep in the frigid, rushing water, fording the river on foot!

"Joan!"

She looks back at you and waves feebly. Just then, a surge in the current upends her. Her head briefly disappears, and then rears back out of the water, gasping for air. You fly immediately to her side.

Let me touch her again, you pray. *Let me hold her!*

When you reach out, your hands close on her cold flesh, but you are touched by wind and wave in turn. Water smashes into your face, blinding you, streaming into your mouth. You cough and sputter, fighting for breathe and balance, remaining upright only by clinging to Joan. For a few terrifying moments, you are as much the drowning girl as the rescuer, as the two of you fight to save each other from the violence of the waters.

"Joan, you must turn back!"

"I am already more than half way across!"

So you struggle on.

Once, you slip again and nearly pull Joan under with you.

I shouldn't have plunged in with her, you tell yourself. *Now we'll both drown, and she might have made it on her own!* However, in the next moment you save her from being carried off by the current, and then are saved by her again. Eventually, you drag each other onto the opposite bank. She stands shuddering violently, shedding water like a burst dam.

"What are you doing?" you demand.

"What God has commanded," she replies through clattering teeth.

"Your family is so worried!"

"I could not trust them with my intentions."

"Pierre guessed. He's following you."

"Pierre!" she cries affectionately. "We will wait. We will wait for him."

The two of you stand on the exposed riverbank, whipped by the wind. You long to return to the temperate nothingness of immateriality, but your touch seems to shield Joan a little from the cold, and so you stay by her. Fortunately, her brother soon appears on the opposite bank of the river.

"Pierre!" shouts Joan. "I am going to Vaucouleurs! Do not try to follow; I crossed the river only with God's help. Tell Mama and Papa that I have gone to – to visit Aunt Jeannette and Uncle Durand!"

Pierre stands there unspeaking for long moments while the river rushes by between them and the wind blows cold on its journey through the world. Then the faint sound of his voice comes floating over the waters:

"Vive la France! Vive la compagnie!"

That night, Durand Laxart and his wife sit at their kitchen table conversing in low tones.

"So, why did she come?"

"I don't know. The poor thing was too worn out to speak. She was asleep before I finished tucking her into the bed."

"Why would Jacques send her out into such weather, alone and on foot? She could have perished!"

Jeannette leans forward.

"Durand! Do you suppose she has had some kind of falling out with them? That she is running away from home?"

"Impossible."

She gives him a questioning look.

"They are good parents," he explains, "and good parents do not provoke their children. Joan is a good girl, and good girls don't run off without cause."

Jeanette leans back in her chair, crossing her arms but smiling.

"Surely it is not that simple!"

"People are what they are. It's why I only do business with good men. I may have lost income by refusing to deal with the untrustworthy, but I have never been cheated."

"How can you be so sure a man is good?"

"Oh, it is obvious!"

She looks at him with affection.

"You can recognize them so easily because you are such a good man yourself."

"Of course I am," he replies. "You would not have married me, otherwise."

After they go to bed, you slip out to make another visit to the castle. Over half a year has passed since Joan's first appearance there, plenty of time for the despair you saw in Sir Robert or the cynicism of that captain who sparred with Bertrand de Poulengy to poison the whole place, or for the nobility of men like Poulengy to cure it.

At first, the signs are good. The guards at the outer gates are as vigilant and well disciplined as they were before, and the grounds and outer halls well kept. You pass though the busy kitchen and the stillness of the armory and out into the open courtyard, where men stride briskly to and fro, as before. From that point on, though, things begin to change. As you approach Sir Robert's council room, you begin to encounter darkened passageways and empty rooms littered with debris. The air takes on a sour smell that increases until you reach the chamber door.

There, you pause as before. No sound comes from within, nor does any light seep out from beneath the door.

Maybe they've already gone to bed, you think, but then hear the crash of shattering glass inside the room and go quickly in. There, dimly lit by a few candles scattered around the room, Sir Robert sits by himself at the table, which is covered with wine bottles. He gropes among them and brings one to his lips. Finding it empty, he flings it away, smashing it against a wall.

The floor is littered with broken glass.

"Boy! BOY!!!" he cries. "More wine!"

He sings a sloppy, drunken song. To your surprise, it's the old litany of French cities, but with a preface you never heard sung in Domrémy:

> *Tell me friend, what doth remain*
> *Of the Dauphin's lost domain?*

> *Orléans, Beaugency,*
> *Notre Dame de Cléry,*
> *Vendôme, Vendôme!*

Are these truly the complete words of the song? If so, it is no joyful celebration, but a lament – perhaps even a taunt – over the diminished holdings of Charles. It's even out of date, for Beaugency and Cléry are now in English hands, with Orléans soon to follow.

You flee from that dark chamber, flying through the ghostly halls and unkempt rooms, but just as you pass through the outer walls of the castle, you hear the last sound you would have expected in this sad place: laughter, easy and assured, ringing out from the ramparts above you. You follow the sound until you come upon the irreverent Captain de Metz, who is walking along the battlements arm in arm with . . . Bertrand de Poulengy!

Have they become friends?

"Really, Jean, you are insufferable!" cries the latter, but with good humor.

"Think about it!" says de Metz. "Dinadan is the only knight who does not have or seek a lady. He's the one who empathizes and sympathizes, the one the others come to for consolation. In one story, he is bested in a tournament and forced to wear a dress!"

"Have you no respect for the old stories of Chivalry?"

Poulengy asks this in a jovial tone, but de Metz goes quiet. He stops and leans against a parapet, looking out into the night. Poulengy stands a little apart watching him.

"You mistake me entirely," says de Metz. "I have a great love for those stories. Tristan, the doomed gallant. Palomides and his hopeless Quest. Lancelot, the greatest knight in all the kingdom…

"Tell me, Bertrand, have you ever pledged your faith?"

"I have not yet married, if that is what you mean."

"No, I mean like the Knights of old, in service to a lord."

"Well, in a sense, certainly! As a nobleman of France –"

"I don't mean mere service to a cause or loyalty to your country. I mean your faith. Your heart!

> *Then laid his hands in the clasp of the King,*
> *And pledged him forever his breath and his strength.*

"So sang an old poet of Lancelot and Arthur. Not the best example, since Lancelot broke faith after all, but…Well. Once upon a time, I pledged my faith so. To Sir Robert."

"The Commander?"

You picture the broken man in the heart of the castle.

"He was not always as he is now. Once, he rode forth upon the singing of trumpets to repel the invader again and again, and I followed him. He fought ever in the forefront of the battle, in a way that commanders no longer do in these latter days, and I stood by his side. It is because of his valor that Orléans remained untaken as long as it did. But now the end has come, to all things."

He bows his head, a shadow framed by night, but the face of

Bertrand de Poulengy glows in the torchlight. He draws himself up and takes one step, formal and processional, toward his despairing friend.

"Orléans is not taken yet," he says.

De Metz turns, his face unreadable in the darkness.

"Some day," continues Poulengy, "I, too, will pledge my faith in the ancient manner. To my king, when he is crowned."

Jean de Metz smiles then, and there is only good will in his voice as he replies, "May you fare better than I did."

The next morning, Joan comes once more to the gates of the castle of Vaucouleurs. Standing on the steps to greet her is Bertrand de Poulengy.

"You are very welcome here, Joan! I am glad you have returned, for as France was betrayed by the actions of a woman –"

"So it shall be saved by a girl! Do you believe it, Sir Bertrand?"

"I do, and hope you will forgive me for my past doubt."

She cocks her head and asks, "What sign was it that convinced you?"

"No sign, but the example of a friend who is mighty in Faith."

A brilliant smile dawns upon her face. She takes a step toward him, formal and processional, and lays a hand on his arm.

"Then I tell you this: Before we are halfway through Easter, you and I - and your friend - will walk together out of the open gates of the free city of Orléans."

When Sir Robert sends back another dismissive note, Joan only laughs and tells Poulengy that she'll be back the next day. The next day, when the commander adds a few choice insults to his message, she shakes her head like a mother over a stubborn child.

"Woe to him who will not believe in God's salvation when it comes!" she murmurs.

Turning to Poulengy, she says, "Well, your lordship. I look forward to seeing you again tomorrow!"

"A moment, if you please. There is someone I would like you to meet. Will you wait while I go find him?"

"Is it the friend you spoke of, the man of great faith?"

"Yes, but I must explain: I did not mean that he believed in you. I do not think he even believes in God! But he is a man of honor who is devoted to the cause of France and the holiness of Truth."

"Then he does believe in me! I will rejoice to meet him."

Bowing, Poulengy retreats into the castle. Joan turns and speaks into the air.

"Margaret, are you there? This man will become one of my most devoted friends. When I am – parted from him, visit him in his solitude. His very life perhaps will be in your hands. You won't be able to speak to him, so you will have to use your wits. God will guide you."

Which man does she mean, and how can she see his future? Do Catherine or Michael sometimes speak to her without your being aware of it? The gates open and Poulengy emerges with his friend Jean de Metz in tow.

"Here she is, Jean, the girl I spoke of. The girl *they speak* of! The Maid who will deliver France."

De Metz smiles skeptically at his friend, then looks Joan up and down.

"A maid, are you? Tell me, my love, would it not it be easier for us to simply stop fighting for a king who does not wish to fight anyway, and to all become English?"

"Jean!" cries Poulengy, but Joan signals to him that it's okay.

"Believe me, my lord, I would rather not be here at all! For my place is by my mother's side, helping her spin, and out in the fields with my father and my brothers. But Orléans will fall by Easter unless help reaches it, and there is no help in the world that will prevail unless it comes from me. Therefore have I pledged myself to this task, to my last breath, to my uttermost strength, in fealty to that Lord whose commands cannot be refused."

As she utters the words "breath" and "strength", de Metz

recoils a little in surprise, but now he looks suspiciously at Poulengy.

"And which lord is this?" he asks Joan, while continuing to stare pointedly at his friend.

"God," she replies.

"Jean, it is true," says Poulengy. "I did not prepare her in any way to speak to you. Nor would I ever reveal to another person anything you have shared with me from your heart. But this girl has been spoken to by God, who knows every heart. Even yours, my friend! And I believe her. She is the salvation of France.

"Therefore, whether or not anyone joins me, I am resolved to bring her to Chinon, and to see the Dauphin convinced of her true call, and to fight by her side as long as there is a single English sword left in this realm."

Jean de Metz looks incredulously at his friend, then bursts into laughter! He laughs until tears begin rolling down his face, until he has to prop himself up against the doorframe. Poulengy's face is locked in an expression of utter bewilderment, but a smile grows on Joan's.

"Bertrand, my friend," de Metz finally says. "You are a mighty knight, by far my better! You have quite vanquished me, and I submit to your will."

He turns to Joan. Dropping to one knee, he places a hand in hers.

"I cannot offer you my Belief, but I will pledge my service to you, as long as my friend believes. He has faith enough for two! I will march by your side (and his) and fight by your side (and his) and never rest until France is her own once more. This I swear, come what may!"

"I accept your service – and your unbelief," replies Joan. "Indeed, should you ever profess Belief, I will consider it a sign that God is a falsehood after all, and run back to Domrémy as quickly as my feet will carry me!"

Rising, de Metz gazes upon her as if for the first time, a smile growing on his face as well, while you look on with Bertrand de

Poulengy, pleased but also a little aghast.

For the next two weeks, Joan settles into a regular routine. Every morning, she goes to the castle and leaves a message for Sir Robert that is quickly rejected. After a pleasant chat with Bertrand de Poulengy and Jean de Metz, she spends the rest of the morning and all of the afternoon receiving the people who flock to the Lax- art house to see her.

"The Maid! The Maid!" they cry, and she speaks to them from the front porch of the house.

"God has not forgotten France! He will never abandon anyone in His care. Know that He has promised me that I will deliver Orléans from the English, and see our Dauphin crowned the right- ful king of this land. Do not despair, but rejoice, praising God who holds all the nations of the world in His hands!"

Evenings, she helps with the cooking and cleaning, and after- ward, sits by the fire with her aunt and uncle discussing the family news.

You're surprised by how little they talk of Joan's incredible call, but come to see that this silence springs from separate sources in Durand and his wife.

Durand accepts Joan's claims without question, but since he has little interest or expertise in war, politics, or religion, he has very little to say to her about them. Only once did he hold forth about any of it, when he overheard Joan refer to Sir Robert's fool- ishness one morning.

"He's no fool. In fact, he is a very shrewd and right-thinking man. But something in him has died. I only met him once, but it was obvious to me. His men see it, too."

Jeannette also believes in Joan's call, but doesn't really want to. "It's monstrous!" she confides one morning to a neighbor, but she remains silent in the company of Joan or Durand. Sometimes when they're working side by side on some task, you'll catch her brushing the hair gently out of Joan's eyes, or laying her hands upon the child in her womb as if wondering what horrible fate God might have in store for it if He can so curse Joan.

Occasionally, Bertrand de Poulengy and Jean de Metz visit the house. One evening, de Metz walks in with several ceramic bowls and dishes in his hands.

"Have you brought me – some empty flower pots, my love?" asks Joan.

"I will bring you nothing less than the Kingdom of France in these hands!" he replies.

"We found them set in front of the door," says Poulengy a little stiffly, as uncomfortable as you are with their easy banter.

"Yes," says Durand. "People leave them to be touched by Joan."

"What virtues does she imbue them with?" asks Poulengy solemnly. De Metz continues to stand casually by the door with the items in his hands, but you can see that he's gone still and his eyes are fixed on Joan.

"See for yourself," says Durand, gesturing toward Joan. Poulengy takes the things from de Metz, then pauses a moment, unsure how to approach her. Finally, he lowers himself to one knee, lifting the bowls and dishes to her.

"Uncle!" she cries in good-natured exasperation. "Stand, my lord. I was not sent to perform such tricks, but to deliver France."

De Metz smiles from where he stands by the door.

"But what about the poor souls who are expecting a blessing?" he asks. "Wouldn't it be a cheat of sorts to return these things untouched?"

"Touch them yourself, then" says Joan. "Your touch will do as much good as mine!"

At that, even Poulengy laughs.

"In truth," says Durand, "she does touch each item, but only because that is what the people ask. She also prays for those who come to see her or who leave such things: the greater boon by far, in my estimation."

"Amen," says Jeannette, and you realize she's been in the room all this time but silent.

"Well," says Durand, "if you will excuse me, I must bring in some firewood for the night."

Joan makes to go help him, but de Metz says, "Allow me!"

She bows to him, and he and Durand go out the door. Once it's shut behind them, he turns to the older man.

"I suppose you have known her all her life."

"Pretty much," replies Durand. "We don't get down to Domrémy often, nor are they able to come up very regularly, what with all the work of the farm. But all that I have heard about her from her parents confirms what I see when she does visit."

"And you believe her claims."

"Of course. Do you not?"

De Metz pauses, then replies, "Let us say – I am on her side."

They reach the woodpile, where Durand looks long into the captain's face in the fading light.

"Well," he says. "You are a good man."

"Um. Thank you."

Durand begins loading him up with wood.

"Tell me," says de Metz. "Have you believed in this call of hers all her life?"

"No, no! She herself did not know it until about a year ago by her account, and she did not tell me until the first morning of her visit, two weeks ago."

"At which point, you believed her at once."

"I did. I think this will do."

He adds one more stick of wood to the bundle in de Metz's arms, and they start back for the house. Just before they reach the door, the captain turns to face him.

"May I ask why you believed her so readily?"

"She is a good girl, and good girls don't lie."

A few days later, de Metz and Poulengy visit the house during the day so they can hear Joan speak to the crowds, but instead, become themselves the focus of attention.

"You two, you are officers of the garrison, are you not? Why haven't you sent the Maid to Chinon yet?"

"She must reach the Dauphin by mid-Lent or all is lost!"

"What is Sir Robert waiting for?"

"Good people," replies Poulengy. "You must have patience. The Commander must consider many things before he can make a decision."

"What is there to consider? Doesn't he believe in her visions? Has he not heard the prophecy?"

Poulengy is at a loss, but de Metz steps up beside him.

"It does not matter!" he cries. "This noble gentleman, Bertrand de Poulengy, and I, Jean de Metz, have sworn to bring the Maid to Chinon, and to do all that we can to persuade the Dauphin to send her to Orléans. This we will do – with or without the Commander's blessing!"

As the people cheer, he looks over at his friend's face, which displays shock at first, but then nods in confirmation.

"The marketplace!" cries Joan, "We must go to the market-place!"

"Joan, what is it?" asks de Metz.

"Quickly! We must go!" she replies, and at that, the crowd bursts into motion. Joan dashes off the porch to make her way to the head of the procession, sliding easily through the gaps in the press while her two friends bump along behind her, trying to keep up.

"To the marketplace!" she cries, and the refrain is taken up by all. The surging mass of townsfolk ripples through the streets, picking up passersby as it goes along. By the time it reaches the marketplace, it must number more than a hundred. Joan leads it part way down the main street, then stops.

"We will wait here!" she calls back to the crowd.

"For what?" de Metz asks her.

"You'll see!" she teases.

So they wait. Before them, buyers and sellers come and go, some of them noticing the crowd and wandering over to inquire what is going on, and some of those joining it. A girl comes running down the street chasing a ball. A supply cart forces them to squeeze aside to let it pass. A cloaked, bent beggar emerges from a side street and, seeing his way barred by the crowd, turns the other way, hobbling further into the marketplace.

"Good sir!" cries Joan. "Do not walk away from us! I have waited long to speak to you!"

The man stops for a moment, then resumes his slow shuffle without looking back.

"Sir Robert!" shouts Joan. "I really think you should stay and speak with me!"

The crowd gasps. De Metz and Poulengy stare at each other in disbelief. The beggar comes slowly out of his hunch, rising to a great height, then turns, shedding his cloak. He is indeed Robert de Baudricourt, commander of the garrison!

"I have heard he sometimes escapes the castle like this," whispers de Metz to Poulengy.

Baudricourt strides up to Joan. She drops to one knee before him. Gradually, so does the rest of the crowd. De Metz and Poulengy remain standing, saluting awkwardly.

"I might have known you two would be here," he grumbles at them.

"You!" he says to Joan. "You are the girl who has been pestering me. I will thank you to leave me and my men alone! When you are not begging at my doors, they carry on your crazy talk in council. Well, I have told you before and I will tell you again: go away! Go back to your sheep! We are serious men here, with serious responsibilities, though some –" he glares at his two officers "– would rather believe in the fairy tales of their childhood."

The crowd murmurs in disapproval, but falls silent as Joan rises to her feet.

"Your lordship," she says, "I would not pester you except for dire necessity. I could not go back to Domrémy if I wanted to, for the thought of what would happen to the people of Orléans would break my heart. You have been their champion in the past, rescue them once more!"

The crowd cheers and people begin calling out, "Send her to Chinon! The Maid to Chinon! Down with Robert!" They press around Baudricourt and Joan, both of whom call out for order, and the commander begins to scuffle verbally and physically with those around him. The cries of the people coalesce into a regular chant, "Down with Robert! The Maid to Chinon!" and you fear that bodily harm will soon come to one or both of them.

The sound of swords being drawn from their sheaths silences the crowd. Those closest to Baudricourt and Joan back quickly away, opening a small circle of cleared space. Jean de Metz and Bertrand de Poulengy stand within it beside their two commanders, swords held before them. Before anyone else can speak, de Metz resumes the chant in a modified form:

"Robert for the Maid! The Maid to Orléans! Robert for the Maid! The Maid to Orléans!"

The people take up the new chant, cheering and clapping.

"Good people!" cries de Metz after the crowd has had time to chant for a while. "We must go to the castle now to take counsel. Return to your occupations and wait for word of our plans."

Cheering and resuming the chant, the crowd slowly disperses.

"Quick thinking," Baudricourt tells his captain when they're alone again, but you aren't sure if it's a compliment or an accusation.

"My lord," says de Metz. "Why not send her? What is there to lose?"

"My reputation! My commission! Perhaps even my head."

Bertrand de Poulengy speaks for the first time, in a low voice that only his commander will hear.

"Robert, if no help comes to Charles in the next month, Orléans, and then France, will certainly fall. I would sacrifice reputation, rank, and life itself rather than see that day."

The next morning, before Joan can leave the house for her daily pilgrimage to the castle gates, Jean de Metz and Bertrand de Poulengy arrive breathless with the news that Sir Robert has consented to send her to Chinon. As they embrace and talk excitedly of their plans, Catherine appears beside you.

"Catherine! Do you know the news?"

"I do indeed."

"So we're going to Chinon?"

"And beyond!"

Clasping hands with her, you jump up and down, shouting for joy, joining the celebration of the others. Then you catch sight of Jeannette Laxart standing in a doorway watching the goings on with one hand clasping the cross she wears around her neck, a stricken look on her face.

"Sir Robert has granted us two other horsemen," reports de Metz later that morning, "plus his best archer, but you will have to provide your own gear. I don't think that will be difficult. I am sure the people of the town will gladly contribute. You won't need armor or weapons yet, but there is the question of clothing. Were you thinking of wearing that dress?"

Since coming to Vaucouleurs, Joan has only worn the dress she arrived in, a frayed but sturdy farm dress that she wore both in the fields and in the church in Domrémy.

"I have another, but I didn't bring it with me."

"Actually, I was thinking about a shirt and surcoat and trousers."

"Jean!" says Poulengy. "I don't think that would be proper."

"Maybe not proper, but prudent and practical. We will face many dangers on the road, and even on campaign it would be good to give the men serving you a way – well, to think of you as a man. And I don't like to think how we would fit armor over a dress!"

"Well," ponders Joan, "it's a sensible idea, but on this matter, I will have to consult with my voi-"

"Joan!" interrupts Catherine. Joan stops speaking mid-word and swivels her gaze in Catherine's general direction. Poulengy gasps and crosses himself, looking upon her almost fearfully, while de Metz glances searchingly around the room. Durand Laxart continues slicing an apple he had offered his guests, but politely averts his mild gaze from his niece's private conversation.

"It will be all right for you to wear men's clothing," continues Catherine. "Indeed, it has been so decreed."

Joan returns her attention to the others.

"I will wear the men's clothes," she says.

The townspeople donate more than enough money to supply Joan with clothing and a horse. Her old dress she gives to Jeannette.

"For the little one someday" she tells her.

Jeannette shifts the garment in her hands uncomfortably, biting her lip.

"Don't worry, Auntie! She won't follow my footsteps. She will never go to war when she grows up because there won't be one then! She will be wise and strong, and you will marry her well, and her children will become builders and healers and far travelers. Her heritage in this world will be the envy of queens!"

"I thank you," says Jeannette, bowing her head, "but what about you? You could have all that, too, but you are turning away from it. What will *your* heritage be?"

Joan lowers her gaze, half closing her eyes, as if listening to some voice that is neither yours nor Catherine's.

"The ways of God are a darkness and a delight," she says. "No one can know how far they lead, and into what strange lands, until she stands at their end."

On a bright morning in the first week of Lent, the company assembles outside the gates of the castle of Vaucouleurs. Bertrand de Poulengy sits splendidly upon his mount in full dress uniform, a saber hanging by his side and a signet in his hand that proclaims the royal authority behind the expedition. Jean de Metz positions himself beside him, chatting merrily with anyone within earshot and leading his horse in an intricate standing dance. Behind them, Joan stands by her horse fiddling with the last few ties and wrappings of her male attire. It took her almost an hour, with Jeannette's assistance, to put everything on that morning.

The other two horsemen and the archer stand behind her, speaking gravely and occasionally casting a curious look in her direction.

Poulengy turns his horse around.

"There is no use in waiting any longer. Prepare to ride!"

The others mount their horses. Joan's rears up whinnying, and Poulengy makes to dash over to her aid, but de Metz forestalls him. Then you see that she's in no distress. Rather, her face is fierce and exultant.

"The Maid rides to war!" cries de Metz.

The others echo him – "The Maid rides! Long live the Maid!" - but just as they begin to move off, the gates of the castle open. Robert de Baudricourt emerges and stalks over to the company.

"De Metz!" he snaps. "Write down these words, to be delivered to the Dauphin."

The captain pulls pen and paper from his pack.

"To my Lord Charles," begins Sir Robert. "I send to you this girl who *claims* she comes to you with help from God. I *do not* vouch for her claim, except to report that she has persuaded many of the townsfolk and some – some *few* – of my men. I send her to you that you might *more rightly* judge this matter. Yours ever in faith and service."

De Metz finishes writing out the words and is about to cap his ink bottle, then dips his pen once more and underlines all the words the commander emphasized in his dictation. Smiling to himself, he blots the letter dry and hands it down to Sir Robert, saying, "I thank you, my lord."

Sir Robert does not reply, but quickly signs the letter and thrusts it back at de Metz.

"Go!" he growls. "Come what may."

Turning his back on the party, he strides back into the castle. The gates crash shut behind him.

The Palace of Dreams

The spires of Chinon rise into a hazy sky, rose-tinted in the morning mist. You see them for the first time after a night in which you soared through the air among clouds of butterflies, and you feel like the dream is stretching on into the day.

Still like a butterfly, you float above the company as they walk up a road of smoothly fitted multicolored stone. The voices of Jean de Metz and Bertrand de Poulengy as they confer with the guards at the city gates, and the rustle of parchment as they hand them the letter from Sir Robert, brush against you like the papery wings whose beating tickled your ears throughout the night. Finally, as you pass into the city, you awaken truly, touching down to walk alongside Joan through the streets of this last refuge of the rightful king of France.

When the company reaches the inn where they plan to stay, a royal delegation waits for them.

"Are you the men from Vaucouleurs?"

"We are," says Poulengy. "We have come by permission of Robert de Baudricourt with great news and help for the Dauphin."

"He sent us to meet you," says their leader. "Is this – is she –"

Joan steps forward.

"I am the Maid."

His men exchange hopeful glances.

"You and your company are most welcome here! If you will come with us, the Dauphin has granted you lodgings in the palace."

"The 'palace' they speak of is the old summer residence," explains Poulengy to the others as they follow the escort through the streets of Chinon. "It has no fortifications, but it is the farthest major city from the English advance, and so has proven to be the best refuge the Dauphin could have chosen."

"If his goal was to avoid battle as long as possible," notes de Metz.

The leader of the escort pauses and turns as if about to speak, but then seems to think the better of it and resumes his brisk march.

"Whatever the Dauphin's motivations," says Poulengy, "you must agree they have turned out for the best, since now he will meet the Maid."

"I agree that much will depend on what he makes of her when they do."

The company is assigned a suite of apartments that, collectively, are finer and more spacious than the grandest house in any city you've ever been in. Every member of the company is given his or her own room, every bedroom has an antechamber where visitors can sit, and all the apartments are arranged around a common room with a balcony that overlooks the east side of the city. De Metz settles himself into a thickly padded chair while Poulengy gives instructions to the servants concerning the baggage, but Joan gets right down to business.

"I will see the king now," she tells the escort.

They look uncomfortably at one another.

"I have been told only to bring you here and see to your needs," says their leader. "I believe – I don't think you will be able to see the Dauphin yet."

"Why not?" asks Poulengy, "Is he away?"

"No."

The man pauses, then continues in a lower voice.

"I have heard he wishes others to question the Maid first, so he can be more certain that she is not – that she is all she claims to be."

"By my honor as a gentleman!" huffs Poulengy.

"Just let me see him!" cries Joan. "I will erase all his doubts in ten minutes!"

"We're sorry!" blurts one of the guards. "We have heard rumors of your feats and rejoice at your coming, but the Dauphin is too timid! He never –"

"He is cautious," interjects his superior. "As any good lord should be."

The man lowers his gaze and steps back.

"It's the Commander all over again," laments de Metz.

"No," says Joan. "Sir Robert was stubborn, and will suffer for it, but the king suffers honestly from his fears. He will pass through."

"Very well," she says to the escort, "I will take his tests! So it is that I must fulfill all the formalities."

That night as you sit by Joan, you are caught up into a dream of splendor and brightness. You stand at the back of a magnificent cathedral, bathed in light that streams from high windows to redouble off polished wood and golden fixtures. Filling the pews are nobles and knights and great lords, as well as ordinary folk dressed in their finest apparel. A contingent of courtiers arrays itself behind you, and before you, at the head of the center aisle, a priest waits for your approach.

Is this a wedding? Some fantasy of Joan's about the alternate course her life might have taken?

Trumpets sound. You take one step down the aisle –

And find yourself in the open air, standing on the uneven ground of a riverbank, beneath an overcast sky. The dancing light of the cathedral gives way to a dismal and uniform gray, and the trilling music is now the flat roar of a high wind. Behind you are gathered, not courtiers in their silks, but knights in dull armor. Before you, a bridge spans the short breadth of a muddy stream.

At its other end, a man stands waiting for you, flanked by two attendants who are lightly armed but unarmored. As you take your first step onto the bridge, your knights rush past you, drawing their swords and falling upon the man at the far end. His cry and yours echo together, "No!" and you wake flat on your back on the floor, looking up at Joan's arm dangling over the edge of the bed.

She remains asleep. Her face is calm. She rests upon the feather bed as lightly as a butterfly upon a thistle. She murmurs, "Good throw, Pierre!" and smiles, having moved quickly on, it seems, to some innocent memory of her childhood.

You remain awake the rest of the night, but detect no sign that she dreams again about either the glorious cathedral or the horrible scene of ambush and murder.

A week goes by with no word from the Dauphin. De Metz rails against the sluggishness of bureaucracies and chains of command. Poulengy writes letters and seeks out old contacts in an attempt to secure Joan an audience. The other men grow restless and are allowed to return to Vaucouleurs. Only Joan remains calm. She spends most of her time on the balcony gazing up at the passing clouds. Catherine often visits her there, bringing each day's news from Orléans.

None of it is good.

"An English supply train was spotted approaching the city with only a light escort. (So confident are they that they have thoroughly broken the fighting spirit of your people!) This time, however, the French decided to attack, at the urging of certain bold lords they still have among them. They mustered such numbers that the men of the convoy saw at once that they had no hope of flight or rescue, and resigned themselves to bear the assault as well as they could, and either die or be captured in the end.

"However, the French held back. They could not agree on the

best plan, and one of their dukes made the others promise not to
attack without him, and then was late! The men in the supply wagons debated whether to flee after all, but in the end, decided that
this was just a trick to draw them from their defensive positions.
The English laying siege to the city refrained from going to their
aid for the same reason. If they had only known that it was no trap,
but indecisiveness and timidity! Then things might have gone better for the French.

"Eventually, one company broke ranks from the rest and rode
against the circled wagons, but when the English saw how small this
company was, they rode out themselves to attack their attackers and
turned them to flight! They pursued them this way and that, achiev-
ing a mighty slaughter, and might have utterly destroyed them had
not another lord – the Duke of Vignolles, whom it would be good
for you to seek out when you arrive – ridden out to their rescue.

"Such is the state of France that even opportunities for small
victories turn to ignoble defeat. You must renew the spirit of your
people; you must rekindle their resolve! If you fail, they will surely
perish from the Earth."

Catherine's face is grave, but Joan smiles back at her.

"Don't worry, Catherine. I will soon be on my way to Orléans.
That will be the last defeat we suffer for a year!"

Despite her sunny daytime disposition, Joan's dark dreams
continue. Again and again, she stands at the back of the cathedral,
but never makes it all the way to the priest waiting for her at the
altar. Always, before she can get half way up the aisle, the scene
shifts to the bloody bridge where her knights ambush and kill the
man coming across to meet her, usually while she cries out to them
to stop. Occasionally, however, she herself leads their attack.

You find that what fills your mind at those moments is not
bloodlust or hatred, but horror at what you're about to do. You try
to hold back from charging across the bridge, and then from striking your bewildered enemy with your sword, but can't. Often, the
dream will go on from that point, until you stand over the unmov-

ing body of your victim, your hands slick with blood, thinking, *I am a murderer! I am a murderer!*

You become so distressed by these nightmares that you stop trying to enter Joan's dreams, but it does no good. Night after night, you are drawn into them anyway. You take to spending nights in her antechamber, and then in the common room or out on the balcony. You try visiting the dreams of Jean de Metz or Bertrand de Poulengy instead. No matter what you do, the moment always comes when you stand in that cathedral again, and then on the blood soaked bridge.

You wake from these dreams to find Joan sleeping peacefully. She never speaks of them to the others or to Catherine. Once, you ask her about them directly, but she replies, "I don't remember anything about a bridge or a cathedral, but I did dream two nights ago that Katie was getting married, and though it was only in the village church, the place was packed with well-wishers and wonderfully lit by candles and torches."

When you ask Catherine about it, she only exclaims, "Margaret! You can enter people's dreams? I never even thought to try!"

Finally, one morning, an escort appears requesting that Joan accompany them to visit a certain nobleman residing in the city.

"What does he want from me?" she asks. "Is this the first test?"

"It is not a test planned by the Dauphin, but it may well serve to grant him a sign of your true call by God. The duke is very ill, and asks if you can heal him."

"This duke," says Poulengy. "He would not be the Duke of Lorraine, would he?"

"Yes, he is."

"Do you know him?" asks de Metz.

"I know *of* him. And from what I know, I would say he deserves to be ill!"

"Bertrand!" cries Joan. "No one deserves to be ill!"

"I ask your pardon," he replies, bowing to her. "Those of us who are not called by God can be often be carried away into sin by our passions."

She walks up to him and, pulling herself up by his shoulders, kisses him on the cheek.

"We are *all* called by God," she says softly. "I apologize for scolding you. It seems we must all learn patience!"

"But what is it that you know about the man that's so bad?" asks de Metz. "It might prove useful to know before we meet him."

Poulengy settles into a chair, thinking it over.

"Let us say that he has not been entirely honorable toward his wife."

"Did he abandon her? Or have her put away?"

"No. She still lives on his estate and retains all the honors and power of her position, but he is usually not there. Even before he became ill and began going from city to city seeking a cure, he spent most of his days elsewhere: in a chateau he kept for another woman. A younger woman, with whom he has had several children."

"Ah. But where's the terrible crime? After all, marriage is marriage, but –"

"Jean!" whispers Poulengy, gesturing toward Joan, but she's paying them no heed. She stands a little aside with a thoughtful look on her face.

"I think he is a good man at heart," she says. "I will see him."

"I cannot heal him," she adds, to the escort as well as her two friends, "but I think it would be good for us to meet."

It's a short journey on foot to the Duke's residence. Standing in the entryway is the priest of the local church, dangling a small gold crucifix from one hand.

"You, Joan of Domrémy!" he intones as the party approaches. "If there be any evil in you, depart at once from this place! Or if you have come from God indeed, kneel and make obeisance to this sign of His salvation."

"This is silly!" cries Joan. "You know the state of my soul already. Wasn't that you hearing my confession just last night? I've committed no mortal sins since then, I promise you!"

"I am sorry," whispers the old man, "but the Duke insisted. He will not let you in otherwise."

"Very well," she sighs, and kneels before him. She cradles the crucifix in her hands, looking down for a moment at the supine figure of the Christ, then kisses it and enters the residence. As Bertrand de Poulengy enters, he, too, brings the cross up to his lips.

Jean de Metz hesitates.

"You two go on," he says. "I will wait here for your good report."

Joan turns and stamps her foot, looking very much the young village girl you often forget she is.

"Jean! You must come!"

"I am sorry, my love, but on this occasion, the command of the Maid must go unheeded!"

"Very well," she tells him. "But if France falls now…"

He smiles and pats himself on the chest as if to say, "It will be my fault."

The priest looks at them in alarm. Poulengy goes over to his side.

"So the angels must jest in the innermost courts of Heaven!" he tells the fretting cleric, and then turns to follow Joan into the house.

The Duke of Lorraine lies coughing in his bed as you enter the room. A doctor hovers over him, mopping his brow but doing little else. When the fit subsides, he goes back to a chair in one corner of the room, leaving Joan and Poulengy to make their own introductions.

"I am Bertrand de Poulengy, and this is – the one with whom you have asked to speak."

The Duke stares at her. He's a large man whose arms and legs are unnaturally skinny, worn away perhaps by his illness. His face is bony and, again, oddly small in proportion to the rest of him, and crowned with a wisp of white hair.

Freeman Ng

"If you are truly sent from God," he whispers, "then heal me. I beg you!"

Poulengy sniffs at this, but Joan replies tenderly.

"*As* I am truly sent from God, I tell you this: you ought to be more concerned about the health of your soul than the health of your body."

"My soul?"

The Duke appears genuinely puzzled.

"I am a patron of the church. I am fully confessed. I have harmed no man to my knowledge that I have not made restitution to."

"What about your wife?" asks Joan.

"My wife? I have never dishonored her, but have given her all that custom demands and more in the way of wealth and titles. She rules my household and my lands, and will inherit all that I have."

"Foolish man!" cries Joan. "Don't you know she cares nothing for these things? It is you she loves!"

The Duke's eyes come wider awake than you've yet seen them as they gaze upon her. In a thousand, thousand years, they will remain among your most vivid memories: the look of a man who has just realized he has been wrong his whole life about that which mattered the most. He begins what seems at first like another coughing spell, but turns out to be a fit of ragged sobbing.

"Ah! Ah! Ah!" he cries as the spasms wrack his body. Poulengy slips silently into a chair by the bed and takes one of the Duke's hands in his own.

"Ah! Oh! Ah!" continues the old man.

The doctor makes no move, but only continues sitting in his corner.

"Ah!" cries the Duke, more weakly now. The sobs become softer, and more spread out.

"Ah . . . agh . . . agggghhhhhh . . ."

Finally he lapses into silence, lying on the bed staring blankly into the air like a ship wrecked upon a rocky shore.

"I am sorry you suffer so," says Joan.

"I, too," he breaths. "May God forgive me."

"Of course He will."

The old man struggles to raise his head again and find her in the darkness.

"Will you – heal me – after all?" he asks.

"I cannot," she replies. "I have no such power. I would if I could."

"I . . . understand," he manages, and then his head falls back onto the bed and his eyes close.

Joan and Poulengy wait several minutes, and when the Duke doesn't rouse again, they nod to the doctor and begin to withdraw.

"I thank you!" comes the voice of the Duke from behind them. "You are an angel. You are an angel sent from God!"

The next day, a messenger appears in the company's quarters bearing a letter sent by the Duke to Charles.

"The Dauphin wishes you to hear all that is reported by those you will be speaking with," he says.

"That is a most honorable course," says Poulengy.

"First, let us see what it says," retorts de Metz.

He takes the letter and reads.

"Most noble Dauphin, I thank you for sending the Maid to me in my sickness. I tell you truly that she comes from God, for she saw my heart and my sin. And though she told me it was too late to recover my health, yet will I repent. I have sent for my wife. If God's judgment finds me before she does, I pray that the Maid speak to her and tell her all that she revealed to me. Your unworthy servant, he who was the Duke of Lorraine."

He lowers the letter and looks at Joan.

"I wish I had been there, after all!"

"That is not what I said!" she protests. "I didn't tell him he would not get well. I didn't tell him his illness was a judgment from God!"

"Perhaps not," says Poulengy, "but God spoke to him nonetheless, through your mere presence if not your words. You may have

Freeman Ng

saved the man's soul! A matter of greater importance, perhaps, than the fate of entire nations!"

That night, you stand in a smoky, candlelit chamber that smells of incense and sickness. An enormous, disheveled bed sits in the middle of the room, and on it, an old man lies raving. You can't make out half of what he screams, and find no meaning in the words you can distinguish.

"They come with fire! They come with fire! Mountains of fire, burning!"

You think he must be dying, but can't tell if this is the cause or effect of his madness.

His wildly roaming gaze fixes on you.

"You! Who are you? I don't know you! You are no son of mine!"

You try to back away, but only seem to draw closer to the bed. The man's face, covered with sweat and spittle, red with rage, looms larger and larger.

"Weakling! Blunderer! I cast you from me! Would that you had died as well!"

You sit with Catherine in one of the pagan temples of Antioch. Before you, a female figure rises from a pile of rocks, as if stone were being transformed into a living soul. Even after you became a Christian, you often came here to gaze upon this sculpture, which you came to think of as a symbol for salvation.

"Is Joan's father well?"

"As far as I know. Why do you ask?"

"It's probably nothing," you tell her. "More dreams she's having."

"Would you like me to make sure of it?"

"Yes! Thanks."

She rises and lays a hand on your shoulder.

"I do not know when I'll be able to speak with you again, but when I do, I will give you a full report."

You thank her again and she fades from sight. The temple surrounding you does not, to your delight. You return your gaze to the stone woman, grateful for the chance to rest and think before you're sent back to Chinon. Could the dream really be about Joan's father? You're suddenly sure it's not. Meanings and appearances can shift in dreams, but that man was simply not Jacques d'Arc, nor was the person through whose eyes you saw him Joan or any of her brothers.

Who, then, was Joan dreaming about, if not herself? The Dauphin, perhaps?

That would fit in much better with the dream of the nobles gathered in the cathedral, but what about the others? Was Charles' father mad? Did he once ambush a man on a bridge?

You wish you had paid more attention to Catherine's history lessons in the distant meadows of Domrémy.

"You want to test *what?*"

Jean de Metz stands at the door of the common room, facing a delegation of noblewomen.

"I have been asked by the Dauphin to examine the Maid," repeats their leader. "To see if she is indeed a maid."

"That's ridiculous!" cries de Metz. "What does that have to do with –"

"Welcome!" interrupts Bertrand de Poulengy, stepping in front of de Metz and bowing. "You are Queen Yolande of Aragon, are you not?"

"I am."

De Metz steps back in amazement.

"She is the mother-in-law of the Dauphin," he whispers to Joan.

Joan steps forward and shakily executes the full bow they practice at the court.

"My lady," she says.

"I am glad to meet you," the Queen replies. "Though I'm sorry it must be under such uncomfortable circumstances. Let us take care of that chore quickly, and then we can perhaps chat at greater ease."

Joan gestures toward her rooms and they enter. Back in the common room, de Metz complains to his companion, "You were very friendly to this latest examiner. Aren't you outraged that Joan is being tested so?"

"I did not like the Dauphin placing Joan before the likes of the Duke," replies Poulengy, "but this is a Queen, and a right-minded sovereign by all accounts. Her involvement here can only result in good for us, and for Joan, and for France."

When you enter Joan's room, you almost don't recognize her. For the first time since you've known her, she appears shy, sitting rigidly on the end of the bed with her hands folded in her lap and her head bowed. The Queen sits in a chair opposite her, with the elegantly attired women of the delegation standing behind her.

"I am told you are from Domrémy," the Queen is saying.

"Yes, ma'am."

"You are lucky to live there. I think the region of Lorraine is the most beautiful in all of France."

"Thank you, ma'am."

"What did you do in Domrémy?"

"We farmed."

The Queen sits back in her chair smiling but silent for a moment.

"That cannot be all you did. What did you do when you weren't farming?"

Joan bites her lip, then replies haltingly.

"I went to church. I idled in the meadows. I played with my brothers."

"It sounds like a good life. Were you happy?"

Joan raises her eyes to meet the Queen's, and her voice conveys emotion for the first time in the interview.

"Yes."

"Believe me," says the Queen, "there are great kings and lords of mighty realms who would envy you that."

"Like Charles?"

The attending women gasp at that, but the Queen only nods sadly.

"Indeed. I love him as if he were my own son, but my heart breaks for him sometimes. Sometimes, I worry he will never be happy."

"But he will!"

The other women react with shock at every new utterance, but Joan and the Queen pay them no mind.

"I think," continues Joan, "that he is the kind of man who can only be happy when doing the work he has been called to do. And it is not even pleasure that he would take from it, but..."

"Fulfillment?"

"Yes!" says Joan, smiling for the first time.

The Queen leans forward in her chair.

"*You* are such a *woman*."

Joan's smile fades, but she meets the Queen's level gaze.

"I am."

"That is why you are here, is it not, and not idling happily in the meadows of Domrémy."

"Yes," says Joan, her voice a little bit atremble again.

"Well," concludes the Queen in a business-like way, "we had best get on with this, then. Now..." She looks over Joan's male attire, full of ties and straps and overlapping layers. "Where in God's name do we begin?"

Joan bursts into laughter!

"I thought my own royal garments were complicated," says the Queen. "And this is the garb of an ordinary man!"

"It took me a while to figure it out," says Joan. "And nobody could help me except my aunt Jeannette, from watching my uncle dress in the mornings. Here...and here..." she notes, as she begins to undo the various fittings.

"They certainly like to keep themselves well bound," murmurs

Freeman Ng

the Queen. "How do you feel when you are wearing all this?"

"Not very different," shrugs Joan as she works at a stubborn knot. "Like myself."

She blushes as the last bits of clothing come off her, but the Queen maintains a steady stream of talk throughout the examination.

"Myself, I do not see what difference the state of your virginity should make, either in this matter or any other, but it seems to hold a grave importance to men. (Not that this particular examination can even tell for sure, I hope you know!) I suppose it is important to the Church, but isn't that only to say *the men* again? Except, it seems, for the fellow who greeted us at the door. That was the captain from Vaucouleurs, was it not? I liked him! He is the kind of man I wish my son-in-law would listen to more than some of those 'advisors' of his."

"Both Jean and Bertrand have been great friends and protectors to me," says Joan.

"Bertrand de Poulengy I knew of before today. He has a noble reputation. You could not have found two better companions."

The Queen sits back in her seat.

"Well," she says, "it is my privilege to inform you that you are a virgin!"

Joan smiles warmly, and you find your own heart overflowing with gratitude toward Queen Yolande of Aragon.

"Listen," she says, after a glance back at her retinue. "If you ask it, I will see to it that Charles sends you home. I will confirm you are a virgin, but will find some other reason that he should refuse your help. It is easy enough to dissuade him from anything, the poor skittish boy! I have every faith that God will send some other help for France, or I will simply persuade him to go fight for himself.

"It is not that I doubt your call. Rather, I believe it enough to wish to spare you from it."

The naked girl takes the hands of the richly attired Queen.

"I cannot. My voices have told me that I am the only hope for

France, but even if that were not the case, I could not disobey the call of God."

The next morning, you wake from a muddled dream of a mother casting her children out the door into a driving blizzard where they perished one by one, to find Joan already up and out of her bed. You find her in the common room gathered with the others around another messenger, who has brought the report that Queen Yolande wrote to her son-in-law.

"The Maid, Joan of Domrémy, is all that she claims to be. Of her call and her courage I have no doubts. You may trust utterly that she will bring to you all that she has promised. Nevertheless, beware. If you accept her guidance, you must follow her unreservedly down the road she would lead you. If you fall short, you will be forsaking a true servant of God most high, to your great jeopardy."

"She is a noble lady," says Poulengy. "A better help to the Dauphin than his own mother ever was."

"First a Duke and now a Queen," says de Metz. "Who will be next?"

The messenger clears his throat.

"The Dauphin requests that the Maid be brought to the University in Poitiers, to be examined by the learned men there."

It's a day's journey to Poitiers, and once the party arrives, they have to wait two more days for the examiners to assemble. On the road and in the rooms of the university, Joan's dreams return to their normal lightness. For three nights, she dances once more in the meadows of her childhood. Clouds of butterflies swirl around her. She flies among them, and then beyond them, rising high into the sky to look down upon brilliant cloudscapes of mountainous whites and grays.

She's finally on the move, you think to yourself.

The university itself supports this new buoyancy you feel. Its buildings stand quietly gray amongst walkways lined with blossom-

Freeman Ng

ing trees. From within its grounds, you can hardly see anything of the city around it. It's a sequestered place, like that favorite pagan temple of yours in Antioch, or the great Library Catherine has told you about in her home city of Alexandria. Bastions of the mind that have always existed wherever men have lived, and which always will, untouched by their wars and catastrophes.

Though her companions worry about the upcoming examination, Joan is already looking beyond them, and you share her confidence.

"We must prepare to ride for Orléans," she says, as she walks along a shaded path one morning with Jean de Metz. "Once the king receives the report of these learned men, I think he will act quickly."

"*If* they rule in your favor," he replies.

"How could they not?" she asks. "Are you beginning to lose faith in me, my love?"

"Never, dearest! But I am not as confident about the clergy. *They* might fail the test."

She stops and looks up at him in surprise.

"Anything and anyone can fail," he gently reminds her.

The next day, Joan and her companions walk over to the university library, where the examination is to take place. The men are invited to wait in the main hall, among shelves and piles of dusty books, while Joan meets with her examiners in an adjacent classroom.

"You must maintain the gravest solemnity with these men," advises Poulengy. "They are not just priests, but scholars. They may be of higher rank than the noble lady who visited us last week, higher perhaps even than the Dauphin himself in their own way, for their authority comes not from the power of governments or the customs of men, but from God and their own long learning."

She takes his hands.

"I thank you for bringing me this far," she tells him. "Soon, we will go farther yet!"

Six examiners sit in a half circle with an empty chair at its center. They are dressed in black robes of fine linen with golden clasps in the shape of half opened scrolls. They're all gray-haired or graying, except for one younger man whose jet-black hair makes his robe look almost gray.

"Welcome, Joan of Domrémy," says the oldest of the men. "Please sit."

She walks over to her chair, but before sitting in it, curtsies to them. It's not the courtly bow she attempted with Queen Yolande, but the slight, pretty dip of a country girl. The man with the jet-black hair smiles.

"Do you understand why you are here?" asks the head examiner.

"I do," she replies. "To put the king's fears to rest, which I am happy to do, for he is a good, though cautious, soul."

The examiners murmur in surprise, except for the younger man, whose smile only broadens.

"Young lady," says their leader. "We are here to judge the truth of your claims. If we deem that you have been lying to the Dauphin, the consequences for you could be very serious."

"It won't come to that," replies Joan. "A friend warned me you might fail this test, but I see already that you are good men, too, though also overly cautious."

Her questioner sits back in his seat, dumbfounded, but you see a smile form on at least one other face.

"Perhaps we should proceed with our questions," says the black haired man.

"Very well. Tell us about your upbringing, young lady."

So the examination begins. Joan tells them about her family and her life in the fields and meadows of Domrémy.

"My mother taught me the prayers and creeds, and also how to cook and clean and sew. I doubt there is a woman in Poitiers who could teach me more about sewing. In fact, I see that you have a tear in your robe there. If you'll bring me some thread and a needle,

Freeman Ng

I could fix it for you while we talk."

At that, even the elderly leader of the group has to smile.

The examiners turn next to the question of her faith.

"Do you believe in God?" asks one of them.

"Better than you!" she replies smartly, and her words elicit not shock, but smiles and chuckles. She tells them about the visits she received from you and Catherine and Michael, repeating in amazing detail every word you ever spoke to her.

"These voices," asks one man in a very different dialect than the others, "when they speak to you, do they speak in French?"

"Better than yours!" is the reply, and the whole group bursts into raucous laughter.

"She has you there!"

"This is the pure French! It is you who have strayed!"

When they settle down, their leader flips through the pages of his notes, obviously skipping over many questions they had planned to ask. He stops at a page and shows it to the others, who nod in agreement.

Turning back to Joan, he asks, "Can you recite the Lord's Prayer for us?"

"Yes," she replies, but rising from her seat, begins, "Let us pray."

The men turn to one another in surprise. Some of them bow their heads or stand, while the others look on uncertainly, as Joan leads them in that model prayer.

When they ask her to recite other prayers and creeds, she responds the same way, not merely parroting the words to show that she knows them, but truly praying the prayers and proclaiming the creeds. When she gets to the end of the Apostles Creed, her examiners rise to their feet as one to join her.

> *I believe in the Holy Spirit,*
> *the holy catholic church,*
> *the communion of saints,*
> *the forgiveness of sins,*

the resurrection of the body,
and life everlasting.

"Amen," they all say together, and silence descends upon the gathering.

"Miss," ventures one of them out of the stillness, "is there some sign you can give us or point to – that we can present to the Dauphin – that would prove your true call from God?"

Joan steps forward and looks around the semi-circle from man to man, that expression of ferocity you once saw in a sunny meadow of Domrémy back on her face.

"Send me to Orléans!" she cries in a passion of impatience. "*Then* you'll have your sign!"

The night the company returns to Chinon, Joan's nightmares return. You're overtaken by them before you can even enter her room. It happens the moment you pass through her door to join her for the night. When you get to the other side, you find yourself not in her room, but at the back of the cathedral again. This time, before you can reach the bishop, the mad dying man rises from the pews and begins raving about how you aren't his legitimate son. Drawing a knife, you rush at him, stabbing him again and again. Then you stand beneath the cloud-shrouded sky, lashed by the wind, with your dying enemy at your feet reaching out his hands to take hold of you. You try with all your might to escape that grasp, but can't lift a foot off the planking of the bridge. You thrash and strain, and wake just as you're giving up the struggle.

It's still night, but Joan is not in her bed. You return to the common room, which is also empty, but find her out on the balcony deep in talk with Jean de Metz. She's dressed as she was during the day, and the remains of a meal sit on a table behind them.

"No, no," he says. "They were not all men. There was the sister of Percival, for example. She joined the three Grail Knights for a time, and if it had not been for her, they would never have achieved the Quest."

"What was her name?"

"Well, um, the accounts don't name her."

"I see. And how did she save the Quest?"

They're clearly in the middle of some long discussion or dispute. Joan has clearly not been to bed. Then you realize what has been happening. All this time, you've been inside someone else's dreams!

The next day, the judgment of the examiners of Poitiers is received by the court, and then relayed to the company.

"Most noble Lord Dauphin, after examining the girl Joan of Domrémy who is called the Maid, we find no evil in her, but only goodness, humility, honesty, and simplicity. Her claims we cannot judge with certainty. It may well be that she brings divine help to your Highness. It is also possible she could help deliver France by entirely natural means. If the Dauphin wishes for our counsel, we would urge him to send her to Orléans and so put the question to a true test, for we see no other hope for France otherwise."

De Metz hands the document back to the squire that delivered it.

"Surprisingly reasonable!" he marvels. "Now, I wonder what the next test will be."

"There are no more tests," replies the messenger. "The Dauphin asks that the Maid appear before him in the Great Hall this afternoon."

At the appointed time, Joan is escorted to the royal hall. Only you are with her, for neither Poulengy nor de Metz were invited. When you reach the entrance to the hall, you find Catherine waiting there.

The escort instructs Joan to step just inside the door and wait to be invited further in. She obeys and then stands looking curiously around the room.

At the far end of the hall, the Dauphin sits upon a throne. He's a large man with deep-set eyes and a streak or two of gray in his beard. Around the perimeter of the hall stand courtiers and clerks and armored knights, looking back and forth from their lord to Joan. You recognize among them the messenger who first greeted you when you entered the city, and the captain who escorted you to the Duke of Lorraine. And is that the guard who expressed his belief in Joan when you arrived at the palace? You're glad he did not, evidently, get into too much trouble for criticizing Charles in the hearing of his superior.

Standing near the back of the room is a man you can't quite place. You're sure you know him, and yet equally sure you've never seen him before. He's average in height, but skinny in an angular, bony way that you would not have forgotten had you seen it before. His face appears to be not quite put together correctly, and wears a hunted, or haunted look. Who could he be? Someone you knew from before Chinon, perhaps?

Then his gaze crosses yours for an accidental second, and you realize in a rush of confusion who he is: the *dreamer* whose dreams you've been sharing!

Who is this man who dreams of coronations and murders and madness? He's dressed in ordinary clothing, neither a noble nor a soldier, but apparently just another servant or clerk of the palace.

"Be welcome to the court of the Dauphin, Joan of Domrémy!" cries a squire. "You may approach his royal majesty."

Joan takes three steps into the hall, pauses, and then turns and walks right up to your dreamer! She kneels before the man and says, "God keep you, gentle king!"

Shocked murmurs echo throughout the chamber.

"I am not the king!" protests the man. At the other end of the hall, the Dauphin rises from this throne and clears this throat loudly.

Joan laughs!

"Did you think I would not recognize my sovereign? You are Charles, heir to the throne of France, whom I have come to help and guide!"

The crowd bursts into exclamations of delight and wonder. The man in the royal finery steps away from the throne and gestures for the Dauphin to take his place, but Charles shakes his head shortly. He looks ruefully at Joan.

"Well done!" he says. "Nevertheless, I did not lie. I am not your king yet, nor is it likely I will ever be. And that might not prove so ill, might it not? For it may be that I would not be a very good king, after all."

No one reacts with any surprise or shock. They all simply hang their heads.

"They have grown too accustomed to this!" mutters Catherine.

"For that which God wills to not be accomplished would be ill, indeed," Joan tells the man. "Come, noble prince, let us speak privately and then we will see."

Charles points her to a curtained side chamber. You make to follow them, but Catherine restrains you.

"It has been decreed by God that no one in Heaven or on Earth should learn what she is about to tell him."

So you watch with the rest of the court while Charles and Joan withdraw behind the veil of thin gauze. You can still make out his face, though you can't hear anything that's said.

Joan does most of the talking. At first, Charles stands before her with his hands clasped behind his back and a patient smile on his face, but the smile is soon replaced by a frown, and then a look of genuine attention. Joan speaks to him calmly, with her gaze fixed steadily upon his face, looking just like Catherine does when she imparts information and instruction.

The Dauphin's face blooms into a look you can only describe as radiant. Those in the hall who can see it gasp, while the rest crane for a better view. He kisses both of Joan's cheeks and makes to reenter the hall, but she stops him. As she continues to talk, his smile disappears. He paces back and forth, disappearing and reappearing in the veiled doorway, and speaking now as well as listening. Finally, he kneels briefly before her, provoking more gasps, and emerges from the side chamber.

Looking at him, you change your word from "radiant" to "exalted". You're reminded of the distant, timeless face of Michael. He walks with a formal grace over to the throne, brushes a hand lightly across its surface, and sits upon it.

The crowd erupts with cries of joy and shouts of acclamation. Charles sweeps his gaze slowly around the hall from his high seat. When he speaks, his voice vibrates with suppressed excitement.

"We welcome, and accept with thankfulness to God who rules all the nations, the presence and help of this Maid, Joan of Domrémy, and we command that an expedition be assembled with all dispatch to accompany her to the succor and rescue of our city of Orléans!"

By the time Joan gets back to the rooms, her companions have heard about the results of the audience.

"Did he believe you right away?" asks de Metz. "How did you convince him?"

"I think he believed in me even before I appeared in Chinon, and was only afraid to play the part that God had called him to. When I set him at ease concerning those fears, he was ready to be king at last."

"Those I have spoken to tell it differently," says Poulengy. "They say you performed a Sign."

"Did I? I don't think so. I only spoke with him."

"Did they not set up another man in royal dress upon the throne, and did you not ignore him and go straight to the Dauphin?"

"Well, yes, but –"

"How did you know it was him?"

She pauses.

"Was it your voices?" asks de Metz.

"I don't think so. It was just obvious. But it could have been something my voices, or even one of you, told me in the past about the Dauphin's appearance or his manner. All I know is that I saw at once that the man on the throne could not be the king, and when I looked around the room, it was just as clear who was."

The next day, the company readies itself for departure. It includes a large number of knights to aide in the battles to come, and several wagons loaded with food and other supplies for the relief of the long besieged populace of the city. Additional weaponry is provided to Joan's two companions, who traveled from Vaucouleurs with only their swords, and armor is found for them all.

"Well," says Jean de Metz to Joan, rapping a knuckle against the burnished metal that encases her, "you look safe enough."

"I plan to be anything but," she replies.

At dusk, when all the preparations are in place, Joan takes a final walk through the streets of Chinon with Jean de Metz.

"Tell me," he says. "What was the Dauphin so fearful of, and what did you tell him to dispel it?"

"Why do you ask, my love?"

"All anyone can speak of is how you recognized him in the hall, but you said that was not the thing that persuaded him."

"That's true."

"So, I am curious. What persuaded him?"

She stops, a thoughtful look on her face.

"I do not think I can tell you. Maybe I received the words from my Voices, after all, because I feel certain now that I was also commanded never to reveal them."

"The mysterious ways of God!" laughs de Metz, and turns to continue their walk, but Joan reaches out a hand to stop him.

"I am truly sorry! I see now that this is more important to you than you are saying. I am more sorry than *I* can say. I would tell you if I could. I would tell *you* if I could tell no one else!"

He looks at her in wonder.

"Perhaps you are simply a mind reader!" he says.

He gestures toward a stone bench, and they sit.

"I have long had doubts concerning the Dauphin, and thought that if I could just meet him, I could finally disabuse myself of them and pledge my service to him with an untroubled heart. Now that you've met him – and read his mind, it seems – I thought I could learn what I needed to know from you."

"What do you need to know?"

He takes a deep breath before he continues.

"There is a story. He was engaged in negotiations with the Duke of Burgundy. They met once, to no avail, and agreed to meet a second time. The appointed place was an old bridge near Poilly. Charles and his men returned from that meeting saying nothing of what transpired. The Duke did not. He and his men were never seen again.

"Now, it could be that they had an accident or ran into some other enemy on their way back from that meeting. Or it could be they never even reached the bridge. Or maybe they did reach the bridge and encountered treachery there.

"If a man invited his enemy to a parlay and then ambushed him when he arrived, I don't think I could serve him. And here I am, about to ride to war for the Dauphin, and I need to know what he is."

Joan gets up from the bench and walks a few paces away.

"Margaret, Catherine," she whispers. "He is a good man, and needs to know for the sake of his own good conscience. What can I tell him?"

You have no answer for her, and Catherine does not appear. She returns to the bench.

"If the Duke of Burgundy was killed on that bridge," she tells her friend, "it was not by the command of the Dauphin, nor was it in accordance with any wish he had. He is no murderer."

He nods in cautious relief.

"Bertrand always said so, but I had my doubts. Maybe there really is a God and he speaks to you, or perhaps you simply see the hearts of men more clearly than most. Either way, I will trust you."

He smiles triumphantly at her, but Joan frowns.

Freeman Ng

"Jean," she says. "Anything and anyone can fail. The hands of Charles are clean now, but they might not stay that way forever. You must promise me that you will remain loyal to his service no matter how he might betray you or anyone you love. For he will be a good king for France, and all that I do is for France."

On your last night in the palace, you follow Charles to his bed to see how his dreams might have changed following his encounter with Joan. This time, the coronation plays out to its completion amid the cheers of the crowd and the ringing of trumpets, but just as the bishop places the crown on your head, the thunderous noise echoing through the cathedral is swallowed up in darkness, and the feel of metal upon your head becomes the weight of shackles on your wrists.

You're in the prison cell again!

First Joan and now the Dauphin. The same dream, down to the feel of the rough stone floor and the certain knowledge of your complete abandonment. Could it be that this is actually *your* dream, born of your own experience of martyrdom? But you were never held in a place like this. Your trial was swift, and your execution immediate.

From somewhere in the dark comes the flat splatter of slowly dripping water. The air is heavy and still. Above you, around you, beneath you, is stone, stone, stone.

The Towers of Orléans

"Twelve towers gird the walls and ways of the city of Orléans: five on the west side and three on the north. One lone bastion, the St. Loup, far down the eastern road, and to the south, across the river, the towers of St. Jean and St. Augustin. And finally, the Tourelles, where you will find the English at their greatest strength, for it guards not only the main gates of the city, but the bridge that leads to it and the river passage below."

So spoke Catherine on a sunny terrace of the Dauphin's palace in Chinon. Now, you strain to orient yourself in the darkness through which you march, led by a detachment from the city that met you when you were still two days away.

"Joan," you whisper. "Do you know where we are? They say we're almost there, but I haven't seen any towers, much less the city. I tried looking ahead, and there's only a river in our path."

"That will be the Loire," says Joan. "The city stands beside the river, so that is all right, but I think we must be well to the east of it right now. Perhaps we are going to attack the tower of St. Loup first."

Jean de Metz, marching ahead of her, turns.

"Did you say something, my love?"

"I was wondering when we would finally reach the English," she says.

"Ah, you young soldiers!" he declares. "Always so anxious to enter your first battle. You should rather be grateful for any delay, for no one is ever as eager to see his second."

You come to a camp of darkened tents by the river, and your guides announce that you've arrived.

"Arrived where?" demands Joan. "I see no towers anywhere. No walls."

"This is a base where we have been stocking supplies for the relief of the city," they explain. "From here, we will sail under cover of darkness to its eastern gate, which the English have left unguarded because they control all the dry ground around it."

"Clever!" chuckles de Metz, but Joan is furious.

"I have no need to enter the city. We have come to free it, not to cower within its walls! Take us to the English positions!"

The men look uncomfortably at one another.

"We are sorry," they say. "We have no authority to do anything else but bring you here."

"Very well," replies Joan. "Then who does? Who commands here?"

"I do," comes a mild voice out of the darkness. A slender man steps forward and bows elegantly.

"I am Jean Dunois, in temporary charge of the city's defenses, and I rejoice at your coming. The people of the city have desired greatly to look upon the Maid of whom they have heard such marvelous –"

"Why did you have us brought here, rather than to where the English are?"

"The land approaches are too dangerous," he explains, showing no sign of offense at having been interrupted. "This is the safest way into the city."

"But we are here to fight the English! Take us to their towers, and we will make *all* the ways safe in no time!"

"That would not be prudent. The English have many more men than we do, and they would be defending strong towers while we attacked in the open. Indeed, we have more to fear from their attack than they from ours. Supply and reinforcement are the indicated courses."

Joan walks right up to him, so that she has to crane her neck to look into his face. Dunois continues looking kindly upon her as she demands, "Indicated by what?"

Some of his men chuckle openly at the sight of their commander called to account by a girl, but he answers her earnestly.

"By the calculations I referred to, as well as my own judgment and the counsel of those wiser than I."

"Good sir!" cries Joan. "I bring you better counsel than anything you could hear from the wisest advisor. I bring you greater strength than you would receive from a company of men or a hundred cannon. I bring help from the King of Heaven! For he has taken pity on the people of Orléans, and will not permit them or their city to fall to their enemies. You have only to strike boldly, trusting in His care. Or is it so hard to believe that our Lord might wish you to live and not die?"

Dunois' men stop laughing, but he doesn't alter his polite, solicitous manner at all. The man is a bastion of courtesy!

"The more welcome are you, then, Maid sent by God. If it be His will, we will attack. However, let us first bring these provisions safely into the city, for the people suffer greatly from hunger. That alone may be a feat more difficult than you would guess, for we have had no wind for three days now, and no expectation of... any..."

His mouth remains open and his eyes turn up to the heavens. The leaves of the trees begin to rustle, and from the direction of the river comes the sound of creaking wood and flapping canvas. A great wind arises, howling above you in the darkness, blowing in the direction of the city.

All the men aboard the lead ship, even her friends Jean de Metz and Bertrand de Poulengy, regard Joan with something like awe. They stand silently behind her while she gazes out over the prow into the darkness through which the miraculous wind propels them.

You, too, remain speechless. If you once felt like a bystander in the temple when the baby Jesus was brought to be blessed, you now feel like a passenger on the storm-tossed boat who saw the man that baby grew into stride across the waves and take the weather in hand with a word.

Poulengy finally breaks the silence.

"Commander, perhaps you could tell us something of the situation here."

"Yes," replies Dunois. "Yes, of course. Do you see that tower to our right?"

You can just make out the silhouette of battlements against the gray stars.

"It is the bastion of St. Loup, the easternmost tower held by the English. Though it is farther from the city than any of their other strongholds, in many ways it causes us the greatest problems, for it lies along the best route for bringing supplies and reinforcements into the city. Until we can increase our strength, we cannot attack the closer English positions, but no reinforcements can reach us in any great numbers while St. Loup stands. And we dare not send the army out so far against it, for that would leave the city under defended."

"Would you really need the entire army to take one tower?" asks de Metz.

"That is what my calculations indicate, though one of my commanders begs me every day to be allowed to attack it with just his company."

"The Duke of Vignolles," murmurs Joan, causing the men to start.

"Yes!" says Dunois. "How did you know?"

She doesn't answer, and he looks long at her before continuing.

"Well, he is a mighty knight and the boldest commander we

have, but to attack a stronghold defended by more men than you can bring against it is simple folly!"

The men continue discussing the strategic outlook for the city. As they talk, you become aware of another voice sounding in a gentle counterpoint to theirs: Catherine stands beside Joan at the prow.

"So, dear child, the day has come. You are about to begin the work God has called you to do. Do you remember all that I have taught you about what must be done? And do you still accept the charge that has been laid upon you?"

"I do," says Joan, and you whisper it breathlessly with her, "I do," still caught up in the power of the raised wind.

"But Catherine," she continues, "there is one thing you and Michael must understand."

Jean de Metz glances over at her, having overheard her whisper, perhaps. After he turns back to his talk with the other men, Joan finishes her statement: "I will not kill."

"That is well!" says Catherine. "For your place will not be to take life, but to preserve it, just as our purpose is not to destroy England, but to save France."

Joan enters the city of Orléans wearing a golden doublet over her male attire and riding a white horse. Four footmen walk alongside her, while a fifth follows close behind bearing a war standard on which are painted two angels surrounded by fleurs-de-lis. There's a collective "Ahhhhhh" by the crowd at her appearance in the open gate, but a profound silence takes hold as she moves slowly into the city.

She brings her horse to a stop at the center of a small square, but the crowd keeps its distance around her. Some of the women begin to hold out their hands in gestures of yearning or adoration, but no one enters the circle of cleared space. Then a child bolts from her mother and runs right up to Joan's horse. The crowd gasps but Joan only laughs and, reaching down a hand, pulls the beaming child up onto the horse and sets her in the saddle in front of her.

Others approach then, to welcome her, to hear her words, or simply to touch her. One man bearing a torch gets too close and sets a corner of the war standard on fire, but before anyone can react, Joan swings her horse neatly over and damps out the flames with her bare hands. Then the crowd finally erupts into cheers and shouts of acclamation.

"The Maid of Orléans! Vive la Pucelle! Long live the Maid!"

Joan dismounts. The people surround her, lifting her up on their shoulders and carrying her away down through the streets of Orléans like a gentle but insistent river.

"Today was quite a day, was not it?"

You're alone with Joan in her quarters. She's just thrown herself onto the bed, and lies staring up at the ceiling. Her tone is lighthearted, but you still feel the weight of the wind's roar on the river and the crowd's awe in the square.

"I am not sure yet about this Dunois fellow," she continues, "but he had a good idea about the entrance!"

The robe and horse had been the commander's idea, and while Joan showed little enthusiasm for them at the time, she made no objection and only asked to include the banner, which she had had made in Chinon. So arrayed, she seemed like a different person from the girl with whom you idled in the meadows of Domrémy, and even like another kind of being entirely: an archangel like the inhuman Michael, or a Figure from History, or a Saint.

"Joan? The wind…did you…how did you…?"

She laughs.

"I know nothing of the wind! Perhaps Catherine arranged it. If so, we must thank her the next time we see her!"

"The people in the square. I've never seen a crowd – welcome a visitor like that."

You almost said "worship."

"Margaret!" Joan exclaims, sitting bolt up in the bed, suddenly earnest. "Do you know what? I love them! I love these people!

Their faces were so beautiful!"

"Soon," you declare softly, "you'll set them free."

"Yes! We must be strong and bold now, and inspire the soldiers here to boldness, and soon our work will be done."

That night, Joan has the strangest dream you ever experienced, either through her or in your own past life. It is a dream of sensation alone. There are no sights or sounds, but only pain. It throbs just above your heart, sending waves of agony through your body. You wonder if she's not dreaming at all, but suffering from some kind of illness or wound, but can't wake yourself to see. The pain lessens as the night wears on, but then, just as it's about to disappear entirely, explodes again, like a smoldering log bursting into new flame when turned. Once again, it slowly dies away, only to spring to life again a short time later. The pattern repeats itself throughout the night, playing out more and more quickly until it's like a terrible heartbeat you have no power to stop or slow.

Wake! you tell yourself. *Wake!*

Wake! Wake! Wake!

And then you do.

It's morning, and Joan lies in her bed panting, her face slick with sweat, clutching her left shoulder.

"Joan!" you cry. "What was that? Are you all right?"

She starts at the sound of your voice.

"Margaret!"

She looks down at her shoulder and slowly removes her hand to reveal the sweat soaked cloth of her nightdress.

"Just a dream," she says. "Just a bad dream."

By the time she recovers sufficiently to dress and venture out of the house, it's almost mid-day and she's seething with impatience to find her companions.

"Joan, you're still trembling from that nightmare!" you tell her. "Stay and rest. The others will find us."

"They are certainly holding a war council as we speak. I must be there!"

"How will we find them? This city is enormous! We'll get lost."

However, when you exit the house, you're greeted by an attendant posted there to be your guide.

"The commander is away from the city again," he tells Joan. "but I can take you to your companions."

He leads you through the streets to the city garrison, where you find Jean de Metz and Bertrand de Poulengy in a large hall bent in earnest consultation over a map laid flat on a table. Off to one side, a mountain of a man paces back and forth. He wears a commander's uniform, but it's tattered and stained with dirt and blood, and the long, unkempt hair of his head and beard catches the light around his face like a halo. He's heavily armed, and every once in a while, swings the biggest sword you've ever seen in easy loops through the still air of the chamber.

"What about this island in the river?" asks de Metz. "Could we land on the opposite side and then cross over where the river is narrow?"

"No!" replies the unknown commander without stopping his pacing. "The bank is steep and muddy, and in plain sight of the tower. Too few would reach the top."

"What if we sailed down river to where we first met Dunois and attacked from the east?" suggests Poulengy.

Just then, de Metz notices Joan's approach and calls out, "You're late, my love!"

The unknown man stops, glances briefly at Joan, and then resumes his pacing.

"I am sorry," she replies. "I've been a slug abed this morning. Have you already held council? When do we attack, and where?"

De Metz and Poulengy look at each other. Poulengy speaks.

"I am afraid there is no definite plan yet. The Commander has gone to bring back more supplies and reinforcements. Once he returns, we will talk again."

Joan huffs impatiently.

"All he is doing is increasing the time the city can remain untaken. It will never be *freed* unless we attack!"

The large man halts his pacing again and looks at her with greater interest than before.

"You speak for the Wrath!" he says.

De Metz steps forward.

"Joan of Domrémy, allow me to present 'the Wrath.'"

"That is what they call him here," explains Poulengy. "He is the Duke of Vignolles."

"You are the Maid!" cries the Duke.

He strides swiftly forward, his unsheathed sword still in one hand, so that you dart forward yourself with a cry of alarm, but when he reaches her, he plunges just as swiftly to his knees before her, holding out the handle of his sword.

"The Wrath is yours to command, Maid sent from God!"

Joan takes the sword, which is almost as long as she is tall, and attempts a short swing with it.

"Rise, my friend. I have two commands for now. First, call me Joan. Second, find me a sword more suited to my stature, for I will ride soon to battle!"

There's no battle for a while yet, though. Dunois remains away from the city, and no one can be persuaded to take any action in his absence. Joan resumes the daily rhythm she established in Vaucouleurs while waiting for Sir Robert to change his mind, spending her mornings with Jean de Metz and Bertrand de Poulengy and her afternoons among the people.

In the evenings, she speaks cheerfully to you about her impatience for the fighting to begin, and your own spirit begins to revive through the inspiration of her lighthearted words. However, you avoid entering her sleep again for fear of the dream of pain, though she shows no signs of experiencing it again.

One day when she tires of waiting for Dunois' return, she has a letter sent to the commander of the English siege, dictating it to Jean de Metz.

"To the King of England and to the Duke of Bedford, who call yourself the regent of France: Our Lord God in Heaven commands that you render to the Maid the keys to this and all the cities of France that you wrongly hold, for she has come on behalf of the rightful king to reclaim all that is his. She is ready to make peace, if you will return to your own country and bring no more death and destruction to this kingdom, but if you will not, we will strike against you wherever we find you, and bring such calamity upon you as France has not seen in a thousand years."

De Metz finishes the last line and passes the letter over to Joan to be signed. Just then, Bertrand de Poulengy enters the room.

"You can write!" he exclaims, but blushes when she and de Metz turn to him with smiles on their faces.

"I apologize if I offended," he says. "It is just that I have never heard of a girl from the villages knowing how to read and write. How did you come by those skills?"

"I can only write," replies Joan. "And only my name. And even then, I still have trouble with that big 'J'. But you can blame all my shortcomings on my teacher, who stands before you."

"You?" Poulengy says to his old friend. "When did you teach her?"

"In Chinon," answers de Metz. "During those interminable days when you were trying to secure Joan an audience with the Dauphin. She decided that she needed to be able to sign military orders and letters like this one, once we were on campaign."

"It seems you had more faith or foresight than I that we would eventually win the Dauphin's trust."

"We also worked out a trick," says Joan. "I will always sign any orders I give, but if I also mark a document with a cross, that means that the order is not to be heeded."

"What would its purpose be, then?" asks Poulengy.

"To fall into the hands of the enemy!" says de Metz.

Poulengy laughs, but then grows serious.

"It's a good idea," he tells Joan. "A very good idea. It seems you have a knack for military thinking."

Dunois returns the following week with the reinforcements, and the French commanders finally meet in council.

"Do you judge that we can now attack St. Loup and still have sufficient forces to defend the city?" asks Poulengy.

"I do," begins Dunois, "or I did, when I had secured the extra men. However, while in Blois, I received reports that a mighty English army, numbering more than five thousand by some accounts, with a large part of them bowmen, landed on the coast six days ago. They are led by Sir John Fastolf, a commander of considerable repute. If this is their intended destination, they could arrive any day. Until we can be more certain of their whereabouts and movements, I judge that we must remain in a defensive posture."

The Duke's face is frozen in an expression of disbelief. Poulengy bows his head.

"This is absurd!" cries Jean de Metz. "If English reinforcements are on the way, that only means we must strike the more quickly!"

"Alas," replies Dunois. "We cannot risk any significant losses even in victory. We could retake one or more of the towers only to lose the entire city once Sir Fastolf arrives. Therefore, be patient! We will send out scouts in search of this new English army. Then we will know enough to make a better determination."

Dunois adjourns the council, but Joan and her companions stay behind. The Duke of Vignolles also remains in his seat, a brooding look on his face.

"Who thinks he will order an attack – ever?" asks de Metz.

"His heart is in the right place," says Poulengy. "He is cautious with the lives of his men and his people, as any commander should be. He will never attack as long as his calculations indicate otherwise."

"You don't agree with him, do you?" asks de Metz.

"No. In this case, delay is the greater risk. The English can bring more force to bear on the city than we could ever raise in defense of it, so we must strike while we have some hope of success. But it is hard for a man like him to see things this way."

The four of them sit around the table in silence. Then Joan walks up to the Duke.

"*You* must attack St. Loup!"

He stares at her in mute surprise. De Metz springs out of his seat.

"We were told you thought you could succeed with just your company," he presses. "Do you still believe that?"

"I do, but the Commander will not allow me."

"You don't need his permission!" says Poulengy, rising in turn. "You are a nobleman. You have the authority to raise armies and fight on your own! The company you command consists entirely of your own men, does it not?"

"It does. Nevertheless, the Wrath has never disobeyed the orders of any man he pledged to serve."

They lapse into silence again. This time, it's de Metz who breaks it.

"Joan, do you still wish him to attack St. Loup?"

"Yes."

"Based on your own judgment alone, or is this also the desire of some…higher authority?"

"Saint Catherine has told me over and over that the city's time is short, that we must attack as soon as possible after my arrival."

"And she speaks for God."

"Of course."

"There you have it," he says, turning to the Duke. "Would you not agree that orders from God should take precedence over the Commander's?"

Early the next morning, Joan starts awake from a peaceful

dream of tending the family sheep.

"Margaret, a battle is about to begin, but I cannot tell if it is because Sir Fastolf has arrived, or the Duke has ridden out! Go and find out while I dress!"

You fly immediately upward so you can take in the entire city, but detect no movement anywhere around its walls. You circle around to each of the eleven towers that surround it, and still find nothing of note. Finally, you turn your eyes to the east, to the distant twelfth tower, and see what seems to be a plume of smoke or dust around its base. Could it be a battle? Then from the direction of the tower sounds a dull boom like the crash of an enormous stone fallen from a great height.

"St. Loup!" you call out to Joan. "There's a battle going on right now!"

"Vive la Hire!" she cries as she dashes out of the house. "Long live the Wrath!"

She wears the golden cloak over her armor and carries her banner of war. Mounting her horse, she spurs it into motion and is off like a bright streak through the streets of the still slumbering city.

Six hours later, Joan walks her horse back toward the city along the eastern road that connects it to the St. Loup. Beside her is the Duke of Vignolles, and behind them march his men. At the very end of the procession, a large number of English soldiers trudge along under guard, prisoners captured in the destruction of the tower. The first small battle for the liberation of the city has been won, and Joan and the Duke are in high spirits, but you are in an entirely different state of mind. You float high above the celebrating soldiers, unwilling to descend back down among them.

"Catherine!" you pray or cry into the depths of blue above you. "You have to find someone who can take my place. I can't do this!"

Once – a thousand years ago! – you were in the room for the birth of an aunt's baby. Once, a man had an arm crushed by a mishandled stone while you were visiting your father on a work site. Once, twice, you experienced the cries of those in pain to the limits of human endurance.

Today, you heard them again, only multiplied many times over, and unending. There were no healers to staunch wounds or set bones, and for every sufferer who found some relief or oblivion on his own, two more immediately replaced him. This cacophony of pain, more than the gruesome sights you saw – you could at least shut your eyes to those – drove you quickly from Joan's side, and then from the battle entirely. You lost all thought for your mission, or for France, or for Joan. You fled high into the air, never looking back until the sounds of the battle were a murmur. From a great distance, you saw Joan's war banner reach Vignolles', and watched the battle unfold from that point like a harmless pantomime.

It's only now that the fighting is long over that you let yourself descend close enough to see and hear the men marching back up to the city. You're terrified that at any moment, Joan will glance up and meet your gaze with a look of…what? Anger? Accusation? Disappointment? Below, she laughs at some jest of the Duke's and claps him on the back.

Catherine! you pray. *Speak to me! Help me!*

Dunois waits for the returning company at the eastern gate of the city. Jean de Metz and Bertrand Poulengy are with him, and when de Metz spots Joan, he lets out a whoop and races out to embrace her. The Duke strides up to his commander and bows low.

"I rejoice to see you return in victory, and with so few losses," says Dunois steadily.

"I rode forth on my own authority," replies Vignolles. "Nevertheless, I ask your pardon for disobeying your orders, today and in the days to come."

"The days to come?"

Dunois looks from the Duke to Joan.

"We are pressing on, to the tower of St. Jean," says Joan. "Send the rest of the army to join us!"

Freeman Ng

"That would be most imprudent!" cries Dunois. "Even with the full army. The English are much more concentrated in that area, and we have been unable to determine the whereabouts of Sir Fastolf."

"Nevertheless," says Joan, raising her voice, "the soldiers will go forth as they have before – is that not so?"

The men of Vignolle's company roar in confirmation.

"And they will prevail – as they have before!"

The men cheer again, striking their swords against their shields.

"My calculations!" pleads Dunois. "They clearly indicate defeat! I beg you to reconsider!"

"Didn't they indicate defeat for the Duke at St. Loup as well?" asks de Metz, but before Dunois can answer, Vignolles speaks again.

"They did. And they were right! I, the Wrath, was wrong. We *were* defeated. I was sounding the retreat when the Mai – when Miss Joan appeared. Then it seemed to me that my men became possessed by the spirit of Roland himself. They fought as they never had before!"

"What happens to your calculations if you double our numbers?" Poulengy asks Dunois. "What happens if every man fights with the strength of two, because he fights for the Maid and knows that he must prevail?"

Dunois' gaze turns inward for a moment. Then he looks up and says, "They still come short. However – they come close enough!"

So it is that the battle for Orléans resumes sooner than you expected, before you have a chance to speak with Joan, to explain your absence from that first victory. There's a brief period when she's entirely occupied devising a hasty plan of attack along with the other commanders, and then they're on the march again.

I mustn't leave her again, you tell yourself. *I must be strong this time!*

But when you see the walls of the St. Jean rise before you, your will is overcome by a panic that seems to come from a place outside yourself, as on the day of your earthly life when you broke a finger and found yourself simply unable to place it in the hands of the healer who needed to set it, and before you know it, you're once again floating high above the battlefield.

To your astonishment, as the French forces begin their charge against the tower, the English pour from its gates, but in the opposite direction, abandoning that stronghold to join their fellows in the St. Augustin.

They, too, have no stomach for the coming fight!

The French forces press on to the St. Augustin, and this time, the English stand their ground. Despite your distance from the action, you can't keep yourself from imagining the horrors that are surely playing out below. In your brief exposure to battle at the St. Loup, you heard and saw – and *smelled*, and felt in your bones – enough to supply your imagination for a thousand years. You try to calm yourself by thinking of the battle as a game like the one you saw many playing in Chinon. A war game to be sure – played with knights and kings and castles – but one that was carried out in quiet contemplation, an exercise in strategy and tactics entirely bodiless and bloodless. You begin to follow the battle below like you used to follow those games as an impartial spectator, seeking only to comprehend its secrets: the clash of advancing forces, the breakthroughs, the retreats.

There, on the fringes of the battle, is the most important piece of all: the Queen.

Joan's banner of war remains for a long time planted solidly at the very edge of the fighting, but soon begins a pattern of rapid but shallow advances toward the tower followed by equally swift retreats. You realize that her position must reflect the progress of the French forces as a whole, and your hopes begin to rise and fall with her every movement.

The battle winds on through the day, and over the course of the hours, you notice that the back-and-forth of Joan's banner

Freeman Ng

leaves her always a little farther back than she began. Soon, there are no longer any thrusts forward, but only a side to side slippage farther and farther away from the English tower.

The peace you gained through your distant contemplation of the battle as an innocent parlor game begins to slip as well. What will happen if the French fail to win this battle? Could you be the cause of their present struggles? Is Joan distracted or distressed because of your absence?

You begin to steel yourself to face your fears and go down to join her at last.

At that moment, however, her banner begins advancing on the tower again, and this time, does not turn immediately back into a retreat. It moves inexorably forward until it reaches the very walls of the St. Jean – and then it enters them! Within the hour, the fighting ends. Joan and the French have the victory.

Late in the night, you descend onto the battlefield. The fighting has been over for a long time, but as you come within range of its lingering signs – the smell of smoke and blood, the moaning of some wounded man – it's all you can do to maintain your intention and not flee once more. You make your way to the largest and brightest lit of the tents, and it turns out to be the command tent as you suspected, but Joan isn't there.

Dunois leans over a map on a table, his brows furrowed. With him are de Metz, Poulengy, and the Wrath.

"It is our best chance by far," murmurs Poulengy. "Today is the day."

"Always do the hardest thing first!" urges the Duke.

"And anyway," adds de Metz, "this is what Joan wants. Do you really think you will be able to persuade the men to take any other course? Let's just get on with it!"

Dunois sighs, still looking down at the map.

"Very well," he says. "Tomorrow we will meet our fate, whether it be deliverance or death."

You withdraw and continue your search for Joan.

You find her banner next, at the stables. A groomer brushes the white horse she rode into Orléans and then into battle.

"Brave heart," he murmurs. "Valiant heart. You bore your precious burden well, did you not? And still you long to see the dawn and another day in the field. Soul of France! Soul of a warrior!"

Looking out over the dark camp, you spot a few tents still lit from within, and try them one by one. Outside one of them, you come across a man making a report to an officer.

"A dozen dead, and more than fifty wounded. Of these, half will be unfit to assemble tomorrow, though some of those may be able to help run supplies."

"Are you in need of supply yourself?"

"No, we still have a good store of herbs and dressings. More hands would be the greater help. If I had an aide, to say nothing of a second physician..."

"We will need every able man for the next attack. But take heart! It may well be the final action."

"That is good to hear. In the meantime, what should we do with these poor fellows?"

"The men are weary, and there will be many more tomorrow. Let them lie."

"Very good. God be with you in the morning!"

You leave them, not quite understanding that last bit of their conversation about "these poor fellows," but within a dozen paces find yourself among them: twelve dark bundles laid out in neat rows along the ground.

You feel no fear, but only a heaviness like that of the stone cell you've encountered in the dreams of two separate dreamers now, and you wonder if the dream was not, after all, a prophecy of any one person's destiny, but the shared nightmare of every living soul.

Many more will lie here at this time tomorrow, and those who escape will only be putting off the day when they must finally relinquish all thought and motion, all hope and all desire. Even I who can no longer die, who thought I would awaken to endless Day beyond the shadows of the world, am here again, standing among the quiet dead.

Freeman Ng

Is there no final escape from this place? Will my renewed life on this earth eventually set me down to lie here once more, perhaps when my duties to Joan have been discharged? Will she lie here herself some day?

Above you, around you, beneath you, the darkness makes no reply.

You finally come to a tent that emanates the sound of Joan's voice cheerfully humming the song of French cities, and you pause before entering. Was she not shaken at all by the carnage that drove you from her side?

At the St. Loup, you had to abandon her the moment you arrived on the terrible scene, and she didn't come back into your view until after the fighting was over, so you only ever saw her riding exultantly into the battle and then celebrating the winning of it with the Duke of Vignolles afterward. You have yet to see her *in* a battle.

"I will not kill," she told Catherine, and the thought comforts you, but what did she think of the killing – and dying – that she inspired others to do?

You enter.

She's preparing for bed. Her sword and armor sit by the entrance of the tent. Some of the clothing she's taken off and set by her bed is stained with blood. Though her face bears the same bright expression you've known for so long now, you find yourself a little afraid of her.

She kneels by her bed to pray.

"Lord in Heaven, I thank you for the victories we have had today, and for your guidance through the teachings of Catherine. I thank you for the friends who brought me here, and for the brave soldiers who have longed to fight as they are doing now. But more than anything, I thank you for Margaret, for how she helped me through this day."

For how she helped me through this day?

She looks up and queries the air, "Margaret?"

You make no answer.

She sighs and returns to her prayer.

"Send her again tomorrow, I beg you, for it is a certainty that I could not stand in the midst of the battle without her!"

She didn't suffer from your absence.

In fact, she thought you were with her all the time!

You ponder this through the long night.

You also ask yourself why you failed to respond when she called out for you, but the reason comes immediately to your mind: If you had, you would have no choice but to stay for the next day's battle. Now you're still free.

But what other choice could there be?

I promised to stand by her, to see her task completed.

And yet, everything went well even without you. Why did Joan think you had been with her?

Maybe Catherine heard your prayer, after all, and sent her some other help. Or maybe she was upheld by her own unsuspected strength.

Catherine! Catherine! I must speak with you!

You sit by Joan all night, but Catherine never appears.

At dawn, as the cock crows and Joan begins to stir in her bed, you fly from her side once more, streaking high above the still slumbering battlefield before you can be forced to ignore her call again.

Later that morning, you watch the French forces muster and make their way toward the Tourelles, the strongest and most important of the towers of Orléans. Then you understand the debate that must have occurred the night before. Dunois undoubtedly preferred to target one of the lesser towers, but Joan's desire prevailed.

Deliverance or death.

Will the question really be answered so quickly?

The battle plays out as before, with Joan's banner bobbing like a fallen leaf that reveals the swirling currents of the river. Back and forth it goes, approaching the tower one moment and retreating the next, and then, around midday, beginning the unchecked advance it made the day before, which in every other battle so far signaled the final French push to victory.

She's going to accomplish everything without me! I won't have to go down into the battle!

You thank God and Catherine and Michael in your heart. All the French needed, it seems, was to be pushed into fighting!

"Vive la France!" you call out, wondering if Joan will hear you. "Vive la Pucelle!" However, at that moment, your left shoulder explodes with pain.

All sight, all sound – every sensation – is obliterated by the waves of agony that spread through your body. You manage to hold on to a single thought: that this is the dream you shared with Joan her first night in Orléans. For a moment, brief and yet packed with whole lifetimes that might be lived upon this earth, you're torn between the raw imperative to flee, to save yourself at any cost, and another impulse that, wordless and nameless, rises up in the Void to oppose it - and then you're streaking toward the battlefield, toward Joan, toward the source of pain.

This time, you don't avert your eyes from the fighting. You look full on at the maimings and killings, the broken bodies, but their horror doesn't slow you. All across the battlefield, the English are issuing forth from their defensive positions in a sweeping coun-terattack, shouting that the Maid is dead. The demoralized French fall or flee before them. You watch one captain cut down while he distracts himself straining for some sight of Joan's banner and call-ing out for news of her. You know she can't be dead, though. The pain that grows in your shoulder by the moment tells you that she still feels. You increase your velocity, racing toward the place you ought to have been all along.

You find her lying with her armor removed in a small culvert near the base of the Tourelles. She screams and thrashes, but her men hold her down while one of them examines the arrow that protrudes from her left shoulder.

"There is nothing we can do for her here," he tells the others. "It would have been better if it went all the way through. Then we could cut off the tip and pull out the shaft. As it is, we should bring her back to the base."

Joan's distress increases at that, and she grabs the young man's arm, but isn't able to make herself understood to him.

"You must calm yourself," he urges her. "We are going to take you back to the base. You will be fine!" But she only becomes more agitated, screaming from the pain multiplied by her own exertions.

"Joan!" you cry out to her, "you have to calm down!"

"This is bad," the young man is saying. "We cannot carry her when she is in this state, and she will only hurt herself further if she keeps this up!"

Catherine! you cry out in your mind. *You must help us! Or show me how I can help Joan!*

You think about the fording of the river when Joan ran away to Vaucouleurs, and how you were able to save her (and be saved by her) from the violence of the waters. You think about that morning in the Laxart garden after her failed first attempt at the gates of Vaucouleurs, and feel again her tears on your shoulder. You think about the night of the English raid on Domrémy, when you assented to be her friend and guide through all.

"By the love of God that holds you," you say to her, and reaching out a hand, lay it on her wounded shoulder.

The second explosion of pain blinds you once more to all sight and sound, but you enter it willingly this time, and for what seems like an eternity, float once more in the timeless void between your death and your waking, the heart of the unshaped stone, the light on the meadows of Domrémy. When the pain subsides, Joan is no longer screaming, but speaking with the young man in a weak but clear voice.

"Pull it out! You must pull it out!"

"I cannot," he replies. "The arrowhead could cause more harm on its way out, or worse, break off! I am not a surgeon; I have only helped at times."

She looks steadily back at him.

"I will trust in God – and the sureness of your hand. Pull it out! There is no time for anything else!"

The young man nods soberly. Crossing himself, he takes firm hold of the arrow. Softly, he whispers, "One, two, three!" and pulls.

Joan screams and nearly wrenches herself free from the grasp of her men. The spot where the arrow entered her shoulder erupts with new blood. The men get her down again and begin to staunch the wound and dress it. Joan's cries slowly die down, until she lies quiet and dazed.

The young man, thrown backward by the force of his own pull on the arrow, rises unsteadily, holding up the arrow with its intact arrowhead in one hand as if it mustn't touch the ground.

"Rest now," he tells Joan. "You will be safe here, and we will stay by your side. When you are ready to move, we will get you safely back to the city. Okay?"

She reaches her good hand up to grasp his, then settles back onto the ground, closing her eyes.

Dazed yourself, you take stock of your surroundings for the first time. You're so close to the walls of the Tourelles that you can make out the triumphant expressions on the faces of the soldiers atop its ramparts. Yet, Joan and the men are completely hidden from their sight in the culvert. She's safe for the time being, but it's a precarious safety. The French forces seem to be standing their ground here better than in other parts of the battlefield, but that could change at any moment. And now that Joan's armor has been removed, a single stray arrow could finish the job begun by the first.

"Send word to the city at once," an officer is telling a young messenger. "Tell them the Maid has been injured, but is alive and safe, and we will bring her back when she is strong enough to be moved."

As he speaks, Joan opens her eyes again and begins calling out to you in distress.

"Margaret!" she whispers. "Find the commanders. Before the messenger reaches them, if you can. If they decide to call off the attack because of me, do all that you can to turn them from that course."

"Joan! Retreat might be your best chance. A successful attack might be the worse thing that could happen, because then the center of the fighting would have to come right here!"

"Let it come! Is that not why we were sent here? You have seen all that God has done so far. Do you doubt he will bring this work to its completion?"

You have no answer for that, but make one more attempt to dissuade her.

"If they do decide to retreat, what can I do? I've been sent only to you. Only you can hear me."

She laughs!

"Who told you that? Did you not know that there are helping spirits everywhere, speaking to people all the time? It is only that most will not hear them. But I know you will find a way!"

You reach the commanders well ahead of the messenger. They stand on the high ground at the base of the St. Augustin anxiously scanning the battlefield.

"Where is she!" bellows the normally mild Poulengy. "Why can no one tell me what happened?"

"Bertrand!" says Jean de Metz. "We should ride out to where she last stood. If she's in trouble, she will need our help. I have already assembled some horsemen."

Poulengy turns to him and cries, "Let us ride!" but Dunois speaks up then.

"Stay, gentlemen! The attack has spent itself. We must call for a retreat!"

Poulengy and de Metz begin to object, but Dunois says only,

"See for yourselves!" and sweeps his hand across the field.

Below you, the retreat is no longer just a losing game of chess, but a human catastrophe, terrible and chaotic. The English cut through the French defenses so easily that you glance involuntarily around the hill you stand on, worried that the still orderly scene will soon be swallowed up by the rout as well.

"We cannot abandon Joan!" shouts de Metz.

"As long as we keep fighting, we increase her danger," replies Dunois. "When we withdraw, so will the English."

"You are right," says Poulengy. "Signal the retreat, and may God bring her safely back!"

"No!" cries de Metz, but just then, a roar goes up among the French forces, beginning near the base of the Tourelles and spreading swiftly outward in a wave. It's like the rumble of thunder that washes across the land, and when it reaches the high ground where you stand, you shiver despite your bodiless state.

"The Maid!" shouts de Metz. "The Maid for France!"

Looking toward Joan's culvert, you see her banner held high once more and advancing swiftly against the tower.

"Gentlemen?" declares Dunois. "I believe we will ride after all!"

You streak past scenes of French soldiers shouting victory and pressing forward once more, and English defenders retreating in dismay. When you reach the culvert where Joan was hidden, you find it abandoned. Her banner stands boldly near the base of the Tourelles, but when you get there, you see it in the hands of the young man who pulled the arrow out of her shoulder a mere half hour ago. He's surrounded by the other men of Joan's command, and for a moment, you're afraid something terrible happened to her after all, but in the next, realize that she's standing among them, completely unarmored, with a siege ladder in her hands!

Arrows whistle down around her, but none of them come close to hitting her. Looking up at the battlements, you see the reason. The English are in a froth of panic. Archers appear, take one glance at the robed figure below them, and let loose their arrows almost at random, dashing away before even seeing whether they hit anything.

Joan turns at the approach of her friends.

"I am glad you have come," she calls out to them, "for I am wounded and cannot climb."

"Now!" she cries to her men, and shrieks with exertion or pain as they raise the ladder and slam it up against the wall of the Tourelles. When it hits the edge of the battlements, you see the defenders manning that position scatter as if it carried some deadly disease.

Jean de Metz leaps immediately from his horse.

"Then allow me the honor!" he cries.

She salutes him as he dashes past her and up the ladder. Dunois and Poulengy follow close behind him. Soon, more ladders materialize next to Joan's, and a battering ram begins pounding the tower gate. In mere hours, a startlingly swift denouement to the days of fighting since your arrival, the weeks of testing and travel before that, and the year since you first delivered to Joan God's promise of this outcome, the French control the tower of the Tourelles, and therefore the river passage and the main gates of the city. Though the English still occupy eight of the twelve towers surrounding Orléans, their siege is effectively broken.

Freeman Ng

The Road to Rheims

The English abandon their remaining positions the very next morning, so no further fighting is necessary. Orléans lies wholly in the hands of the French once more. The commanders meet in council to decide what their next step should be, with Joan among them, pale and subdued with her left arm in a sling.

"Prudence," begins Dunois, "would suggest that we remain here and defend the city. The English who withdrew today still constitute a formidable force, and Sir Fastolf remains unaccounted for. The indicated course is to repair the towers and send for more men to help defend them. As long as we hold Orléans, the English will not be able to make any further progress, and the Dauphin will remain safe in Chinon.

"Therefore, as the commander of the city defenses, I ask the council: Which city of the English shall we attack next?"

There's a moment of silence during which you ask yourself, *What did he say?* Then the company bursts into laughter. The Duke of Vignolles, whose scowl was growing more and more pronounced as the commander spoke, nearly chokes in his surprise.

"You might have said so from the start!" he sputters.

"I ask your forgiveness!" replies Dunois with a smile. "In truth, I do see some danger for the city yet, and we must remember this in any plan we make today. But I also know that the calculations I would once have made no longer hold in this new world, wherein walks a Maid who brings the help of God!"

"Vive la Pucelle!" assents Vignolles.

"In peace and happiness," adds de Metz. "Well, one way to deal with any new English army is to draw it to the defense of some English-held city elsewhere. I suggest Beaugency, then Meung, then Jargeau."

"Those are lesser strongholds," objects Vignolles. "Always do the hardest thing first! The Wrath says: Paris! Or better yet, Rouen."

"Either would be a major undertaking," says Dunois, blanching a little. "Even with the Maid, they may be beyond our reach at this time."

You expect Joan to object to this, but she continues to sit quietly.

"But tell me," continues Dunois, turning to de Metz, "what are your reasons for Beaugency and the rest?"

"Rheims!" interjects Bertrand de Poulengy, turning to his friend with a smile. "Of course!"

"Yes," says de Metz. "The idea is to clear the way to Rheims, so the Dauphin can be escorted there in safety."

"But Rheims would be a much more dangerous base for him than Chinon is," objects Dunois. "I hardly see what the purpose –"

"He cannot be *crowned* in Chinon," says Poulengy.

Silence descends upon the gathering.

By your sword will the English be driven from Orléans. Your hands will set the crown of France upon the head of the Dauphin.

The Duke of Vignolles speaks out of the stillness.

"I would see my king crowned!"

"It is why we came from Vaucouleurs," says de Metz.

"I believe," begins Dunois slowly, "I believe it is a sound plan. It may do more for our cause than any other victory we could win.

Many cities may return their allegiance to the Dauphin of their own accord once he is truly king. Yes, I believe it is the plan we should follow. Are we all in agreement?"

"There's just one thing," says Joan, and everyone turns to her for the first time. "We should start with Jargeau, and then move on to Meung and Beaugency."

"Well, that seems fine, too," says de Metz. "Any particular reason for it?"

Joan just shrugs, but the men instantly comprehend.

"Ah," says Poulengy.

The Duke frowns.

"You might have said so from the start," he grumbles.

Despite Dunois' valiant words, it proves difficult for him to completely abandon his cautious ways. It's several weeks before the army finally sets out for Beaugency, after enough reinforcements are brought into the city to satisfy him of its future safety. (For this, you are thankful, for it gives Joan's shoulder a chance to heal.) All that time, the scouting parties continue to search for Sir Fastolf, to no avail. You begin to wonder if the rumors of his arrival in France were just that.

"No," Joan tells you on your first night in the field again. "He is out there. I am sure of it. But I had hoped *you* would tell *me* where he was!"

"Do you mean that Catherine hasn't?"

"I have not heard her voice since the night we entered Orléans."

You haven't seen or heard from her since then as well.

"Don't worry," you say. "I'm sure she'll appear again soon. We must be doing well, for her to have no need to give us more instruction!"

Joan smiles and nods, but you begin to worry. She's been relying on information she received from Catherine in Chinon, and even before that, in Domrémy, but that knowledge will soon run out. You can remember nothing about what Joan should do after the retaking of these three cities, and many more stand between them and Rheims.

Catherine! you call out in your mind. *Where are you? Why are you silent?*

On the evening of your second day on the march, you reach Jargeau. The walled city is surrounded by suburbs, and the French attempt to occupy them in preparation for an attack on the city proper the next day. However, rather than stay behind their walls, the English ride out to contest every street, and so you enter into battle alongside Joan for the first time.

With no wall between them, the English and French lines come together with great force, and the horrors of battle begin to crowd in on you from every direction once more. You keep your eyes fixed firmly on Joan. She brandishes her sword and shouts commands to her men with assurance that reminds you of her father issuing orders to the village watch in Domrémy. Her face reminds you of the mountains in Michael's domain of Light: shaped from immovable stone, and yet alive with an inner fire.

In this way, you manage to remain by her side despite the horrors around you, though other anxieties soon begin to press on you. Immersed in the fighting as you now are, it's impossible to grasp the ebb and flow of the battle as you did when you floated high above it. Joan and the other commanders seem to know exactly where they are and where they want to go. She directs her men here and there, sometimes in response to commands shouted toward her by Dunois, and sometimes on her own initiative, and never hesitates for a moment. You on the other hand become more and more distressed by all these maneuvers whose meaning you can't comprehend. Are you attacking or retreating? Are the French winning or losing? Your uncertainty gnaws at you.

Around midday, you find yourself rising a little into the air above Joan. Not to flee, but simply to gain a better view of the battle. You don't stray so far that you can no longer see or hear her, only enough to also see the flow of the fighting around her.

Below you, Joan cries, "Into the breach!" and her men rush to probe a gap in the English lines. Dunois shouts, "Back to the hill!" and they return to the high ground they occupied before their feint. Joan leads her men in a test of the English defenses around an outer tower of the city before racing back to join Dunois in bolstering the defenses around the few archers put afield by the French.

Watching these maneuvers, you think again of the games of chess you saw played in Chinon: the advance and clash of the pawns, the dance of the bishops and knights among them. Suddenly, the inner life of this battle becomes clear to you.

"Joan!" shouts Dunois yet again. "To me! To me!" But seized by your sudden insight, you cry out to her, "No!"

She looks at you in surprise.

"You must attack!" you tell her. "Press forward, whatever the Commander says!"

"Margaret!" she cries, looking searchingly around her. "Has Catherine returned? Have you finally heard from her?"

"No!" you proclaim. "I just know that you must."

"This word comes not from God?"

You don't know how to answer this, but in the next moment, Joan's face brightens.

"Your word is good enough for me!" she cries, and then to her men, "Forward! Forward to the walls!"

Joan was not the bobbing leaf, but the Current itself. Her position did not change according to the fortunes of battle. Rather, her position determined them. You saw this as soon as you rose far enough above the battle to see its flow while not losing touch with Joan and the other commanders on the ground. Then you saw how every time Joan advanced, the French army followed, until she was recalled by Dunois in his fear for her safety. Now, she presses forward relentlessly, and Dunois, after a futile attempts to call her back, plunges ahead after her.

Within the hour, the English are forced back behind their walls, and the French occupy the suburbs beyond them.

Jean de Metz, Bertrand de Poulengy, and the Duke of Vignolles come galloping over to Joan.

"Are you all right?" shouts de Metz, and Joan in answer raises her sword, though her expression is clouded.

"Come," says Poulengy. "Let us find a quiet place to talk."

Joan makes to follow them, but Dunois interrupts.

"Where do you go?" he asks.

"To take council," replies de Metz. "About…the disposition of the English prisoners we took."

"Very good," says Dunois. "What do you propose?"

"Let us find a private place to speak," says Poulengy, but Dunois replies, "A private place? I do not understand."

Puzzled yourself, you glance at Joan – and see that her face is about to crumble! – and then it does! She bursts into loud sobs and collapses to the ground.

The men dismount and stand around her in silence. You stand with them, uncomprehending.

Dunois turns to the others in confusion.

"What is wrong? What is happening?"

"We came too late this time," says de Metz.

That only bewilders Dunois the more, but Poulengy explains.

"She cries so after every battle."

"But why? After every battle?"

"They are the tears of God!" breathes the Duke.

You go over to Joan and kneel beside her, placing an arm around her.

"Be comforted Joan. Be comforted."

Soldiers gather. They stare in silence at the weeping girl.

"She weeps for those who have died," Poulengy tells Dunois, "and for the horrors she must witness. We have managed to get her out of the sight of the men after every battle so far, to spare her the shame."

"There is no shame!" insists the Duke.

De Metz steps forward, telling him, "You are quite right, my friend. Would that we all could weep so!" Then he addresses the soldiers.

"Remember well what you see today! Remember, and know that what we do is a terrible necessity! Remember, and know that we fight not to destroy, but to build! Remember, and know there is a cost!"

That night in the field, you speak with Joan frankly and at length for the first time in many days. She tells you how much she has been missing her family, and you tell her about your ancient conflict with your father. She speaks of the terror and grief she feels even as she leads the army in its victories, and you finally confess how you abandoned her during every battle up until the final attack on the walls of the Tourelles.

"Did you really?" she exclaims. "But I was so sure you were right there by my side the whole time!"

The next morning when the commanders meet to plan their attack on the city walls, Joan speaks before any of the others.

"You must let me bear my standard at the fore of the attack this time!"

"That would not be prudent," replies Dunois.

"I must disagree," says Bertrand de Poulengy. "It may well be the epitome of wisdom. We have all seen the effect it can have on a battle."

"Yes, yes, I see it, too," says Dunois, turning to Poulengy and lowering his voice. "But she is only a child, and a girl! After last night, that should be abundantly clear!"

"She is a warrior!" cries the Duke of Vignolles. "She braves the hardships we all do, each in his own way."

"And she has God's protection," adds Poulengy. "That, too, is clear. She has been called for just this purpose, to lead us to victory. Let us not stand in the way of that."

Dunois bows his head in thought.

"Very well. But she must remain by my side at all times. I will be responsible for her safety."

With that, the commanders move on to discuss their strategy. A half an hour later, when they've finalized their plans and left the council room, Joan catches up with Jean de Metz.

"What is the matter, my love? You never spoke your mind about whether I should ride at the head of the attack."

"Well," he says with a sigh, "I am pledged to serve you, and so your wish is already, to me, a command, whatever I might think about it. But yes, I agree with the others that it is the right choice. The lives it will save by shortening the battle alone make it so. But unlike the others, I don't have the comfort of belief in a God who will protect you!"

Four hours into the next day's attack, she certainly seems safe enough. The English remain behind their walls this time, and the French remain at a distance while they bombard the city and its walls with their cannon. Joan stands with Dunois at the head of the French forces indeed, but it makes no difference when they are not engaged in any fighting at close quarters.

"Commander!" she shouts above the roar of the cannon. "Is it not time for the ladders?"

"Not by my calculations," he shouts back.

"The cannon have done their work," she retorts. "This is not a siege, but an attack!"

Just then, de Metz, Poulengy, and the Duke of Vignolles ride up.

"Why do we delay?" demands the Duke.

"I do not judge the time to be propitious as yet," says Dunois. "There are many factors that must be taken into account."

Poulengy approaches him and speaks in a low tone.

"I know what 'factor' most concerns you, but you must not let fear for her safety cloud your military judgment. We must stay true to the decision we made last night. We will attack, and she will lead us."

In desperation, Dunois turns to Jean de Metz.

"Do you concur?"

The captain sighs.

"I do. Come what may."

The French storm across the intervening space, with Dunois and Joan at their head. They reach the base of the city walls with no difficulty and begin raising their siege ladders. Dunois dashes over to the first ladder and begins climbing, but then pauses, looking down at Joan, who is right behind him. Arrows and stones thrown from the battlements rain down all around them.

"Do not hold back on my account!" she cries. "Go! Now is the time!"

More ladders hit the walls. Men begin climbing them.

"Very well!" says Dunois, and continues his climb. As you look fearfully up at the men defending the top of the wall, you hear a loud crack of stone on metal, and Joan is tumbling down to the ground!

"Joan! Joan! Are you all right?"

You hover over her still form. Her helm is dented and her eyes shut, but she's still breathing.

Men gather around her. Dunois slides down the ladder and runs over.

"God forgive me!" he cries. "I should never have let her march at my side!"

She opens her eyes.

"I'm all right," she says. "It was just a stone. A small stone. Continue your attack! This is the moment. I don't know what will happen if we fail to seize it."

At first, the men don't move. She shakes herself loose from their grasp and pulls herself onto her feet again.

"Look! I am fine! Now go!"

After a wrenching look back at her, Dunois shouts to his men,

"Back to your positions!"

Joan picks up her standard and waves it high in the air, eliciting a roar of triumph from the French forces around her.

"Go on!" she tells the commander. "I will stay down here."

The attack is over within the hour, as Joan predicted. After a brief defense in which they lose nearly half of their numbers, the remaining English quickly surrender.

You walk with Joan up the main street of the city.

"So," you say. "What awaits us next? Didn't Catherine say something about a different tactic we should follow in Meung? Well, I'm sure you remember it."

She doesn't answer, but only walks on, with a look of slight concern on her face. Could she be having trouble remembering Catherine's instructions? She stops at a cross street.

"Margaret?"

"Yes?"

She says nothing, but looks searchingly around her.

"Margaret?"

"I'm here, Joan."

She continues looking up expectantly, and you realize she doesn't hear you. She waits a little longer, then shakes her head and resumes her walk.

Your contact with her remains broken the rest of the day. Fortunately, when the commanders meet in the evening to plan the next stage of their campaign, she remembers what Catherine said about Meung.

"We should leave the city alone, and attack only the bridge fortification."

"The bridge *is* the really important target," says Jean de Metz. "But I am surprised. This is the first time you have backed away from any fight. Don't you believe we could take the city easily as well?"

"My reports indicate that the English presence there is

extremely light," adds Dunois.

"Therefore," says Bertrand de Poulengy, "they are no real threat to us."

"And once we take Beaugency," says Joan, "the people of Meung will oust the English occupiers themselves, with no need for bloodshed."

Dunois nods thoughtfully.

"And all this is promised by your voices?" he asks.

"Yes," she replies. "And it is predicted by common sense, too, don't you think?"

The battle for the bridge at Meung plays out as every victory has so far: with Joan's war standard at the head of the attack, inspiring the troops to press forward more boldly than ever before. The English defenders still in Meung then abandon it without a fight, exactly as she predicted.

"Never in all the history of war that I know of, have there been so many victories won so swiftly in so short a span of time!" marvels Dunois.

That evening in Beaugency, the commanders hold a small celebration, setting aside their usual field rations in favor of some small pastries and a pheasant prepared for them by the cooks of the city, and opening some rare bottles of wine. Joan joins them, though her attention wanders. You suspect she's looking and listening for some sign of your presence, as you've been unable to communicate with her for two days now.

"Ah!" sighs Jean de Metz, holding his glass up to the light.

"What do you think of our land and its 'poor fruits' now?" asks Bertrand de Poulengy with a twinkle in his eyes.

"Did I once say that?" replies de Metz. "You must be mistaken. That was some other fellow, in a time so long ago it is all but forgotten."

The next morning, you test your contact with Joan once more, and finding it still broken, go out in search of the other commanders. You find Poulengy and Dunois standing on the battlements over the main gate, looking out across the hills and woods to the west of the city.

"Are you sure of this?" Poulengy is asking.

"The reports are to be trusted."

"It is a pity the news is so old."

"Still," says Dunois, "there can be little doubt that Sir Fastolf is coming this way, and every reason to believe he is within a day's march by now."

Poulengy peers into the distance.

"Good," he says. "We will clear the way to Rheims, or fail, with one final battle."

"Not necessarily," says Dunois. "We could still escape if we wished."

"Turn tail? Would that even be wise? For the first time in this campaign, we will be the ones behind the walls. Let *them* smash themselves against *our* defenses for a change!"

"Retreat would be more prudent," says Dunois. "As strong as the walls of this city might be, they will not be enough to withstand so great an army. Of course" (and here he smiles) "I have had to alter many of my usual formulae."

Poulengy looks around.

"Where is she, anyway?"

As if waiting for this prompt, Joan appears at that moment, climbing up the steps to the walkway where the men stand.

"Good morning!" says Dunois. "You have come just in time for another council of war."

They explain the situation to her. She asks for more information about the English numbers and arms, which Dunois supplies, and then stands with her eyes closed and her head slightly bowed. You wonder if she's waiting (in vain yet again) for some word from you or Catherine.

"Well?" says Poulengy smiling. "What do you advise us to do? Fight or flee?"

"I think you should put on your spurs with all speed."

Poulengy is crestfallen. Dunois is surprised himself.

"Well," he stammers, "I judge that we have the rest of the day at most. If we are to escape without a fight. I will alert the captains –"

"Escape?" says Joan. "I said nothing about escape. We are going to ride out and attack them first!"

Later that morning, the French commanders debate the plan in formal council.

"To attack, in the open field," says Dunois, "a force vastly greater than your own, is foolhardy beyond all measure. Why not let them come to us, so we can make use of the city's defenses?"

"You said it yourself," says Bertrand de Poulengy. "They would still defeat us."

"How will it be better outside these walls? Think of Crécy, of Agincourt! You cannot attack so many bowmen when you have no cover for yourself!"

"I fought at Agincourt," says Poulengy, "and you are right. You cannot attack bowmen once they have dug well in, but if you can catch them by surprise, you can easily overrun them. That is our best hope."

As the army rides out of Beaugency later that day, you find yourself worrying about Joan's plan. Did it come from Catherine, or is Joan acting entirely on her own judgment now? You can't remember whether Catherine ever said anything about riding out to meet Sir Fastolf's army, and you can't ask Joan now.

Catherine, Michael, you pray. *If you won't appear to her, at least let me speak with her again!*

Dunois sends out dozens of scouts in an attempt to locate the English army. You follow one of them deep into the woods. As he works his way on foot along the banks of a small stream, you float above him, scanning the area. As he approaches a bend in the stream, you spot them: an enormous company of bowmen, maybe a thousand or more, moving silently through the woods. Looking ahead, you see that their direction will take them to a narrow pass near the small village of Patay, where the French are headed themselves. If they reach it first, your friends will never get past them. And even if they don't meet each other in the open field, it will be a terrible blow to the new balance of power if all these bowmen find their way into the remaining English held cities to bolster their defenses.

You look back at the lone French scout. When he reaches the bend of the stream, he'll be about a hundred yards away from the English company. Will it be close enough for him to detect them? You watch as he approaches, then reaches the spot. The English continue walking through the wood, trying to remain silent as before, but clearly unaware of his presence. He pauses, looking around. He bends down to dip a hand into the water for a drink. Then he moves on.

"No!" you cry out to him. "Stop!"

You hurtle through the woods after him, passing right through the trunks of the trees, and at one point, startling a deer, which jerks its head around to look at you then darts away just before you can pass through its body as well. You reach the scout and shout at him, urging him to turn around again.

"Stop! They're right over there! Turn around!"

Let him hear me! Please, let him hear me!

The scout continues moving away down the river.

"Please! You must hear me! Joan said you should be able to!"

Then it dawns on you: You startled the deer!

You race back to it. When you emerge into the clearing where it stands, it looks up at you again. When you take a step toward it, it backs away one step.

That's right, you think. *Run away from me!*

You maneuver carefully around it, and then when you get to the right place, jump out at it, shouting and waving your arms. It bolts immediately away! You race along beside it, flanking it on one side and then the other, steering it through the woods – "Yah! Yah!" – and straight into the English company!

There are shouts of surprise and panic when it crashes into their lines. You do your best to keep it darting and leaping among them, but eventually lose control of it and watch it bound away into the woods. You look back at the stream, but there's no sign of the scout. Did he hear the commotion, or did he continue on, following the river away from the critical area? You hesitate for a moment, unsure what to do next. You could continue along the river in case the scout never spotted the English, but what more could you do to steer him back toward them? You could seek out Joan in the hope you'll be allowed to communicate with her again, but you find yourself disbelieving that possibility. You finally decide to stay with the English army, though you can't think what more you could do from that position, either.

The bowmen emerge from the woods near Patay and march on toward the pass. Rising into the air and looking ahead, you see a company of heavily armored English knights approaching the pass from the opposite direction, and your heart goes cold. Not only will the bowmen reach the pass in time to establish their defenses, but they'll have the support of these knights as well. You picture Joan riding to her death at the head of an attack against these forces.

Why won't you let me speak to her? you cry out to the heavens.

At that moment, the English bowmen cry out in distress and begin to run, ragtag, back to the woods. You turn and see the French cavalry roaring across the plain, with the Duke of Vignolles at its head, and by his side…the scout you saw by the river! The bowmen pause to fire a volley of arrows back at the charging French, but while a few riders fall, the main company is not slowed.

The bowmen begin dropping their packs in an all out sprint to safety. The French thunder across the level ground between them. For a moment, you're certain the English will escape. The French seem to move in slow motion, while the distance separating the English from the woods shrinks by the second. But in the next moment, it's over. The horsemen streak across the path of the flee-ing bowmen just before they gain the woods. Arrows fly into their ranks, taking a toll, but they round swiftly on the unprotected arch-ers, and there is no second volley.

So it is that when the French meet the army of Sir Fastolf at last, the English are already fatally weakened by the loss of their archers. The battle does not revolve around a single point of defense as before, but is scattered across the terrain between the pass and the village, so Joan is unable to ride at the very front of the battle. Instead, she gathers men to herself as she can, and leads them this way and that as need demands.

With the battle as unfocused as it is, it's hard to tell whether the French are winning, but you're encouraged by everything you see as you follow Joan. Wherever she appears with her men, the English quickly fall or flee before her.

"The Maid!" they cry. "The Maid!"

Toward the end of the day, Joan is marching into battle with a troop of reinforcements when they pass a line of English prisoners being led back to the French base. One of them, a young man who looks to be no more than fifteen years old, is so badly hurt that he can barely walk, and soon stumbles to the ground.

"Get up!" commands the guard, but the boy does not move.

"Get up, scum!"

When the boy remains motionless, the guard kicks him sav-agely. When that fails to elicit a response, the guard shakes his head and draws his sword, setting its point against the boy's throat.

"Stop!" cries Joan. Flinging aside her standard, she races over to the guard and knocks the sword out of his hand with her own. Swinging it around, she slams the flat of it against the man's helmet, knocking him to his knees. She stands over him, sword drawn back as if to strike a final blow. He looks up wide-eyed at her, unresist-ing.

"Go!" she commands in a voice shaky with rage or tears.

The man makes to rush off, then turns and bows deeply to her. However, she has already forgotten about him.

"Go on without me," she calls out to her troop of reinforcements. "You will find Captain de Metz by the river. Place yourselves under his command." Then she looks down again and asks the boy, "Are you all right? Can you hear me?"

When he opens his eyes, he cries out in alarm and tries to push himself away from her with one hand, while clutching a cross that hangs around his neck with the other.

"You're the Maid! Leave me alone, in God's name!"

"Be still," she tells him. "I won't hurt you."

"Witch!" he cries. "Devil!"

Removing her helmet and laying down her sword, she kneels beside him, cradling his head in her hands.

"Do I look like a witch to you?"

He stares at her face. His breathing slows and his eyes flutter.

"It hurts," he says.

"I know. I have sent for the doctor."

"But – you're the enemy."

"No, no. Our kings are quarrelling, that is all. We are brother and sister."

His gaze falters as he's overtaken by a fit of violent shuddering. When it subsides, he looks up into her face again.

"You're crying. Don't cry."

"I will try," she smiles, wiping away a tear. "You and I, we must be brave."

He settles back into her arms. His breathing slows and roughens. He shuts his eyes.

"I'm scared."

"It is a hard time," she tells him, "but it will pass. This very day, maybe, you will see our Lord! You will be with Him in Paradise. Think of that!"

He doesn't speak again, but continues to breathe thinly, sometimes stopping for so long you think he's finally died, only to resume with a cough or a sputter. The doctor arrives, takes a brief look, and declares that there's nothing he can do. That evening, Poulengy, de Metz, and Vignolles pass by and call out to Joan to enter Patay with them, for the battle is over and the victory won, but she waves them away.

All around her, men trudge back to the city, or are carried back on stretchers, but she pays them no heed. She continues to cradle the boy's head in her lap, looking down into his face.

"I envy you," she tells him. "You go to where there can be no more doubt, no more darkness, but it seems I am only just entering the valley of those shadows. Will you see Margaret, I wonder? And Catherine? If you do, tell them…tell them I am doing my best. Tell them I am doing well! Tell them I miss them."

Late in the night, she bows her head over the unmoving body of the boy, and picking up her sword and her standard, goes finally to join the celebration in the village.

The French army enters Chinon to the music of trumpets and ringing of church bells and the acclamations of the people of the city. Joan strides purposefully through the crowds with her companions, accepting their thanks and praise but not lingering among them. They walk up the main avenue of the city until they reach the gates of the palace courtyard, and pass within, leaving the crowds behind. Soldiers run over to them, stopping at attention and saluting. They return the salutes and press on. They enter the palace and pass by the rooms where they once stayed. They follow the brightly lit passages until they come to the door of the Great Hall. They enter.

Charles sits on his throne. His courtiers burst into applause when Joan enters the room, but he silences them with a gesture. She and her companions approach the throne.

"Noble Prince," says Joan. "We come to bring you to Rheims. Are you prepared?"

"I am."

Two days later, the French army is camped just outside the

walls of Auxerre, the first major city on their way to Rheims. The commanders meet in council as usual. This time, though, they're joined by Charles.

"Like all the other cities we will pass through," explains Dunois, "Auxerre has not replied to our messages calling upon them to return their allegiance to the Dauphin. However, that may be due to the English garrison stationed there. The people may have feared reprisals if they showed us any friendliness while we were still far off, but may open the gates to us freely once we appear before it."

"And the English soldiers?" asks Jean de Metz.

"They will probably flee," says Bertrand de Poulengy. "There are not many of them in any of these cities."

"A pity," grumbles the Duke of Vignolles.

"All is clear, then" concludes Dunois. "With his majesty's permission, we will march on the city at first light tomorrow. Should the English decide to fight, we will deploy our forces –"

"Wait! I beg you."

It's the panic-tinged voice of Charles.

"You decide matters so quickly!" he exclaims. "I suppose that is how you have so swiftly brought me this close to my crown, and I am thankful. Nevertheless, I must be more certain of a few things."

"Of course, your majesty."

"You said that the English soldiers would flee at our approach. Are you absolutely sure of that?"

"Not absolutely, your majesty, but it is very likely," says Dunois. "What is certain is that they cannot prevent us from entering the city however they respond. If they choose to fight, we will defeat them easily. Our strength is so much greater that we would suffer only slight losses."

"But some would be injured or die, is that not so? And many more of the English?"

"Certainly."

"I see."

He rubs his chin, his gaze turned inward. The others look expectantly at him, except for Joan, who has sat quietly in her seat with her head bowed through the entire meeting.

"You said also that the people would most likely welcome us. How can you be sure of that?"

"It is always more difficult to predict civilian responses, but I believe it is reasonable to assume they have not yet expressed their true dispositions. Though the English force is small, it does not take much armed strength to cow a city's population."

"Also," adds Poulengy, "we have seen the people of all the cities we have retaken freely return their allegiance to France."

"But these were cities with a much greater and more hostile English presence among them, were they not?"

The commanders are silent for a moment, and then Jean de Metz says pointedly, "His majesty is astute! There is a chance the people of this region are genuinely allied with the English. But what if they are? What can they do to oppose us, call us names?"

Charles actually flinches a little at this. Poulengy hastens to intercede.

"Your majesty, the plain truth is that they are very, very likely to welcome you as their king. Just as it is overwhelmingly likely the English will simply flee. You must trust our judgment on these matters; it has been tested and refined throughout our long campaign. And then there is the Maid! Joan, do you not agree that we should march immediately on the city?"

She finally raises her head and nods. Charles leans toward her.

"Is this what your voices say?"

She stares levelly back at him.

"I am sorry, good Prince. My voices have not told me what the people of the city or the English soldiers will do."

"Nevertheless," says Dunois, "if God wishes us to enter the city, we may trust that the outcome will be as He desires."

"Very well," declares Charles, and assembled company begins to rise from their seats with sounds of relief, but Joan interrupts.

"My voices: they have not told me anything at all about Auxerre. I have no command either to go forward or hold back, and no assurance about the outcome of either."

Her words, spoken in the flat tones of a dreaded admission drawn finally from a reluctant witness, leave silence in their wake. Poulengy and Vignolles gape at her in surprise, and Dunois in confusion. Jean de Metz bows his head, so you can't see his expression. The Dauphin is crestfallen.

"Well," he finally says. "If there is no word from God, I would learn more on our own before committing to any action. Let us send another message to the people of the city. Now that we are camped so close to them, they may find the courage to answer truly where their loyalties lie. Let us also contact the English garrison, and ask them directly what they intend to do if we attempt to enter the city."

The council is adjourned. Joan immediately heads back to her tent, but Jean de Metz follows her.

"Joan! Wait!"

She stops and turns.

"I hope you know that it is not your responsibility to produce answers from God whenever they are required of you by weak-willed sovereigns."

She smiles.

"I thought you did not believe in God."

"I don't," he replies, returning her smile. "Which makes your predicament all the more unfair in my eyes!"

Joan remains largely in her tent for the next few days, during which a long negotiation is carried out by messenger between the Dauphin and the people of Auxerre. She eats her meals alone, and spends most of her time lying in her bed looking up at the drab canvas roof of the tent.

"Catherine? Margaret? Why have you left me?" she asks of the silence one evening, and it breaks your heart that you can't answer. "Has the time of your help and guidance come to an end? Will you be returning?"

The negotiations finally end, and the French enter Auxerre under an agreement that they will allow the English soldiers safe passage out of the city, and that the Dauphin will not hold it against the people of the city that they switched their allegiance temporarily to the English. They in turn pledge their loyalty to him anew.

"Isn't this exactly what would have happened three days ago if we had simply marched on the gates?" asks Jean de Metz.

"Think of it as a good development," says Bertrand de Poulengy. "We have left behind the days when decisions had to be made quickly, in the field, under the threat of imminent destruction. Now, there is the luxury of greater deliberation. This is a good thing."

"Maybe," says de Metz. "But it really depends on the decisions we make with this new bounty of time."

The same scenario plays out in the remaining cities between Auxerre and Rheims. The French approach them but stop short while Charles corresponds with the city leaders and the English commanders. In every case, just as with Auxerre, an agreement is reached that allows the French to regain control of the city and the English to safely depart, but the process is slow. Joan stops attending the war councils, but you continue to go to them on the chance that some important information might come out that you can communicate to her later, should your contact ever be restored.

In these meetings, you learn that the army is running low on supplies. The road to Rheims has turned out to be much longer than they anticipated when they left Chinon, and they've been unable to replenish their stocks sufficiently from the small, war-impoverished towns they've passed through so far.

"Conditions have become extremely difficult," Dunois reports on the night before the army is to set out for Rheims. "However, I believe we can endure until we reach our final destination. Once there, we should have no further problems, for a city such as Rheims could easily house and feed an army twice our size. Only let us be swift about it!"

When you return to Joan's tent, you find her exhibiting an even greater impatience.

"Catherine! Margaret!" she fairly shouts, showing something like anger for the first time. "Where are you? I sit alone in my tent night after night. My king and my friends look to me for guidance, but I can tell them nothing! When will you speak to me again?"

The army reaches the outskirts of Rheims three days later, and there they halt once more, delayed by the most difficult negotiations yet. A week goes by with no progress, until the army has to start foraging in the woods for sustenance.

"Whatever our own desire might be," reads Dunois one night from the latest message from the city, "we must be be careful not to anger the English soldiers among us. Furthermore, there are those among us who will choose to leave the city if the Dauphin enters, and the loss they would suffer will be no small matter."

"Leave the city?" puzzles the Duke of Vignolles. "Loss they would suffer?"

"They are telling us that there are some in the city who are loyal to the English, and who would leave the city if it returned its allegiance to Charles," says Bertrand de Poulengy.

"And that they are largely rich men," adds Jean de Metz wryly, "who wish to be compensated for the goods and property they would have to leave behind!"

"Villains!" shouts the Duke. "They should be content to get away with their own skins!"

"True," says Dunois, "and yet, it will not be that easy. I fear we will have to negotiate with them, and we may have to concede a great deal, for the food shortage is now acute."

"Perhaps," ventures Charles, "Perhaps we should withdraw. Return to Chinon. We have made excellent progress, but the recovery of Rheims may require a diplomatic effort we are not prepared to prosecute out here in the field."

Jean de Metz glares in open disdain at the Dauphin, but says nothing. The Duke of Vignolles sits in his place as stoically and silently as ever. Dunois and Poulengy look to each other, but neither takes the initiative to speak. Then an assured voice declares:

"There is no need for retreat or further delay!"

It's Joan, in full armor and with her sword and standard in her hands, standing at the door of the council room.

"This very night, we will take up arms and encircle the city, and they will surrender to us, as every other city has before. The king himself will command the army, and the people will flock to hail him as their good lord, come at last to reclaim their allegiance."

Charles looks up at her in hope.

"Have your voices spoken to you at last? Is this their counsel?"

"No!" she declares triumphantly. "But long before I heard them for the first time, when I was a child in the fields of Domrémy, I still had to act and choose and do what was right. Long after they leave me, I will share this burden with every other soul on Earth, in every place, at every moment. As do you.

"You have been called to be king. Now you must boldly seize your crown. No one can do it for you!"

So came the Dauphin at last to Rheims, where the kings of France are crowned. The gates were opened to him without opposition, the burghers of the city rushing out to greet him and pledge their faith, and on the seventeenth day of July, in the fourteen hundred and twenty ninth year of the Lord, he was crowned king amid pomp and splendor in the cathedral of the city.

The Maid stood by him, her standard in her hand, as he bowed his head before the Archbishop to receive the Church's blessing, and then his crown.

"Vive le Roi!" shouted the crowd. "Long live the King!"

Bertrand de Poulengy was the first to kneel before him then, laying his hand in the hands of the king and pledging his faith, but Jean de Metz beside him peered up into the face of his new sovereign the whole time, as if he were a jeweler examining a diamond for flaws. Jean Dunois, the commander of Orléans, came in his turn, and then the Duke of Vignolles, who provoked gasps and then cheers from the crowd by clapping the king on the arm and gripping his hand in a hearty handshake.

Yolande, the Queen of Aragon, appeared last of all. She went first to the Maid and took her hands, and they spoke long in lowered voices in the silenced church while the king looked shyly on. Then she turned to her son-in-law and embraced him, kissing him on both cheeks.

The ceremony was over. The king turned to the girl who had brought him to this place. She had not spoken or played any role in the crowning, but now she looked sternly into his eyes, like a mother admonishing a child or a teacher driving home a crucial lesson to a student, and said, "For the good of your people, and the glory of God!"

The Maid in the Court of the King

When Joan and her companions return to their apartments in the new royal palace in Rheims, Bertrand de Poulengy enters the common room and exclaims, "My young friends! What brings you here?"

"We've come to join you!" replies a familiar voice.

Following Joan into the room, you see that the visitors are her brothers Pierre and Jean!

"It *is* you!" she cries. "I am so glad you are here!"

"We were in the cathedral, too," says Pierre. "Way in the back. You will never guess who was with us, sent by Mama."

"A priest!" says Jean. "She found him in Tours and sends him to be your pastor and confessor as long as you are away from home."

"We, too," says Pierre. "We've come to join you."

"If we may," adds Jean, looking to Bertrand de Poulengy.

"Today is a good day for France!" says Poulengy.

"And Papa," asks Joan. "What does he send?"

Pierre takes her hand.

"His permission. I think it is the hardest thing he ever did. He acts as though he's condemned you to death, but we have heard about your many victories, and Mama says that God will preserve you through all."

Bertrand de Poulengy takes Pierre and Jean to the garrison the next day to have them outfitted and inducted into the army. Joan and Jean de Metz go to speak to the king.

"I think we should attack Paris as soon as possible," she tells de Metz as they walk through the passages of the palace. "Our job will never be easier. I think the people of Paris could rise up against the English on their own, if we would just appear outside their gates."

"You may be right," he replies. "If I were the English regent, I would do everything I could to reinforce Paris and Rouen, even at the cost of relinquishing control of other cities."

They reach Charles' council room. The young guard at the door steps forward to greet them.

"I am sorry," he says before they can speak. "The king cannot see anyone today."

"This is the Maid," says de Metz. "in case you did not recognize her. We have come to discuss future plans with his majesty."

"I do recognize you," the guard says to Joan, "and I beg your forgiveness. The king has given me strict orders, though. He told me specifically not to let you or your companions in!"

The poor fellow is terrified. Joan lays a hand on his arm.

"That's all right," she tells him. "We understand that the king cannot be available whenever his subjects wish. Only tell him we wish to hold council with him as soon as possible. Tell him there are certain actions it would be best to attempt sooner than later!"

They try again the next day, this time in company with Bertrand de Poulengy and the Duke of Vignolles, but are again rebuffed.

"The king wishes me to tell you that he will send for you when he is ready to speak," says the guard.

"But this is preposterous!" says Poulengy. "We are the ones

who liberated Orléans. We drove the English from the Loire valley. We brought the king to his crowning! With whom is he taking counsel now if not us?"

The young man is distressed again.

"I cannot say, sir. I can only tell you what I have been ordered to say."

They turn to go, but curiosity holds you. Who *is* the king so busy with? You pass fthrough the door of the chamber.

When you get to the other side, your first thought is of Robert de Baudricourt, the commander at Vaucouleurs, for the room is dark and empty, and the king sits slumped over a dimly lit table at one end of the room. However, when you come closer to him, you see that the table is covered not with wine bottles, but papers: letters, it seems, most of them written in French or English, but some in other languages. There's also a stack of blank paper, and one sheet on which the beginning of a salutation has been written.

Charles sits bent over the table with his head in his hands, but his eyes are not dimmed by either drunkenness or despair. Rather, they dart alertly across the pages laid out before him.

"There must be a way," he mutters. "There must be a way!"

Two weeks go by with no summons from the king. Joan and her friends languish in their apartments. Every day, she calls to you and Catherine, but you're never able to respond.

The French cease all military operations during this period, but the English do not remain idle. News comes in about the arrival of reinforcements that head straight for Paris and Rouen.

"Just as I thought they should do!" laments Jean de Metz.

Joan's periodic pleas to you and Catherine become more pressing.

"Catherine! Margaret! Speak to me! Please! All that we fought for is coming undone, and I don't know what to do. Is my job truly over? I wish you would tell me."

Catherine never appears to you, either, and a slow anger grows in you every time you have to listen to Joan's increasingly desperate pleas.

If you won't speak to her, at least let me!

One day, they finally receive a communication from the king, only it's not a call to council, but an announcement that he has ennobled Joan and all her family line.

"You are moving up in the world!" says Jean de Metz. "If I may be so bold as to address the new Duchess du Lys with such familiarity."

Joan is not so pleased.

"Am I really the Duchess du Lys now? Is the tale of the Maid of Orléans really complete? If so, it is not a change I would have wished for!"

"Well," says de Metz to the others a few days later. "I have discovered what the king has been up to, holed up in his council chamber."

They sit in the common room of their apartments. Bertrand de Poulengy and the Duke of Vignolles turn to him eagerly, but Joan continues to look absently out the window she sits at.

"Peace negotiations!" says de Metz.

"What? How do you know?"

"I befriended one of his aides and learned all over a bottle of wine last night. Charles has been involved in written correspondence with the English government and other interested parties. He is trying to convince the English to surrender Paris and Rouen and other cities they hold of their own free will!"

"Fool!" cries the Duke of Vignolles, jumping to his feet and sending the bowl of cherries he held in his lap clattering to the floor. De Metz and Poulengy stare at him, shocked expressions on their faces. It might be the first time you've ever seen him speak ill of any superior.

"Well," says Poulengy. "That explains why he does not wish to see us. He knows we will only counsel war."

"He *is* a fool," says de Metz. "And to think, I once thought him merely dishonorable."

"There is no dishonor in the pursuit of peace," replies Poulengy. "Nor is the preservation of life a foolish desire."

"It is if your enemy has no intention of reaching a settlement. If his only goal is to delay you long enough that he can reinforce his two largest cities!"

You glance over at Joan, but she doesn't stir.

Poulengy sighs.

"You are right, of course. The question is: what can we do?"

"Talk to him! Force our way in if necessary! There is more at stake than just obedience to our sovereign; we must also consider the good of the nation!"

The three men nod in agreement, and then turn to Joan.

"You three go," she says. "I think it might be mostly me that the king does not wish to see. You will do better without me."

After the others leave, Joan sets out herself, in the opposite direction. She exits the palace and goes down to the army garrison, where she inquires after her brothers. She's directed to one of the barracks, where she finds them cleaning some armor.

"Joan!" cries Pierre. Dropping the items they were polishing onto the floor with a loud clatter, they run over to her and embrace her.

"It is so good to see you!" she cries. "I have wanted to talk to you ever since you arrived."

"We're sorry we have not come to visit you," says Pierre. "We won't be able to take any leave until we finish our training."

"That will be soon, though," says Jean. "The drill master says we are going to be excellent soldiers!"

They sit and exchange news of all that has happened since the day Joan left Domrémy. You learn that Joan's old priest is now retired, and that Jacquemin now serves on the village watch under the command of his father.

"Papa is grimmer than ever," says Pierre. "He hardly ever speaks nowadays."

"It makes up for Mama," says Jean. "She can't stop!"

"She boasts about you to everyone in the village," says Pierre. "And she goes as far as Greaux to gather the news. We write her every day, of course, and tell her that we are all well."

"You haven't mentioned Katie," says Joan. "Do you know? I dreamed about her. When was it? Maybe in the early spring when I was at Chinon."

Pierre and Jean look long at one another, their expressions darkened, and Jean finally speaks.

"Joan, Katie died in the spring."

It was an illness that started off looking like a simple chill and then grew worse, until the doctor could do nothing. The funeral was held in the little church of Domrémy, which was packed to overflowing by scores of well-wishers – many of whom the family didn't even know – who came from miles around to support the family of the Maid.

You're not sure if Joan took any of this in. She received the news from her brothers in silence, and then they sat together for a long while without another word being spoken before parting ways. You walk beside her now as she returns to the palace.

"Ah, Margaret," she says. "I wish more than ever that I could speak with you now! I feel I should never have left home. Can it be that a family is more important than a nation? I seem to be doing nothing for either just now.

"If you should meet Katie in the realm you inhabit, tell her that I love her, and that I am sorry I was not there to say my goodbyes. Tell her to stand well for our family in the courts of Heaven, and that some day, I will stand with her."

When she reaches the group's apartments in the palace and enters the common room, the others are there, already returned it seems from their attempt to speak to the king.

It can't have gone well, you think to yourself, and sure enough, their expressions are grim.

"Well," she says, "what happened? Were you able to see him?

Did you persuade him?"

Poulengy and de Metz look long at one another – like her brothers did! – and de Metz finally speaks.

"No, we were not able to see him, but he sent orders out to us. Bertrand and I have been reassigned to the southern army. We must leave tonight to join a detachment from Chinon that is being sent there."

Joan walks with Jean de Metz one more time through the streets of Rheims.

"What will you do?" he asks her.

"I don't know. I have not known for weeks now. I suppose I will stay here and, with the Duke, continue trying to persuade the king to action."

"You could also go home, you know. Or come with us. There is no royal command binding you here."

"No," she says. "But there may still be a divine one. I wish I knew for sure."

"Uncertainty is the lot of man."

"I suppose so. I suppose I have been lucky for a long time."

They come to the square where de Metz and Poulengy are supposed to meet with some others to set out. He takes her hands and kisses her on both cheeks.

"My service and my unbelief remain yours to command, until the day I breathe my last. Only call on me, wherever you may be, and I will come."

"Farewell, my love. Never allow yourself to be consumed by melancholy, for God or no, this world is a bright place, and full of wonders."

Early the next morning, Joan rises from her bed and takes up her sword. She slips out of the palace and strides purposefully through the streets of the city, cold and empty in the pre-dawn light.

"Joan?" you venture, but she still can't hear you. She winds her way through the castle district, exhaling plumes of mist that swirl away behind her, then walks down the main avenue of the city. She stops before the cathedral.

You're visited by memories of her sneaking into the church of Domrémy to pray as she opens the doors a crack and slips inside them. The interior of the church is lit only by the slowly growing morning light, and as Joan walks up the center aisle, you have to strain your eyes and wipe them in disbelief at who you see standing behind the altar.

"Catherine!" you cry.

You fly up to her and throw yourself into her arms. She holds you tightly, whispering, "Dear Margaret. Dear Margaret." You pull away and smile up at her.

"You and Joan have done well," she says.

"Will you be with us again from now on?" you ask, but she gestures at Joan, who has reached the altar, and turns to face her.

Showing no sign that she sees Catherine, Joan lifts her gaze to the cross behind you and begins to pray.

"Lord God," she says. "And Catherine, and Margaret, if you are here and can hear me: I have fulfilled all that you called me to. I freed Orléans, and cleared the Loire Valley of the English, and did away with their mightiest army. I brought the Dauphin here to be crowned.

"Now that he is king, it seems he does not wish to have my help any longer. In truth, I do not know what I could tell him or do for him if he still did. You have not spoken to me in a long time, and I cannot remember any charge that was ever laid on me that remains undone."

She draws her sword from its sheath and holds it up for a long time looking up and down its length. Then she lays it on the altar.

"Therefore, I lay down my sword in thanksgiving for your protection and guidance. I ask that you accept it, for I have grown weary of battles and debates in council. I have grown weary of watching men die.

"My brothers are here, come to join the army, and so my parents are without their help. I wish to return to my duties ploughing the fields with my father and spinning cloth by my mother's side. I wish to pray to you once more from the church of Domrémy. I wish to hear the waters of the Meuse.

"I wish to go home!"

Her voice, breaking at last into an impassioned cry, echoes through the empty space, but she ends her prayer in a calm tone.

"Nevertheless, not my will, but thine be done."

She steps back from the altar and looks up expectantly.

You look to Catherine, but she doesn't speak or make any move.

Joan continues to wait.

"Catherine?" you say. "Will you speak to her? Or am I supposed to?"

She only shakes her head.

"Why have you left me?" cries Joan. "Why won't you speak? If there is more you wish me to do, just tell me!"

"Joan, we're here!" you blurt out, but it does no good. When the echoes of her final plea die away, she takes her sword up in her hand again with a sigh and strides out of the cathedral.

"Why wouldn't you speak to her? Why haven't I been allowed to?"

You walk with Catherine in a place you've never seen before: a city so magnificent in the weight of its antiquity that it makes Antioch look newly built, and the grandest cities of the French like army encampments thrown up in a night. The columns and facades of the mightiest structures are half crumbled away, and yet, the effect is not that of deterioration, but of maturation, like the wrinkled face of a village sage. There are streets trodden so smooth, they seem to be carved from a single sheet of rock. There is marble so worn by time that it feels like soft cloth to the touch.

You guess that this must be Alexandria, Catherine's home city.

"I am sorry," she replies. "Our silence has been decreed by

God; I have spoken of it with Michael himself. Know, however, that though I have not been free to speak or show myself to you, I have watched you every step of your long road. You have done exceedingly well. You have been a good and faithful servant."

Have done? Have been?

"Has Joan reached the end of her road, then? Is our job with her really done?"

The two of you reach the end of the literal road you walk, and Catherine turns down a side street that leads to a wide plaza filled with more people than you've yet seen. You sit together on a stone bench beneath a shade tree.

"I have not been granted knowledge of all that will come to pass," she finally replies. "But would it be such a terrible thing if your task were done indeed, and you could rest finally from your labors? The angels will sing her deeds – and yours – for as long as the light of God brightens the worlds."

You try to be pleased with what she says, but the disquiet that has been woken in you won't go away. You note that she has not really answered any of your questions, and glance sideways up at her serene face.

"Are you also a patron saint?" you finally ask.

"I am! Try and guess what of."

You think about her history lessons to Joan, and of her pedagogical manner even in the most casual conversation, and venture, "Educators?"

"Close! I am the patron saint of those called upon to answer hard questions before the powers of this world, and the vast majority of those who pray to me are students – usually just before their examinations!"

You ponder this for a while in silence, then realize that you failed to laugh at her joke.

"Well," she continues, looking down at you with a smile. "I will send you back to Rheims now. Do not worry. We will meet again soon."

However, you think yourself, *Joan is no student facing examina-*

tions.

"Wait," you say. "Tell me one more thing before you go."

She nods gently, smiling still.

"How did you become the patron saint that you are? Were you a famous scholar or teacher?"

"Oh, I thought you knew my story already. I suppose it had not yet reached Antioch by your time. Well, it is a simple one, similar to yours. The story of Catherine of Alexandria is that of a woman who was brought before the Roman governor because she was a Christian, but who, by her eloquence, succeeded in converting not only his wife, but many of the guards in the prison, before they put her to death by fire."

"So," you say, trying to keep your voice light, "it is not only students who look to you."

"No, though they are by far the most numerous. But I also serve those who are brought to trial unjustly, or who are threatened by death for their beliefs."

In that moment, you come to a terrible understanding, but Catherine and her city are already fading from your sight.

"Catherine! Wait!" you cry, but she only continues smiling, with a hand upraised in a gesture of farewell, and in the next moment, you're back in your rooms in the palace of Rheims.

Catherine! I must speak with you again!

Can it be true? But if it were, why didn't Catherine say anything about it? Could it be that she herself doesn't realize what's about to happen? Once again, you think about how evasive her words and her whole manner have been, and you realize that, yes, she knows. She knows! And has not told you. But you're not certain. You can never be certain! How can you make sure of it?

If only you could speak to Joan. She sits having breakfast in silence with the Duke of Vignolles, both of them shy in their new solitude.

Leaving them, you seek out the council room of Charles again. When you enter, he's in the same state in which you left him: intent at his correspondence. You settle down beside him to watch and wait.

You spend the entire day in that room. Amazingly, so does Charles. Except for brief breaks to eat or rest, he remains at the table, reading, reading, and reading, or writing the occasional reply. Messengers are in and out all day delivering new missives and picking up his.

You begin to read the letters. Again and again, Charles urges a peaceful resolution on the English. Again and again, he is rebuffed. He tries to enlist the help of other neighboring sovereigns, but they mostly respond with puzzlement over why he doesn't simply carry on the war that he's now winning to its likely favorable conclusion.

"Courage, my son!" writes his mother-in-law, Queen Yolande of Aragon. "You are king now, beyond dispute and doubt. You must leave your hesitation behind and boldly reclaim all that is yours. Are not the Maid and her companions giving you this very counsel every chance they get?"

By the end of the day, you know nothing new, nothing that confirms or dispels your sudden fear. Then Charles clears a small space on the table and lays his head down on it in his arms, and you find yourself instantly in the dream of the stone cell.

It's the same as you remember it: the dead air, the cold stone. This time, though, instead of experiencing it all from Charles' point of view, you seem to float just outside the bars of the cell and look in on him: an indistinct gray shadow huddled in a corner.

Is this a vision about him losing the war? Or is he afraid to fight because even if France won the war, he would risk being personally captured?

The figure rises and walks out of the cell, the doors swinging open before it. It turns and proceeds down a passageway. Is the dream about to turn into a fantasy of escape? But no: the passage comes to a dead end. And when the stone at the end of the passage begins to part, no joy fills your heart, but dread. Light streams through a widening crack. The wall swings open to reveal: Fire!

You scream, nearly waking from the dream.

It's me! you think. *This is* my *death! Why are they dreaming about my death?*

Then, in the flickering light, you see the prisoner's face, and it is neither yours nor the king's.

The prisoner is Joan.

You stride through the streets of Alexandria. You arrived here not through the call of Catherine, but somehow on your own. In the moment that the king's dream confirmed your guess about the meaning of all the silences and evasions, you called out to Catherine once more, and simply found yourself here.

You pass through the marketplace and then down a long avenue flanked by rows of small parks. You enter one of them and approach a figure that sits on a bench in front of a fountain.

"Catherine," you say.

She turns and gasps.

"Margaret! What are you – How did you –?"

"Joan is fated to die, isn't she?"

Her face freezes in an expression of dismay.

"That's why you haven't spoken to her, isn't it? Her only remaining task is to die! That's why the king won't fight any more. He knows it, too! He's been dreaming it since the day he sent her to Orléans, and now he's trying to save her.

"How could you hide it from me, Catherine? How could you hide it from *her?* How can you be a party to it?"

"Margaret," she says. "The ways of God –"

"Are a horror! An evil!"

She slumps down onto the bench, turning away from you. You come around to kneel at her feet, taking her hands.

"How can you let this happen? Have you forgotten the Fire? We can't let her die like we did!"

Catherine pulls her hands away from yours and covers her face with them. When she speaks, it's in a small and trembling voice.

"Margaret, I was never brought to trial for being a Christian. I never felt the touch of the fire. These are the stories that have come to be told about me – Heaven knows how – but they are untrue. I was a wife and a mother, and lived a long and happy life. My children grew up to be teachers and lawyers and physicians. I died peacefully in my bed."

You step back from her.

"Liar! Hypocrite! You, and Michael, too! What does he know of death? What does he know of pain? He was never human! Send me to him! I would speak with him! He must answer!"

"I cannot," says Catherine, looking up at you with surprise and fear in her eyes. "He only ever calls me into his presence. I cannot get there on my own."

"Michael!" you cry. "Show yourself! Answer me! Or if not, I will come to you!"

With that, you fly up into the heavens. ("Margaret, you mustn't!" comes the voice of Catherine from below you, already far, far away.) You choose no direction, but think only of the fiery landscape in which you've appeared before Michael in the past. Faster and faster you streak, through realms of nothingness, through darkness and light. A warmth grows around you, as you think furiously about what you will say to the archangel of God.

Why must she die? What would that accomplish? She's already done all that you asked. Why can't she simply go home now? What great plan would that disturb? How can you use her to carry out your purposes, and then betray her to torment and death?

Worse yet, you realize, they would use her one more time, in death, as an example of the beauty of martyrdom. Perhaps she would even be made a saint some day, like you: an inspiration to other girls who would be sacrificed by their families, their kings, their God.

Men look to the heavens for strength to do what's right, but you have no more honor than the basest of earthly tyrants. Men pledge their faith to you, and you break it. You break them, on the wheels of your cruel designs!

Then you're speaking your words aloud to Michael himself, surrounded by the burning hills of his demesne.

"We made a pledge to her when we called her down this path. We have an obligation. Even if we didn't acknowledge it at the time, even if she wouldn't have required it of us!"

Michael stands impassive in the distance as always, neither moving nor speaking.

"We must warn her! We must save her! It's because of our guidance that she's in danger. We can't leave her now! Do you even hear me? Will you deign to answer? You're no angel of Heaven! You're no servant of God!"

Wiping your tears, you see with a shock that Michael is now speeding toward you across the landscape of light. He stands as still as always, but his hair and the flame of his sword stream backward in a long train behind him. He's already twice the size he normally appears and looms larger by the second. Soon, he dwarfs the landscape itself. His feet are mountains, his face a bloated, blazing sun. His sword, as he swings it down upon you, sweeps the stars from the sky.

You throw your arms up before your face, turning away from his wrath.

Let him destroy me. Only let him save Joan.

Long moments pass, and no sword strikes you with a second death by fire. No voice thunders with judgment in your ears.

You open your eyes.

The face of Michael appears before you, not the sky-masking visage of a god, but an ordinary human face mere inches from your own, like your father's when he would bend over you in your bed to wish you a good night when you were a child, in the sweet days before Belief drove you apart. His expression is mild and his voice gentle as he says, "Then do so," and leaning forward, kisses you on the forehead as if you were his daughter indeed.

You return to Rheims the evening of the same day. Joan is already asleep in her bed. You sit beside her long into the night. She dreams of many things: the bright meadows of her childhood; the whistle of arrows through the smoky air of a battle; the cool, airy darkness of the insides of churches. She also dreams of things that seem to come from your life rather than hers – the back room of a bakery, your favorite pagan temple – so that you wonder if it's really you who dream.

In the morning, she wakes and looks sleepily into your face.

"Margaret!" she murmurs.

You walk with her through the streets of Rheims, in close conversation once more.

"But you must tell me first about Sir Fastolf," she says. "Was it you who revealed his bowmen to the scout? I knew it! I was sure it would be you who found them. Did I not say so myself?"

You've been trying to warn her about the dangers ahead, but she is naturally possessed by a desire to catch up on all that you did during the time you were unable to speak to her. You answer her questions as quickly as you can, afraid that your renewed contact could be taken away again at any moment, but once you have an opening to speak, you're unsure what to say. To your chagrin, you realize that not once throughout your encounters with Catherine and Michael did they explicitly confirm or deny your accusation concerning Joan's death.

How could I have let them slip away like that?

Not knowing for sure whether you guessed the future rightly, you can only warn Joan in the vaguest terms. She'll undoubtedly take anything you say as a message from God, but what if you turn out to be wrong? What if her job is not quite done after all, and you prevent her from carrying out some needed final task to secure the freedom of France? Worse, what if you push her onto some path that actually leads to her capture, when she would have been fine had she remained in the place prepared for her by Michael and Catherine?

Did Michael realize I would be hobbled like this? Is that why he granted his permission so readily? Slippery, slippery.

"Joan," you tell her. "Be careful what you do next. You have no more commands from Catherine or Michael to do anything else now."

"That is true," she says. "But they also did not accept my sword when I offered it back to God in thanksgiving last week. It must be that I am to make further use of it."

Do you tell her about your presence, and Catherine's, in the cathedral that morning?

"Wait, then. Wait for certain word of what you should do."

"I will try to be patient. But if I – if either of us – had waited for a clear message from God before acting against Sir Fastolf, there would be a thousand more English bowmen and four thousand more knights in this land right now. Just think what trouble they would be causing!"

The next day, you're woken by someone pounding on the doors of Joan's rooms.

"Miss Joan! Miss Joan!"

It's the Duke of Vignolles.

"The English are about to strike Compiègne," he tells her. "I have been instructed to muster my company. Come and fight by my side once more!"

"Gladly!" says Joan, her eyes glowing. "When do we ride?"

"Not for some days yet, and perhaps not at all, but the king has ordered me to be ready nonetheless by tomorrow morning."

"Not for some days? Perhaps not at all? What is this all about?"

"Humph," grunts Vignolles sympathetically. "The king wishes to negotiate first, but I see no hope in it. I think we will ride soon."

"But will it be soon enough?" asks Joan. "Where are the English now?"

"Margny. They have set up a forward base there. It is small, but the rest of their army will soon reach it."

"Then someone must retake Margny before it gets there!" cries Joan. "Once we hold that position, we will be able to observe the approach of the full army, and maybe even slow it down." She steps forward and looks up into the Duke's eyes. "Will you attack Margny right now with your company, in disobedience to the king, as you once disobeyed Dunois?"

"I will – in obedience to the Maid who speaks for God. Do you so command?"

Joan looks long into his eager eyes. You edge closer to her, but dare not speak. Finally, she says, "No. I cannot. I have no clear command from God."

"Then march with me at the command of the king. I think we will have some good fighting still, and we won't have to wait long for it!"

After he leaves, Joan hurriedly dresses and calls for help to put on her armor. Taking up her sword and her standard, she leaves the palace and makes for the garrison barracks and her brothers.

"Pierre, Jean, have you been assigned to any company yet? Do you know of many others who are presently unattached or on leave? Seek them out for me! Spread the word that the Maid is riding into battle, and calls on all who can to join her."

"What's this all about?" you and they ask all at once.

"The English are moving on Compiègne," she says, after a quick glance at you. "They have already set up a post at Margny, but the king is holding back from attacking it. The Duke will not march against it without the king's permission. Therefore, I am going."

"Joan, can you do that?" asks Pierre.

"I can now," she says with a smile. "For the king was kind enough to make me a duchess. As a noble, I can raise armies and fight battles on my own! Though I imagine it is usually the *dukes* who exercise this power."

All together, she rides out of Rheims with about a hundred men later that day, including Pierre and Jean. Before she leaves, the Duke of Vignolles tells her, "Fare well, but leave some English for me to fight!"

On the road, she explains what she can to her brothers about what to expect in battle.

"They have no walls to hide behind, so I expect that they will set up a defensive line just outside the village. If they have time, they will plant sharp, slanted stakes in the ground that we would do better to avoid. In that case, we will swing quickly around and attack them from the south, even though the terrain will be less suited to a swift charge. If they have less time, they will erect some kind of barrier of wood or stone. That should prove no trouble at all. We will simply attack it at its weakest point. Once we pierce it, the defenders will be in disarray; whatever strength they still maintain along the rest of the line will mean nothing.

Do not allow yourselves to be slowed by doubt or fear. When you see armed soldiers waiting to meet you for the first time, your first thought is to advance carefully, but that is the most dangerous course. The longer they can draw out the battle, the more men will die on both sides. The safest course is to attack boldly, to end the battle as soon as you can."

When they arrive at Margny, the fight plays out exactly as Joan laid it out. The English wait behind rows of defensive stakes, but Joan's small company circles quickly around it and attacks from the side. The enemy archers throw down their bows, and their knights quickly surrender as well.

"Send word to the city that we hold Margny now," Joan tells a messenger. "Tell them that if they will send us some archers and artillery, we will hold off the English attack as long as we can. Tell them to be ready to receive us should we need to retreat, but to be ready also to raise the drawbridge at the first sign of trouble, for the English will be able to do no more than lay siege to the city as long as they can't reach its gates, and that will give the Duke of Vignolles time to come to their aid."

"Joan?" says Pierre. "Maybe we should all go to the city, and raise the bridge right now!"

He gestures to the south and the west. Coming from both directions are English armies that together must number in the thousands. The one coming from the south is close. The horsemen at its head are probably only a half hour away.

"Fight or flight?" Joan mutters to herself.

"Joan!" you cry. "It must be flight! You have only a hundred men, and they have thousands. This is not like St. Loup, or even the Tourelles."

"Mount!" she calls out. "Gather the people of the village. Pierre, Jean, you must shepherd them to safety. You others, flank the line. You, and you, at the rear with me!"

The company is quickly on its way, but the going is slow. The people of the village, with children and elderly among them, can only move so fast. Pierre and Jean ride at their head, with the rest of the company stretched out along the length of the procession and a handful of the ablest knights taking up the rear with Joan.

When they reach the bridge to the city, a sortie of English horsemen bursts out of the nearby woods and bears down on Joan's position. Her men spring forward to engage them. Joan stands with her banner held high near the foot of the bridge calling out to the villagers to be calm and to continue crossing the bridge in an orderly fashion, "for those horsemen will not lay a hand upon you!"

Sure enough, the attackers are beaten back. Only a handful of villagers still wait to squeeze onto the bridge, along with maybe another dozen soldiers.

They're going to make it! you think to yourself, but at that moment, there's a commotion along the bridge, and you see Pierre fighting his way back toward Joan.

"Joan! Joan!" he screams. "You must come! Come now!"

She makes no move, but only looks curiously at him.

"Joan! The dream! This is the dream!"

"What is the matter with him?" she asks, but you have no idea what it could be. He seems gripped by madness.

"Joan!" he shouts when he finally reaches her. "You must cross the bridge. Now! They are going to raise it! You will be be trapped outside!"

"Don't be silly, Pierre. They won't raise it unless they see a danger of the English getting across, and we just chased them off."

He takes her by the shoulders and speaks in a terribly controlled calm.

"Joan. They *will* raise it. Perhaps more English will arrive. Perhaps they will panic. I do not know. But they will raise it and you will be stranded outside. Papa dreamed it! That is why he tried to stop you!"

The dream!

"This is the place!" cries Pierre. "The city, the gates, the bridge! This is where it happens!"

Joan looks at him with eyes wide with comprehension, but says, "I have no choice. I am the commander. I cannot cross until the rest are safe."

"Then I will stay with you," he replies, drawing his sword.

"No! Go with them. Do all that you can to speed their crossing. That is the best help you can give!"

He gazes at her for a terrible moment, then kisses her on both cheeks and whispers, "God keep you!"

"Go! Go!" he cries to the retreating company. "You, carry that man! You! Drop those bags! Are they worth your life? Go!"

He works his way along the bridge, clearing blockages and urging the people to greater speed. Just as he crosses its midpoint, it begins to rise.

"Joan!" he cries, teetering off balance with the others near him, lifted up on the wrong side of the divide.

The few villagers and soldiers caught on the near side race back to Joan.

"We must fly!" she tells them. "Eastward, straight into those woods and then scatter. Meet at the south road. Go!"

As she makes to follow them, an even larger band of horsemen comes galloping down the western road.

"Go!" cries Joan to the others, but remains at her position near the bridge with her selected rearguard. The horsemen do not pursue the others, but ride straight for her. They fan out, cutting her off from escape in any direction.

"Now!" she cries to her men, but instead of trying to get around the English encirclement, they charge straight into it! Their surprised pursuers scatter momentarily, and Joan cries out, "Flee!" Her men break for the woods, but as she makes to follow them, an unhorsed Englishman catches hold of her golden cloak and wrenches her to the ground. Before she can remount, the horsemen regroup around her and cut off her escape. They circle her, shouting in triumph and hurling insults and threats. She remains calm, standing at the center of the whirlwind with her sword raised high into the air. More horsemen arrive, some carrying banners and others blaring trumpets, circling more and more thickly around her, until she's lost to your sight.

The Maid of Antioch

You wake in your bed. Though it's still early, the air flowing in through the window of your room is warm with the breath of summer. Your parents are already up; you hear them moving around in the rest of the house. There's a crash – perhaps a pitcher falling to the floor and shattering – followed by sharp words from your father, and then silence. He walks past your door and pauses to glare at you, looking like he might speak at last, but then shakes it off and continues on his way. Your heart freezes in that moment, but quickly recovers. It's been recovering more and more quickly from his angry slights. Some day, you'll no longer feel them at all.

Your mother's anxious face peers around the doorframe.

"Will you eat before you go?"

You review your day. You have an hour before you have to relieve Sennie, but you want to sneak into the catacombs to pray before then.

"No time," you reply.

"Let me pack you some food," she says. "You can't watch the sheep all day without eating!"

"Mother! I'll be fine!"

She cringes and retreats. You remain in your bed, imagining yourself as she will the rest of the day: alone and hungry in the fields. It's not an unpleasant picture to you, but it will haunt her. There's nothing you can do about it, though. Her weakness is not your responsibility.

The window of your room opens onto the alley behind the house. Though it doesn't offer much of a view, it does allow the morning sun to shine almost directly into your room most summer mornings, and admits the sounds of the neighborhood and the smell of garden flowers.

This is my life, you tell yourself. *And it is good.*

You are Margaret of Antioch, born seventeen years ago as the only child of a hard-working stonecutter and his Phoenician wife, and reborn just last month as a child of God. In that month, you began fighting with your father for the first time in your life, going from screaming arguments to the cold silence that now sits between you, and watched your mother, never a strong woman to begin with, become beaten down even further by this conflict in her own house. On the other hand, you're growing and learning every day in the Faith, and you just got a job watching sheep for a man who's also a secret Christian.

Plans are in the works for you to go live with him and his family. Though your father has disowned you, he has yet to order you out of the house in so many words, and so you've lingered while seeking a place to land. Is he wondering impatiently why you haven't left yet, or waiting for the next big fight to finally and formally throw you out? You hope to be able to leave on your own before finding out.

You dress and make your way through the house. As you pass the kitchen, you see your mother on all fours on the floor picking up bits of shattered pottery. A small basket of bread and cold meat sits on the table, probably a lunch she packed you. You go quietly out without speaking to her or taking the food.

You leave the residential district and start down the main

avenue of the city. At the end of the market area, just where temples and parks begin to replace the shops and animal pens, you enter a bakery. The man behind the counter greets you cheerfully; you ask him about his goods and make small talk about the weather until the other customer in the shop makes her purchase and leaves. Then he gestures for you to join him behind the counter. From there, you slip into the work area of the shop.

In one corner of the room is a small table with a lamp on it. You move the table aside to reveal a low, loose grate in the wall. You light the lamp. Removing the grate, you slide yourself into the space behind it: a corridor of stone that runs behind the shop and along the length of the marketplace.

You pause a moment to let your eyes adjust to the lamplit darkness, and to let your heart expand to take in the faint pressure you always feel here: the weight of the Holy. It's here, in the tunnels and caves left over from the construction of the city, that the Christians of Antioch gather to worship when they can.

You whistle three short notes to announce your friendly presence, but hear no replies.

Ah well, you think. *I'll come again in the evening when there's sure to be a gathering.*

You follow the passage, occasionally repeating your whistle, until it opens out into a small cavern. Digging under a rock, you pull out two sticks of wood and some metal pins, and use the pins to secure the wood against one wall in the shape of a cross. You kneel before it.

O God of all times and places, you pray. *I thank you for bringing me into your eternal family, now when I'm ready to begin my life in earnest. Show me the way you would have me go: where I'll live and what I'll do. In all things, in whatever ways I can, let me serve you.*

Half an hour later, you find Sennie in the pastures outside the city lying on her back beneath an olive tree looking up at the passing clouds.

"Hey you! We're supposed to be watching the sheep!"

"I'm tracking them by their reflections in the sky," she says. She reaches out one hand in a gentle patting motion. "There, there, now, little fella. Don't go straying."

You can't think of a thing to say in reply, but are happy just looking down at your friend's serene, abstracted face. She pivots her gaze over to you.

"How goes the war at home?"

"My father still isn't talking, and my mother hasn't stopped fretting."

"I think it's time for a change, then. Don't you?"

"Well, yes, but…what?"

She gets to her feet to beam at you.

"Anthony decided out of the blue to join the army! He leaves within the week. Marcus and Tullio will take over his room. 'Tra and Aula will move into theirs. And you will move into mine!"

"Sennie!" you cry, embracing her.

"I told you to be patient," she says. "There's always a way, like father says. Listen, come for supper tonight, and we'll make our plans."

"I will. Thank you! Thank you."

She makes to leave, but you take her by the shoulders and look into her eyes.

"You've been my best friend and my greatest help. Long before you brought me to the Light of God, you were that light in my life."

"That's funny," she says. "I thought it was *you* who led *me* to God."

You're alone in the pastures of Antioch. You stand beneath the olive tree, looking down at the flock in your charge. The "little bumblers" (as Sennie calls them) munch away at the tall grass as if they think it's going to disappear from beneath them at any moment.

Are they aware of your role in finding them these good patches for grazing, and in protecting them from accident and predation?

Freeman Ng

Do they praise you in their fat animal hearts?

"The Lord is *my* Shepherd!" you call out to them. "I shall not want. He maketh me to lie down in green pastures. He leadeth me beside still waters. He restoreth my soul.

"Yea, though I walk through the valley of the shadow of death, I will fear no evil, for thou art with me; thy rod and thy staff, they comfort me. Thou preparest a table before me in the presence of mine enemies; thou anointest my head with –"

You pause, puzzled about this psalm you have repeated, aloud or in your own mind, almost every day of your fledgling Christian life.

Thou anointest my head with oil.

Is the psalmist still talking about God as the Shepherd and himself as the sheep? You labor in thought to make sense of those last two lines, but can't avoid the conclusion that, for a sheep, a set table and an anointing with oil can only signal a bad end.

Three horsemen appear in the distance. *That will be the Roman captain*, you think to yourself. The road running by the pasture is not a major one, and in your short time on the job, you've quickly become familiar with everyone who uses it: the watchers of other nearby flocks, a merchant who lives in the country and goes into the city every few days on business, and this soldier who's been riding by almost every day for a week now, sometimes alone and sometimes with a companion or two. You've often wanted to ask him what brings him out here, but have been stopped by a habit of stealth you've had to learn since becoming a Christian.

"Secrecy," the baker once told you, "is not always a simple matter of either knowing or not knowing a hidden fact, for knowledge itself is not an object you can either possess or not, but a living thing that grows and changes and walks its own path through the world. Therefore, we ought to remain as inconspicuous as possible, especially to those in authority, even when we don't think we're revealing any dangerous information about ourselves. Every impression we make adds itself to the rest, pulling the creature of understanding in new directions. The simplest 'hello' on the street could eventually lead to discovery and disaster."

Obedient to his warning, you move to the other side of the tree and stand at the edge of the hilltop looking down at your flock and away from the road. You hear the horsemen approach; soon, they'll reach the tree. Then they'll follow the curve of the road around to where you'll be able to see them out of the corner of your eye. You'll remain in your pose until they disappear from your sight.

It seems a shame. Before you became a Christian, you spoke freely with strangers in the street, and roamed the city at all hours. Your mother wrung her hands, but your father said, "My girl can take care of herself!" You were a child of the Roman Peace, unafraid of any danger.

Now, though – but here you pause. Where are the horsemen? They haven't appeared along the outgoing road, though they've had plenty of time to get that far. Did they turn off the road somewhere behind you? You strain to detect some sound of their movements. Though you could just turn and look, you're suddenly afraid to. The disappearance of the riders takes on a sinister cast, and you have to fight to keep from picturing them creeping up on you across the hilltop at this moment.

You try to shake it off.

I've got to tell Cornelius about this. It's fear *that's the creature with a life of its own!*

Nevertheless, you still can't bring yourself to look behind you. Then you hear the sputter of a horse, and a voice says clearly, "Wait here." When you turn, you see the three horses standing in the shade of the olive tree. The captain dismounts and walks toward you, a smile on his face.

"Good day!" he calls.

"Good day, sir."

You keep your voice low and your eyes downcast.

"I've often seen you out here all alone. This must be a very tedious job."

"No, sir. It suits me."

He takes another step forward until he's standing too close for your comfort. A shiver passes through your body despite the warm sunlight you stand in.

"I find that hard to believe, a pretty girl like you."

What did he just say? The conversation has somehow gotten away from you, and you're certain you mustn't let it go any further.

"Thank you, sir. If you'll excuse me, sir, I must be getting back to my duties."

"Actually, I thought you might take a break. With me."

Now you understand. It seems there's more than one kind of discovery and disaster!

"I have rooms in the palace itself," he continues. "Have you ever set foot on the royal isle? I could show you some things…"

"I – I couldn't leave the sheep."

"My men will stay and watch them, and I'll have you back on the job in a couple of hours."

Even as you strain to come up with another excuse, you realize the dead end you're running down. There must be another way! If you had the time and peace to think, you might find it, but caught by surprise as you are, it's all you can do to stay one step ahead of the pursuit.

"The owner wouldn't like it."

"I'll simply explain to him that you had better things to do. I'm sure he won't be so foolish as to cross the will of a Roman captain."

His voice and expression harden a little at the end of that, and you realize your back is now against the wall.

"I don't – I don't do things like this."

"Then you don't know what you've been missing."

"But – I have no desire for you."

You hold your breath at this last resort. Will he be terribly hurt? Is he a man who would hold a grudge? A Roman captain could make life very difficult for you if he chose to.

He reaches to take one of your hands, and you let him, afraid to antagonize him any further. His grip is hard, and his voice is cold with insistence when he finally speaks.

"I think you'll change your mind."

Darkness washes over you; you teeter on your feet. However, in that darkness, a tiny flame of defiance blazes up. You lift your gaze to meet his.

"If you do this thing, it will be a stain on your honor as a Roman, and a blow to the goodwill that exists between you and the people you govern!"

Rage convulses his face. He raises his voice to a shout that his men can hear.

"Honor? I've watched your comings and goings, and I know your shameful secret. While you blather about good will, you've been working to undermine the morals of the Empire and sanctity of its gods. You are a Christian!"

You find nothing, nothing at all to say. When he gestures to his men to take you, you wrench your hands from his grasp and run.

It was a foolish, useless act of desperation, of course. They catch up with you in ten strides, tie you up, and bundle you back to the city on the back of one of their horses. They take you straight to the garrison, where you stand, briefly and mutely, before a judge while the captain lays out his evidence against you: your frequent forays into the catacombs, your friendship with certain other suspected Christians, and words you supposedly let slip to him on the hilltop.

It's not until they bring you to the Fire that you find your voice again.

"The captain alone knows the true reason I've been arrested and condemned, and yet, I will not claim that any injustice has been done, for I *am* a Christian. I serve the King of Heaven, who rules the nations and who is bringing all peoples to himself. Beware, lest you be found wanting on that day!"

No one pays you any attention. They go about their tasks silently and efficiently, like men who have had long practice with them.

So it is that, four hundred and twelve years after the death of your Lord, you follow Him into the darkness of the grave.

You wake, and for a moment, think you're still in the Fire, beneath the blindingly bright sky of that dreadful day, but then the dazzle fades from your eyes and you begin to pick out the details of your room, washed white by the early morning light streaming in through the window of your bedroom in the small house in the residential district of Antioch.

Was everything you went through really just a horrible dream? But it was so vivid: the crackling of the flames, the numbing cold of their touch. You look down at your arms lying above the covers; they're sunburned as usual but otherwise undamaged, though they do tingle a little, the way the flesh of your right hand did for hours after you held it as close as you could for as long as you could to a fire once.

You lay back in the bed, arms held out to either side, opening yourself to the day. Are the memories already fading, the way all dreams do?

There's a crash from inside the house somewhere, and the voice of your father scolding your mother. You sit up, your eyes fixed on the door of your room. In a moment, your father appears, and then your mother. He refuses to speak, though there's nothing unusual about that these days. She says, "Will you eat before you go?"

You can only stare blankly at her.

"You can't watch the sheep all day without eating," she adds. "Let me pack you some food!"

You remain stunned and speechless until she ducks her head and retreats.

You look at your hand again. It's calloused and red, but unburned. You flex your fingers. You bring them slowly up to touch your face.

On your way out of the house, you peek into the kitchen. Sure enough, your mother kneels on the floor picking up the bits of a shattered pot, and a basket of food sits on the table. As you walk through the streets of Antioch, you try to remember whether the sights you see also occurred in the dream. Were those children playing tag among the fish market barrels before? Was the merchant glaring at them with that exact combination of annoyance and envy? Did a hay cart hobble by just then on one warped wheel?

At the baker's, you linger in the catacombs only long enough to confirm that they are indeed vacant, and then return immediately to the front of the shop.

"Cornelius," you ask the baker. "Would God ever send a prophetic vision to an ordinary Christian?"

"What's an 'ordinary' Christian?" he replies.

In the fields, Sennie delivers her good news word-for-word and goes her way. You stand beneath the olive tree, paralyzed by indecision. If the dream was a warning sent by God, you ought to flee this place immediately, but if you do, the sheep will be left unguarded. You should have asked Sennie if she could stay one more shift in your place, but what reason could you have given her?

What's happened so far, after all? you ask yourself. Your father wouldn't speak to you, and your mother nagged you about food. Your father yelled at your mother. Can these common occurrences really be the signs of pre-ordained doom? Are they worth abandoning your duty? You've just started this job, and your employer is a fellow Christian and your best friend's father, the man who might be letting you live in his home. Will you really risk failing his trust because of a bad dream?

You look up. Three horsemen, the Roman captain and two others, appear around the distant bend of the road.

You pull your cloak over your head and trot down the hill to join the sheep. You linger among them, glancing from time to time at the road where the captain approaches the spot where you were standing, passes it, then turns and comes back to it. He and his men stand there looking down at you, while you busy yourself examining the leg of one of the sheep.

"Go away. Go away. Go away," you whisper, but instead, he gestures to his men to circle around, and all three of them start down the hill.

Do you run or stand firm?

You continue tending the sheep until the Roman looms over you.

"You're a very conscientious shepherdess," he says.

Rising but keeping your head bowed beneath the cloak, you say nothing but only shake your head. You can hear clearly in his voice what you had to labor to finally comprehend in the dream.

"Modest, too!" he exclaims. "And I think you're also very pretty, if memory serves. Come, let's see your face."

He reaches out a hand and you can't keep up your willed still-ness. You slap it away just as it's about to pass within the cowl of your cloak.

"Hey!" he cries, his face darkening. His men close on you and you almost break into a run right then, but he waves them away.

"No matter," he says in a lowered voice. "I already know who you are: Margaret, daughter of Trenus. And disciple of Christ. Don't be alarmed. Only I know it, and perhaps you can persuade me to keep it a secret."

At that, you do bolt. You run straight through the midst of the sheep, hoping to gain a big enough head start to escape all pursuit, but the field is wide and the surrounding terrain level and treeless. There's no refuge or place of concealment you can reach for miles around.

The men simply trot back up the hill, remount their horses, and ride you down.

The rest of the day plays out as you were given to foresee. You attempt to defend yourself in the trial, but your efforts prove as ineffective as your dreamed silence. You try threatening the captain with your knowledge of his improprieties, and finally shout them out to the guards securing you to the stake, but they look right past you as if you're already dead. The fire grows around you, exactly as you dreamed it: the flames you strained to see in the bright sunlight, the numbing cold they spread through your body.

Then you reenter the blackness of death.

You wake.

You lay in your bed on a warm summer morning, trembling from a nightmare that was so vivid, you feel like you died indeed and have woken up in the afterlife. You review the events of the dream in reverse order, from the fire to the trial to the pursuit across the pasture. When you get to your waking at the very beginning of the dream, you sit bolt up, remembering the dream that preceded it and foretold the events of that day. A dream within a dream? If that's what it was, then what's this?

There's a crash from somewhere in the house, and your father's voice shouting, "Stupid woman!"

You stare at the doorway of your room in dread, fighting an urge to run out through it before the way is blocked. Your father appears, looking once more like he might speak at last, but not. When your mother asks if you'll eat before you go, you blurt out, before you can stop yourself, "No time!"

At the bakery, you wait until the other customer in the shop is gone, then ask Cornelius, "If a thing is certain to happen, as certain as if – as if it had already happened, might it be possible to prevent it? Could one person do that?"

He leans back in his chair, smiling.

"I love your questions, little Margaret. This might be the best one yet. I'm afraid I must disappoint you again, however, and answer, 'Yes and No.'

"Consider the prophet Jonah. He leaped into the sea to avoid pronouncing God's judgment on the Ninevites, and was swallowed by a great fish that spat him up – onto the shores of Nineveh! But he was later incensed when the Ninevites were able to change *their* fate and avoid destruction. Among the Greeks, there were philosophers who held the gods to be no more than the blind working out of what must be, while others claimed the gods could change the past itself. Infinite are the arguments of philosophers, and the inferences that can be drawn from Scripture!"

"Cornelius," you say. "Is there any way you could get a message to Sennie in the sheep pasture?"

"Her brother Marcus usually comes by to pray shortly after you. I can ask him."

"Good! Tell him to tell Sennie that I can't watch the sheep today. Tell her I'm sorry, and that I promise to make it up to her. Tell her that I'll explain it all to her tonight."

"I will," he says. "And don't worry. If she can't stay to watch them the rest of the day, Marcus will. And if he doesn't show up, I'll close the shop and go myself. But what's the matter? Is everything all right?"

"I'll tell you tomorrow, if I can."

You sit in your favorite pagan temple, making your plans for the day. You'll stay here until sundown, and then go on to Sennie's. There, you'll tell all to her and her father. He's one of the elders of the small assembly of Christians in Antioch, and though his mind is not as wide ranging or as subtle as Cornelius's, you need to hear something better than "Yes and No" right now.

Or maybe this will all blow over after today. Maybe I've already escaped the danger. Maybe the captain experienced a chance compulsion out there in the fields, and tomorrow, he'll ride right by me as he usually does.

You have a hard time believing it, though. You have hard time believing that Sennie's father will be able to help you in any way. You imagine arriving at his house to find Sennie furious at you for leaving her in the lurch with the sheep. Her father lectures you about responsibility and Christian honesty, and you storm out in a rage, having told them nothing about the horrible trap you find yourself in.

You look more closely at the sculpture of the Emergent Woman in front of you. Is she really coming to life from dead stone? For the first time, you see that there could be another interpretation: that she was actually *escaping* from the stone, but has been caught. The sculpture, then, portrays the moment at which hope turned to despair, when her ascent into regions of light was arrested and about to be reversed, as implacable rock closed around her legs and her thighs and her hips and began to pull her back down into grinding Hell.

You lean back in your seat and close your eyes.

What's happening to me? Why am I thinking these horrible thoughts? It's that cursed captain! Why should he have the power to darken my mind like this? What did I ever to do him?

Keeping your eyes closed, you take a deep breath and feel it filling you, and then flowing from you. You take another, expanding beyond the shell of your self. You inhale once more, and as you let go of that breath, find yourself drawing close again to your own thoughts and sensations.

I must be strong and not allow myself be pulled down by fear. I must meet every challenge with joy in the moment. I must trust God to lead me finally and always to the way of escape, though I walk through the valley of the shadow of death.

You slowly open your eyes to see if your vision of the sculpture has been restored, but find your view blocked by the Roman captain, who stands directly in front of you looking down at you with a grin on his face.

You wake, this time with no confusion about where and when you are. You review the events of the day "before", when you came close to escaping your fate. Caught by surprise, and yet at a moment when your spirit was strong and prepared, you adopted a completely different posture toward the man, rising imperiously from your seat to face him.

"I know why you've come," you declared. "And I tell you now: Let go of your desire, for it will do neither of us any good. The Gods we serve are looking down upon us. Let us do what is right in their eyes!"

The man was stunned by your insight into his intentions, but your mistake was to utter your words too loudly. He nearly backed off in awe and dismay, but then rallied (you now realize) in order to save face in front of his men.

"The gods? The gods? Which gods do you mean?" he began, and from that point on, there was no getting off the path to the Fire once more.

You wake again and again to the same day, and every time, fail to find your way past the encounter in the temple. The next time around, you try building on your previous attempt, uttering the same words but more softly, so only the captain can hear. This seems to rob them of their earlier authority, however, and he's not nearly as affected by them. The day after that, you alter your words, removing any mention of God and invoking the pure virtues of honor and kindness instead, but that only insults him. Next, you downplay your knowledge of what he's about to do, making friendly small talk with him like you used to do with strangers on the street, but that only encourages him the more.

Your frustration grows as the failures mount. You ought to have the advantage in these encounters, for you alone have the opportunity to learn from your mistakes and refine your approach over time. Instead, you aren't able to improve on that first, unpremeditated assay. When you try going back to it, you find you can't recapture your exact tone and bearing again.

Then, one day, the captain fails to appear in the temple!

You sit in front of the familiar sculpture going over every step you took in the morning, but can think of nothing you did differently that might have caused him to alter his actions. Either his will is as free as yours in these repetitions of the day, or it can be influenced by changes so small that there's no way you'll ever be able to control them!

Later that day, he tracks you down in the street.

For a week after that (if that's the correct name for the same day repeated seven times) you lose the will to keep trying. You walk numbly from your waking to your preordained fate: from home to the catacombs to the pasture, from arrest to trial to the fire.

And then you wake again.

How many times do you relive that one last day of your life? Fifty? One hundred? You experience death so many times it begins to take on a distinct taste in your mouth, garlicky and gummy, each time the moment approaches.

You try everything you can think of to escape your fate: fleeing the city, hiding amongst the narrow streets of the residential district, feigning sickness and staying home in bed. No matter what you do, the Roman finds you somehow – he must have been eyeing you for a long time up to that point, and decided that today would be the day – and you can't escape his lewd demand and the consequences of refusal.

Several times, you manage to evade him the entire day, only to have him come breaking down the door of your house in the middle of the night. When you try sleeping at Sennie's, she and her family are arrested along with you. You can't even find safety in the depths of the catacombs. The captain's men come whispering through its branching ways, torches in their hands, and you're eventually hauled before the judge once more.

Once, once only, you agreed to go with him.

"I thought you might!" he happily exclaimed, and reaching a hand down to you, pulled you up behind him on his horse. You clung fiercely to him as he galloped back into the city, your hair streaming backward behind you in the sun, thinking to yourself, *I will live! I will live! I will live!* But once you were in his rooms and he stood by the bed unbuckling his gear, you found you couldn't go through with it. Snatching up his sword, you ran him through – you'll never forget his surprised look, or the surprising volume of blood that slicked the floor – setting yourself on the path to the Fire once more.

That "night", in the darkness of death following your execution, or of sleep prior to your subsequent waking, you dreamed of a girl in bright armor, holding a sword high in the air in one hand and a banner of war in the other. Enemy horsemen thundered round and round her, shouting out threats and insults, but she stood firm, defying them in a loud voice and warning them of the judgment of God.

She was still captured in the end.

You wake to the sounds of the summer morning floating in through your bedroom window. You lie in your bed, in your home in the residential district of your beloved city of Antioch, in the four hundred and twelfth year after the death of your Lord.

You hear your parents moving about the house, and then a crash and your father's angry tones.

You review your day.

When your father walks by your door, you call out to him, "Father!"

He stops, makes to walk on, then turns to face you.

"Do you know what they do to Christians?" he demands in a tense, low voice.

"Yes. I do."

You blink, and a tear escapes one eye. Your father's expression softens.

You continue, "If I should meet that fate, will you take good care of Mother? She's not as strong as you."

"Of course!" he says.

He continues to stand uncertainly in the doorway.

"I love you," you tell him, and a pressure in your chest that you hadn't even been aware of before melts silently away.

He scowls, but answers, "Then be careful!"

You dress and leave the house. As you pass the door to the kitchen, you see him kneeling on the floor with your mother picking up the bits of broken pottery. The food she made you sits on the table. You go in and take it. They both look up at you.

"Thank you," you tell your mother, holding up the basket. "I'll share this with Sennie."

You alter no more of your original behavior the rest of the day. You pray in the catacombs and wish Cornelius a good day. You go out into the fields and say your goodbye to Sennie exactly as you did the first time around. Then you stand patiently waiting for the captain to arrive. The only change you make is unintentional: when he threatens you with death, you find it suddenly absurd to try running again. Instead, you burst into laughter! You laugh until tears roll down your face, until you have to lean against the poor man's chest to steady yourself.

You look up at him, catching him by surprise. His face wears the hurt, bewildered expression of a child who's been left out of some joke and fears he may be its butt.

"I'm sorry," you tell him.

You pull away from him and collect yourself, wiping your tears. You hold out your hands to be bound, saying, "What thou doest, do quickly!"

That afternoon, as the flames rise around you, you see a vision of the girl you dreamed about before. She dances amidst a cloud of butterflies, while singing a simple song that tolls the names of the great cathedral cities of France.

> Orléans, Beaugency,
> Notre Dame de Cléry

"Joan!" you cry, just before death takes you once more.

You wake to the temperate, immaterial darkness of your eternal condition. The face of Michael looms over you, not the dreadful visage of an angry God, but a tender human face like the face of your father.

You remember everything now: how at the capture of Joan you shot up into the heavens in a frenzy of wrath and grief, seeking to come before Michael once more, but instead strayed into a blackness so complete that you lost all sense of direction, and could not regain the least glimmer of light no matter how long or how fast you traveled in the straightest lines you could.

The darkness soon became like that of sleep, and perhaps you slept indeed, before you woke.

"Where is she?" you ask.

"In the city of Rouen, held by the English."

"How long have I been away from her?"

"Nine months. Tomorrow, she goes on trial for her life."

You speak out loud what you instantly know: "And she will be condemned."

Michael makes no answer, but only continues to gaze down upon you.

"Why must she die?" you beg of him (or God, or the darkness) feeling again the heat of your old anger.

"She will live," he replies, bending to you and kissing you on the forehead once more.

The Bishop of Rouen

Rouen is a city of iron. Never have you seen so much metal in one place outside of an army camp or a battle. There are iron gates and statues, and carriages with metal wheels, and even metal window frames in some of the grander houses. The streets are filled with more armed and armored soldiers than even Vaucouleurs was, so that you come to understand that, though this is technically a city that has aligned itself with the English, it could return its allegiance to the true king as quickly as any of the cities of the Loire valley, and the English know it.

Every French city they control is an Occupied city.

Passing through the well-guarded streets, you come to the castle of Rouen, whose enormous main gate is also made entirely of metal. Inside it, another metal door separates the rest of the castle from a prison area, and in the prison, behind a final door of iron bars, you find Joan.

You gasp at the sight of her sitting on the floor of her cell with shackles on her wrists and ankles, not just because of her dire state, but because you instantly recognize the stone cell as the place from the dream, the place beyond the reach of help or hope. Joan's hair and face are dull and dusty, as are her clothes. (The same male garb she wore the day she was captured.) Her eyes, though, when she raises them to you, sparkle as brightly as ever.

"Margaret! I am so glad you are here! Catherine has been with me wherever they've kept me so far, but she said she would not be permitted to follow me here. And she was not sure if you would ever be back."

"I lost my way," you tell her.

"Well," she answers brightly. "You have found it again. Or me, anyway."

You have rarely seen her so light hearted, even as a child in the meadows of Domrémy. You look more closely at her, and realize that her face is not just dirty, but bruised, and one of her arms is heavily bandaged.

"Joan! What happened to you?"

"This?" she says, lifting her arm and causing her shackles to clink. "It is nothing. An accident I had. But do you know? When you are a prisoner, it is not so bad to be confined to your sickbed for a time. Everyone leaves you alone!"

She laughs, then continues more soberly.

"Not any more, of course. Listen." She lowers her voice and you move in closer. "Tomorrow at the trial, there will be a notary recording all that is said. Station yourself where you can look over his shoulder, and make sure he does his job well. Everything depends on it."

You nod automatically, occupied by another question: When was the last time you heard her laugh? After some great victory during the Loire campaign? If not, then certainly after the liberation of Orléans. But no, you can recall no memory of it. Has she not laughed since the company's days in Chinon? Since she left home?

You will hear her laugh just three more times.

That night, you and Joan soar among the butterflies as you have many times in the past, but even as you participate in her

Freeman Ng

dream, a corner of your mind frets over her irrational gaiety. Does she think she's going to escape this net the English have caught her in? Around and around she flies, rising so high at times that her fluttering friends cannot keep up and must circle below, waiting for her return.

The air is clean and cold. The skies of her mind bright and unclouded.

The following morning, a guard walks Joan across the castle courtyard and into its church. You're surprised by this – are they going to let her pray, or even take communion, before going to the courtroom? – but once you enter, you see that this *is* the courtroom. Armed knights are stationed along all the aisles, and a narrow table has been set up in front of the altar for the judges to sit at. Behind the altar, a large English flag is draped across the front wall, bulging a little at its center with the shape of the cross it obscures.

Seven men wearing the tall miters of the bishopric enter from the left and take their seats at the table. To one side, a cleric sits at a small desk with pen and paper. Seeing that he's already writing, you hurry to his side to perform the job Joan charged you with.

Day 1, reads his neat, compact handwriting. *January 9, 1431. Rouen chapel. Duke of Bedford in attendance. Presiding: Bishop of Beauvais.*

The pews of the church are almost completely filled with spectators, most of them English. As Joan is walked up the center aisle, they hurl curses and obscene insults at her. Two or three attempt to strike her as she passes, only falling short due to the girth of the guards at her sides. They sit her down in a small chair at the head of the aisle directly in front of the judges.

"French whore!" the crowd continues to shout. "You will burn!"

"Down with Charles!"

"To the Fire with his witch!"

The judges make no attempt to bring the courtroom to order. The one in the center chair looks out benignly at the raucous crowd, a satisfied smile on his face. Finally, an English lord sitting in the front row cries out, "Cauchon! Get on with it!"

The crowd instantly falls silent. The judge flinches, then rises to speak, bowing pointedly to the English lord.

"This proceeding of the Holy Inquisition will begin. I am Pierre Cauchon, the Bishop of Rouen."

The other judges glance at one another and the notary lifts his head.

"Your Eminence. Strictly speaking –"

"I am the Bishop of Rouen!"

Cauchon glares at the notary until he lowers his gaze. You find his look so withering that you lower your eyes as well, shrinking behind the notary's broad shoulders to hide yourself from his wrath. Then he turns back to Joan.

"I am Pierre Cauchon, the Bishop of Rouen, and I will be your judge, along with these worthy men, all of them high priests of the Church. The notary will be Father Manchon, who will faithfully record these proceedings without interrupting them again in any way."

He shoots a warning look your way again, but Manchon keeps his head down and his pen moving across the paper. The Bishop turns back to Joan.

"Do you swear to tell the entire truth concerning all that you will be questioned about?"

"No."

The crowd erupts in renewed anger – you yourself are stunned and a little dismayed: does Joan plan to say nothing in her own defense? – but Cauchon only narrows his gaze upon her, leaning across the table that separates them.

"If you will not speak the truth," he carefully pronounces, "we will have no choice but to render judgment against you right now."

"I swear to tell the whole truth," says Joan, "concerning all that I may honorably speak of. But you might ask me to reveal a secret I have promised another that I would keep or that God has not given me permission to share, or for information about the disposition of

French forces. I will not answer such questions, for *that* would be the grievous sin."

The crowd murmurs unhappily, but without its earlier vehemence. Cauchon leans back in his chair.

"Very well. Let it be noted that the prisoner swore to tell the truth only on some subjects."

You look anxiously down at Manchon's notes, but see that he carefully records every word spoken between Joan and Cauchon without omission or interpretation. He does write down what Cauchon said, but exactly as he said it: *Let it be noted...*

"Now," continues Cauchon, "I hope you will agree that questions of your faith cannot be evaded, for the court must know if you are in error concerning any of the great doctrines of the Church. If you refuse to answer in this area, we must conclude that you are hiding heretical belief!"

"I will answer any question put to me concerning the Faith."

"Then tell us, who first taught you the principles of religion?"

"My mother taught me the prayers and the creeds, and everything else that was needful to know about the Faith. I could not have had a better teacher."

"Let us find out how good a student you were. Recite for this court the Lord's Prayer."

"No," says Joan, and this time, the murmurs of the spectators are tinged more with puzzlement than wrath. You wonder yourself what her reason will be for refusing this time.

"It would be disrespectful," she explains, "and perhaps even prideful, to utter those words just for the sake of proving I knew them. But if you will hear my confession first, I will gladly say the prayer in earnest afterward."

"Very well!" cries Cauchon, half rising from his seat, but the man next to him lays a hand on his wrist and whispers, "No, your Eminence!"

"Why not?" hisses Cauchon. "She is offering to confess all, right now!"

"But then we would be constrained by our vows as priests never to reveal what she said – and to grant her forgiveness!"

Cauchon settles slowly back into his seat. It was a trap set by Joan for the Bishop!

"Vive la Pucelle!" you cry. She answers you with a grim smile.

"It would not be fitting for me to hear the confession of one so obviously unrepentant," Cauchon finally says. "Instead, simply swear to us that you know the Lord's Prayer and the creeds, and that you hold unreservedly to all that they proclaim about the Faith."

"I know them well, and hold them dear."

"Swear to it, then! Why will you not swear?"

"Because I already swore to tell the truth once, and our Lord has commanded that we not swear much, but let our yea's be yea's and our nays be nays."

Manchon writes out that last sentence with such vigor that his triumphant dotting of the final period sounds clearly in the silence. Cauchon glares at him, then turns back to Joan, working his jaw but finding nothing further to say. Finally, one of the other judges speaks up.

"Tell us how you came to hear the voices that you claim directed your actions."

For the next hour, Joan talks freely about her childhood in the meadows of Domrémy, and about how you and Catherine and Michael came to her with messages from God. Cauchon remains silent through it all, allowing his peers to conduct this part of the interrogation, and as far as you can tell, they set no traps for her, but seem genuinely interested in obtaining as much information as possible. Her calm voice and the gentle scritch-scritch of the notary's pen lull you into the dream-like state of a child listening for the umpteenth time to a familiar bedtime story she never tires of. Your own words strike your ears afresh, as if they had been spoken by the voice of God indeed in some fantastical tale from the days of yore.

Be a good girl, and go to church!

Your hands will set the crown of France upon the head of the

Dauphin. Your voice will pronounce your people's liberation.

Be comforted, Joan, by the love of God that holds you.

When she finishes her account, Cauchon speaks again.

"Why would saints and angels of God need a girl to do their work? Could they not have fought for the French themselves?"

"If God willed it, then they could. Neither they nor I can do anything except by the grace of God, but with God, all things are possible."

"Are you in fact in God's grace, then?"

He asks this last question with a deliberate casualness that jolts you into wakefulness again. He busies himself with his notes, as if preparing to move on to the next round of questions, but the other judges and the English lord peer intently at their prisoner. This must be another trap! What can it be, though? Do they really expect her to answer that she's not in God's grace? Joan remains silent, fixing her eyes upon Cauchon until he can no longer keep up the pretense of rearranging his papers and must finally look back at her.

"If I am not," she tells him, "may God bring me to it. If I am, may God keep me in it!"

Rage convulses the face of the Bishop of Rouen. The other judges sit stupefied in their places. The notary looks up from his papers, startled and smiling.

"We will adjourn for the day!" growls Cauchon, and with a bang of his gavel, turns and fairly flees through a door behind the altar.

The other judges follow him, muttering and disputing among themselves. The English lord bolts from his seat and strides after them. The guards lead Joan back down the aisle of the church. The crowd disperses in discontent. As the pews empty, you notice a figure sitting on the aisle next to where Joan was placed.

"Catherine!" you cry, running down to her and throwing yourself into her arms.

"Yes, it is I," she says. "I am happy to see you, but happier that *you* are happy to see *me!*"

In your joy at being reunited, you let go of your anger at her.

"I'm sorry I left Joan alone all this time," you say. "It was a long journey back from – from where I was."

"I can't imagine," she replies, shaking her head.

"Why is the trial only now starting? It's been nine months since Joan was captured, hasn't it?"

"Yes, but she has only been in the hands of the English for one month. The lord who held her was not English, but a French noble allied with them. He waited long to receive the highest offer of ransom, but in the end, sold her to the English after all."

"How did she get hurt? She told me she had some kind of accident."

"An accident? She had that 'accident' the day she learned she was to be delivered to the English, and tried to escape her imprisonment by jumping out of a tower window, sixty feet to the ground! I told her not to, but she was a little mad with despair. She had already made an earlier attempt, a few weeks into her captivity, by breaking through the wooden floor of her cell with her bare hands!"

"She continued to escape their nets today. Were you helping her all the time?"

"Some of the time, and other times, not. There have been many occasions in the past when she has exhibited knowledge I did not give her, and I assumed it was you or Michael who told her, but now I think she sees much on her own, and has no need for us to tell her everything."

"What was that last trap she escaped, about God's grace?"

"You saw it, did you? It was truly diabolical. They would have condemned her if she had answered No, of course, but had she answered Yes, they would have charged her with presumption. There was no good answer to that question – until she found it!"

She beams as if the trial were already over and Joan freed.

"Did she see the trap on her own, then?"

"I think so. That crafty old man had me fooled at first, but when she refrained from answering right away, I saw the poison in his harmless sounding words. But I only told her not to answer Yes or No. She found an excellent way of saying not less, but more, and yet in perfect safety! A remarkable young woman."

"What she spoke is only what she's always believed."

Catherine looks at you in surprise.

"Why yes, you are right! I didn't think of it that way. I will try to remember that in the coming days. There will be many more attacks, many more traps, but they will have no power to harm her in her honest innocence."

You look into her smiling face. Is she lying to you again? No. She believes what she says. Once, years ago, you wondered if Heaven could be divided against itself. Now you see that Heaven is a mystery. Who can guess what God might decree?

"Will you be with her all the time from now on?"

"Only when she sits here answering her judges. I am the patron saint of those who are tested in that particular way. Your job will be to stay with her in the prison. As you now know, I have no experience in my life that would be of any use there."

She smiles timidly. You take her hand and kiss it.

"I will think of your kindness and your care for me," you tell her, "and that will help me to help Joan."

The following morning, the English guard that escorted Joan to the church the previous day reappears outside her cell. Unlike the guards who watch her in the prison, he's an older man, and kind.

"Good morning, miss," he says as he enters the cell.

"Good morning."

"Are you ready to go to court?"

"As ready as ever."

He chuckles softly to himself as he undoes her chains.

"I don't doubt it!"

Yesterday when you arrived at the church, he turned Joan over to the French guards at the door, but you looked over at him from time to time sitting in the back row following the proceedings intently. He would contort his face in anxious surprise whenever Joan refused to answer a question directly, and labor in thought, cocking an ear, as she explained herself.

They set off across the courtyard, but when they come up to the door of the church, the man continues to walk past it.

"Sir? Aren't we going in?"

"They've moved the proceedings," he replies. "We're going to the courthouse today. It's just this way."

Joan remains standing by the door of the church.

"Miss?"

"May I enter?" she finally asks.

"The church?" he says. "I'm sure you're not allowed. You're on trial for heresy!"

"What would the harm be?" she persists. "If you were in my place, would you not wish to pray for strength before entering the arena of your enemies?"

"I wouldn't be in your place," he says simply.

"But you are a soldier! Have you never wished that you could stop time just before the attackers crashed into your lines, or before you plunged into theirs, so you could say a final prayer, or think for a moment of your family?"

"Well," says the man. "We *are* early. Go on, but only for a minute. There'll be trouble for both of us if you're caught."

"I thank you –"

"Thomas. Tom."

"I thank you, Tom."

Once in the courthouse, you bypass the double doors of a couple of larger courtrooms and enter a small chamber at the end of a dark hall. Within, the layout is similar to that of the church, but on a much smaller scale. The judges must look almost straight down from their high seats to see Joan, and Manchon looks almost like one of the judges, sitting just to their left and on the same level. Although there are enough seats for maybe 30 spectators, only the first row is occupied, by the English lord and a few of his men.

Freeman Ng

Catherine stands by the chair where Joan will sit.

"This Trial of the Holy Inquisition will resume," says Cauchon when everyone is in place. "To begin, the prisoner will swear again to answer truthfully every question she is asked."

Joan pauses, in some doubt. Catherine's face displays uncertainty as well.

"I am willing to do so," she says, "if it is the custom in such trials that the oath be repeated each day."

The judges remain silent and still. She looks over to you, but you have no idea what the correct answer is, either. Will they condemn her for swearing unnecessarily, or for refusing to swear again when it's required?

Then, beside you, the notary Manchon dips his head ever so slightly. Was it a nod, or is he merely bending over his notepad?

"Very well," says Joan. "I renew my original oath to tell the whole truth concerning any subject of which I may honorably speak."

On this second day of the trial, her accusers narrow their inquiry, probing for evidence of magical practices:

Was there not a tree in your village reputed to be haunted by fairies? And did you not dance around it and leave offerings beneath it?

"I knew about the tree, but never thought the talk of fairies anything more than a game the children played. I may have danced around it or near it, for I danced often in the fields. Sometimes, the young married couples of the village would picnic beneath its branches. But I never left offerings anywhere but in the alms box of the church."

What about the items that people brought you to bless in Vaucouleurs?

"I never claimed to be able to imbue them with power beyond that of any useful or beautiful thing. But the people were fearful and disheartened because of the war you have waged against them, and I saw no reason to discourage them further by refusing their requests."

What was the meaning of the crosses engraved on your sword?

"How should I know? They were already there when I obtained it."

Isn't it true that you caused your standard to float through the air at your king's coronation?

"Yes. By holding it high in my hands!"

Did you not have a ring that you often kissed before going into battle?

"Yes. My parents gave it to me and I liked to remember them by kissing it. It was taken from me when I was captured, and I wish you would give it back."

That night, a visitor comes to Joan's cell. It is Guillaume Manchon.

"Father!" cries Joan to the notary. "I am so glad you've come. You have the most important job in this trial, you know."

"Do I? It does not seem so to me. They have been pressing me to alter the facts of the record in ways unfavorable to you, and though I have refused so far, the Duke of Bedford has his own secretaries recording who knows what, anyway. I doubt that anything I have written will be used in deliberations or be sent on to Rome. I think I may resign my position soon. But do not worry. I am here not as notary to the trial, but the chaplain of this prison, and I will continue to come in that capacity for as long as you wish."

Joan hobbles over to the bars.

"Does the Bishop know you are here?" she whispers.

"Well, no," replies Manchon, lowering his tone as well, "but this is what I do for every prisoner, so I am sure he will assume I'm doing it for you."

"Perhaps," says Joan dryly. "Or maybe this will be the last time we speak to one another."

"No, no," says Manchon. "He could not interfere with my official duties."

"Any more than he could keep me in this military prison instead of a church prison, even though I am a woman and a noble and the charges against me are religious? Any more than he could declare himself the bishop of *Rouen?*"

Manchon makes to answer, then stops. When he speaks again, it's in an earnest whisper after a quick look around.

"He has been given temporary jurisdiction over this region in order to preside over the trial, though even that is not strictly proper. I think he hopes to retain the position after the trial is over. He has risen far and fast through the hierarchies of the church, some say by ruthless means. In the matter of Boniface and Gregory, for example – "

He stops abruptly and looks at Joan.

"I think I had best stay quiet about my visits to you."

"It is already too late," she says. "The guards will let him know you were here. Tell me, what region is he really the bishop over?"

"Beauvais. But he lost his seat and had to flee his home in Rheims when – when your king came there to be crowned! Dear God. You are in great danger, my child!"

Joan reaches through the bars to lay a shackled hand on Manchon's arm.

"Father, you must not resign your position, no matter how little good you think you may be doing now. For it will be only by your accounts that my king, and my friends, and my family will ever know what truly happens here."

"I will stand fast," declares Manchon, sorrow in his eyes. "They, and the world, will know."

Over the next few weeks, Cauchon explores a number of different avenues of attack. (Like a prosecutor who has no case, notes Catherine.) One day, the main topic is the propriety of various past actions of Joan's.

Did you not sin in running away from home?

"I did so in obedience to God's command, and later, I apologized to my parents and they forgave me. At no other time in my life did I ever disobey them."

What about when you jumped from the tower? Suicide is a mortal sin!

"I jumped fully expecting to escape, though if I had perished in the attempt, I would have considered it a better fate than to fall into the hands of the English."

Why did you bring your standard into the cathedral of Rheims for your king's coronation?

"It had been through the toils of battle. I thought it only fitting that it should share in the rewards."

Another day, the issue is her wearing of men's clothing.

Why do you wear men's clothing?

"These clothes are the least of things. They are of no importance. I wear them for my own safety, and for reasons of propriety. It would not be fitting to wear women's dress into battle."

You are no longer in battle now, and yet you continue to wear male garb.

"I have not been told by God to relinquish it yet."

Would you put on a dress if it meant you could go to Mass?

"Yes, if I could change back into my old clothes afterward."

No! You must resume female dress permanently!

"Then I will do so if, afterward, I am moved to a church prison to be guarded by women, as should have been done from the start."

You are an enemy combatant, captured while leading armies against us! You will be held right here for the duration of this trial.

"Then I will remain in the clothes I am wearing now."

Finally, they spend an entire day trying to make the idea of Joan's voices seem ridiculous.

When Michael comes to you, is he naked or clothed?

"Do you think God cannot afford to clothe his servants?"

Does he have hair?

"Why should he have cut off his hair?"

Does he speak to you in French?

"Why should he speak in English when he is not on their side?"

Toward the end of that day, their questions take on a scurrilous cast that make you seethe with indignation:

When the spirit woke you, did it do so by the sound of its voice alone, or did it touch you?

> *Have your spirits ever touched you in your private parts?*
> *Have you ever embraced one of these spirits?*
> *Did you embrace its upper parts or lower parts?*

After three weeks of such questioning, the trial is suspended for a time. That doesn't mean that Joan's persecutors are done attacking her, though. Her rations are cut in half, and her chains are no longer removed when she has to leave her cell to go to the latrine. When she's in her cell, an extra chain is secured around her waist, confining her to a sitting position on the floor and preventing her from moving around even in that small space.

Within a week, she goes from the girl who raised a siege ladder against the wall of the Tourelles while arrows whistled down around her, to a shadow shuffling through the corridors of the castle prison, dragging her chains behind her and gasping occasionally in pain.

"I have never felt so weary," she says one day. "Not even the autumn we raced the early snow to bring the harvest in. Will you just sit by me a while, Margaret? I am too tired for conversation."

Soon, that's all you do, day after day: sit by Joan's side holding her hand and letting her lean on you. Manchon does not visit again, and you wonder if he even knows about the alterations in her treatment. He would surely do something about it. Surely, there's something that could be done. There must be some authority above the Bishop that could be informed of his tactics. It could even be that the other judges don't know all of what's happening, and it would be enough for them to learn of it.

You're powerless, though. Even if you could communicate with others, you can't leave Joan for any length of time. Sometimes when she wakes at night, she cries out if you're not right there beside her, and her dreams are dark and unbearably weighty unless you join them and exert all your will to recall the brightness that used to fill them. Then, for a night, or two, you dance with the butterflies as before, but more and more now, Joan dreams (or thinks, unsleeping) only of the cell itself, of fetid damp stone and the weight of her chains, and the echo of the guards' footsteps in passageways unseen.

After three weeks of physical hardship and partial starvation, Joan stands before her judges once more, only not in the courthouse. Instead, they gather right outside her cell and interrogate her from there. She's forced to remain on her feet through the whole of these sessions, and if she falters, court is adjourned for the day and she is placed in a metal box that doesn't permit her to fully sit or stand until the next day.

The judges raise no new issues, but repeat their previous questions over and over, sometimes shouting two or three of them at her simultaneously. Catherine does her best to guide her through the maze of questions, but you come to see that she's simply adding her voice to the tumult assaulting Joan's ears. From that point on, the two of you merely stand by her side, holding her up when you're able to touch her, and comforting her by your mere presence when you're not.

Some days, she's too weak to even speak, and court must be adjourned. Even on her better days, she takes longer and longer to respond to the questions fired at her from every direction, and her answers grow less and less coherent.

"My what? My standard?"

"Yes, wench! Why did you have angels painted on your standard?"

"I think, I think I have already answered."

"You will answer again! Why did you have angels painted on your standard? And why with arms and legs, as if they were ordinary mortals?"

"They will come in clouds of glory." Her voice is as faint as a child's talking in its sleep. "Let all mortal flesh tremble and rejoice. His sword is a flame of fire."

You think often in these days about your reliving of the day you died. No matter what you tried, you couldn't escape your fate. No matter how much longer Joan is able to avoid saying something incriminating, she's sure to slip up in the end, for her body (and therefore, her mind; and perhaps even her soul) is at the mercy of not just one vengeful Bishop, but an entire government, whose resources and lifespan far exceed her own.

They can wait as long as they need to for her to finally stumble. How much longer can she remain on her feet?

One morning, a masked man accompanies the judges to her cell and spends an hour setting up various mechanical devices you can't fathom the purpose of. Joan stands silently watching him at his work. Most of the judges avert their eyes, looking to the left or right down the halls of the prison, or down at their own feet, but Cauchon gazes at Joan the whole time, a look of predatory intensity on his face. The man lays out mysterious tools that might be medical, culinary, or astrological, for all you can tell. Then a brazier of hot coals is brought into the cell, and you understand in a cold flash who he is and what's about to happen here.

Catherine appears at that moment, her face pale with fear, but Joan gestures to her to keep her distance with the slightest bending of her hand where it hangs by her side. She keeps her eyes on Cauchon, like a fencer who must focus all her attention on the feints and thrusts of her opponent.

The masked man nods to Cauchon, who then speaks.

"This court has exercised great patience in striving to teach you the error of your ways, and yet you have resisted us time and time again in your insolence and pride. Today, you will admit to the charges leveled against you, or your body will be put to the trial, that your soul might be saved."

Joan does not hesitate to reply.

"Everything I have done has been in obedience to the commands of God, and in accordance with all that I know of the principles of the Faith. Though you tear me limb from limb, I will never say otherwise, or if I did, it would only be because you forced me into it. You wish to condemn me only so that you might undermine the power of my king, but I tell you now that though I were dead, and though there were a hundred thousand English soldiers in this land, you would not prevail, for the King of Heaven does not wish it."

It's the longest speech she's made in weeks, and it seems to you that it exhausts her last reserve of strength. You detect the beginning of a swoon in her and dash over to her to take an arm and help her remain on her feet.

Cauchon gestures to the masked man to proceed, but can't catch his attention because he's still staring at Joan. He pulls off his mask and continues to look into her eyes, which look evenly back into his. Finally, he turns to the judges with a look of such disgust on his face, it's as if *he* were the noble priest and *they* the vile torturers.

Without a word, he walks out of the cell.

"Praise God!" whispers Catherine in your ear as the judges also leave, but you hardly hear it through the roar of a sudden urgency.

"Stay with her," you say, and leaving the cell, follow Cauchon through the metal door into the castle proper. You trail him through the stone halls, calling out to him over and over, "She's innocent! She's innocent!"

What Catherine praised God for, you see as the beginning of the end, for Cauchon will soon find a man more willing to perform the gruesome task assigned him, or he'll simply continue to worsen Joan's treatment until it becomes just as bad. (Some nights when she's locked in the metal box, she groans for hours at a time.)

This can't be allowed to continue.

"She's innocent! She's innocent! She's innocent!"

Cauchon enters his quarters, slapping aside the helping hand of the guard posted at the door and slamming it shut behind him. He screams in fury and sweeps the books off a table. He hurls a bottle against a wall, shattering it and spraying wine and bits of glass in every direction.

"Damn her!" he cries. "Damn her to Hell!"

"She's innocent!" you shout back at him. "Innocent!"

He throws himself onto a couch and finally lapses into relative silence, lying on his back with his arms over his face, groaning a little now and again.

"She's innocent!" you whisper urgently to him, willing the sound of your words into his ears, and their meaning into his brain. "Joan is innocent. She's truly sent from God. You're persecuting an innocent girl! She's innocent. She's innocent!"

Cauchon sits bolt upright on the couch. His eyes open so wide that you glance in the direction of his gaze to see if some divine vision isn't unfolding before him.

"My God!" he murmurs. "Of course! Of course!"

Flying off the couch, he calls out, "Guard! Guard! What are you doing out there, you worthless lump?"

The guard pokes his head into the room.

"Yes, my lo-"

"Quiet!" snaps the Bishop. "Let me think!"

He stands frozen in thought while the guard looks patiently on.

"Tomorrow," says Cauchon at last, "we go to the Wood. See to the preparations. Work through the night if you have to! Tell Manchon to come here at once."

The guard no sooner withdraws than Cauchon snaps his fingers.

"The Duke! I must tell him the news!"

He races from the room, leaving you stunned in his wake. What just happened? Did he actually hear your words? Did you somehow convince him of Joan's innocence? But the plan he just made is something he believes will please the English lord. You finally think to dash out into the hall, but he's long gone. You try to catch up with him, but the endless branching passages of the castle prove to be too much for you, and in the end, you have to pass completely out through the outer walls and reenter through the main gate even to find your way back to Joan's cell.

She's asleep, and Catherine is gone. You sit, wakeful, by her side all night, wondering what the next day will bring, and whether Joan will survive it.

In the morning, Tom, the English guard, undoes her chains and escorts her out the front gates of the castle. You think for one incredible moment that they're releasing her, but no: the wagon he loads her into has its own set of shackles, which he attaches to her wrists before driving the wagon away from the castle and out a side gate of the city.

Joan leans up against the side of the wagon, looking out hungrily at the plain daylight glancing off the tiled houses of the city, and then slanting through the silent woods around it. She breathes it in deeply, stretching her arms out to the very tips of her fingers. When she speaks, there's a buoyancy in her voice you haven't heard in a long time.

"Do you know, Tom? I had the strangest dream last night. A cleric came to visit me and my mother in our home in Domrémy. He told me that a boy from Toul was suing me for refusing to marry him, except that the boy turned out to be the Bishop! We were frantic over how to escape his trap, but the cleric came to our rescue. 'I tell you what,' he said. 'I will go back and report to the Bishop that you are dead.' We were so relieved!"

Tom makes no comment, either because he has nothing to say or because he didn't hear her words over the rattle of the wagon.

"What do you think, Tom? Will I escape the trap?"

The wagon winds through the woods until the path it's on grows too narrow for it. Then he unchains Joan and lifts her down off the wagon. You're far from the city or any other human habitation. The air is still and silent.

"Tom?" asks Joan as he begins walking her down the path. "Have you brought me out here to kill me?"

"No! No, miss. The judges are waiting for us, not too far ahead."

"And what is *their* intention?"

He trips on a root and when he regains his balance, stands looking anxiously at Joan.

They emerge into a small clearing. The judges sit in a semi-circle at the opposite side of it. To their right, Guillaume Manchon sits at a small table with pen and paper. In the center of the clearing, a post rises from the ground, with a pile of firewood heaped at its base. Standing by the pyre is another masked man, holding a torch.

"Sweet Jesus!" murmurs Tom under his breath.

Joan takes three steps, formal and processional, into the center of the circle to stand by the readied wood.

"Today is the day of Judgment," intones Cauchon. "Today, this court relinquishes its duties to instruct and uphold, and leaves you to the fate appointed you, whether it be salvation or damnation. The choice will be yours."

He holds up a sheet of paper with writing on it.

"This is your confession."

He gestures to a clerk, who sets a small table in front of Joan and places the document on it, along with a pen and ink.

"You will sign it," says Cauchon. "Today. This hour. Or we will have no choice but to deliver you, body and soul, to the divine judgment that awaits you."

Joan looks down at the paper.

"I cannot read," she says. "Will someone tell me what is written here?"

"Of course," replies Cauchon, and gestures to the surprised Manchon. He trots quickly over to Joan and reads the confession out loud to her.

"I, Joan of Domrémy, commonly called The Maid, do confess that I wore men's clothing and fought in the war in disobedience to the teachings of the Church. I renounce these acts, and promise, upon pain of death, never to return to them."

He turns the paper over but finds nothing more written.

Joan looks at him in confusion.

"I promise upon pain of death?"

"Yes," he replies in an animated whisper. "It appears that if you sign this document, your life will be spared! They will not be able to execute you unless you wear men's clothes or take up the sword again."

She looks up at the judges.

"If I sign this, you will release me?"

"No," says Cauchon. "You will spend the rest of your days in prison, that your adherence to your promises may be strictly monitored."

"In the castle prison, or a church prison?"

"You would be transferred to a church prison."

She looks at Manchon.

"I cannot renounce any of my actions, for they were all done at God's call."

"I do not doubt it," he says. "But can you at least promise to never do them again? It does seem unlikely that your king will need you to do any more fighting for him, and if you aren't fighting, there will be no more need for men's clothes, will there?"

She bites her lip, passing her eyes across the lines of the document over and over as if she can read them indeed.

"Sign the paper!" cries Cauchon.

"Sign! You will sign!" shout the other judges.

"Sign that paper or you will be put immediately to the fire!"

Joan looks around in indecision. You have no idea what to advise her, and Catherine is nowhere to be seen.

Finally, she tells Manchon, in a low voice that only he can hear, "It is better to sign than to burn," and takes the paper and pen from him. She practices the initial 'J' of her name in the air a few times as usual, but before she can begin to write it on the confession, Cauchon speaks again.

"You will mark the bottom of the page with an X."

Joan freezes. She glances up at him.

"With what?"

"With an X, you illiterate wench! You will write an X on the paper as a sign of your name! But do not think you will escape the consequences if you break the promise written on the paper, for we are all witnesses to your consent!"

Her face blooming with an incredulous smile, she carefully marks the confession with an X, which can also be seen as a cross. *The sign that a document should not be heeded!* Then, to the utter confusion of not only the judges, but Manchon and Tom, she bursts into laughter!

"Stop that!" shouts Cauchon.

"Joan, what is the matter?" asks Manchon.

She makes no answer, but continues to laugh wildly, joyfully, like a mother who thought her only child lost and dead, only to look out the window one day to see her limping in through the garden gate, years older, bruised and travel-stained but alive. The judges command and threaten, while Manchon and Tom try to persuade her to be more circumspect, all to no effect. Soon, they can only stand around her in perplexed witness, as the sound of her mirth fills the silent wood.

The Fire

Tom maintains a steady stream of encouragement all through the ride back to the castle.

"It won't be so bad, miss. The church prison is hardly a prison at all. It's really more like a nunnery. You'll have your own room, and a real bed. And you'll be able to go to mass as often as you like. You just won't be able to leave. It won't be that different from taking holy orders!"

Joan sits on the floor of the wagon, her head in her hands. She has not spoken since her laughter died finally away in the distant wood.

"I've heard," continues Tom, "that sometimes, a person condemned to life imprisonment can be released. It's usually for reasons of state, but – but that's your case exactly, isn't it? Perhaps your king will bargain with my king to have you freed. Perhaps the Pope will grant you a pardon. Anything is possible."

"Cross or no, I did wrong," Joan finally utters bleakly. "Margaret, what was I thinking?"

"Miss?"

"I did wrong, Tom. I should never have recanted, even in

appearance, even to save my own life."

The wagon creaks to a stop, still well outside the city walls. Tom gets down and comes around to the wagon gate. His face is grave and tender.

"I have a daughter your age, and if she were threatened with death, I would tell her to say anything and do anything to live. You did right, and your father, if he were here, would say so, too. You mustn't refuse the gift of life that comes from God."

Joan goes to the bars of the wagon and lays her hands over his.

"I thank you, Tom. I think you're right about my father. But are you certain that there is no fate so terrible that you would not prefer that your daughter died rather than have to face it?"

Upon their return to the castle, Joan is brought to a small ante-chamber. On a table is a double ration of hot food. Slung over a chair is a yellow dress.

"They say you have half an hour to eat and put on the dress," says Tom. "Then they'll come for you. Once you're wearing the dress, you must never go back to wearing men's clothes! If I don't see you again, I wish you Godspeed."

"I thank you, Tom. God's blessing be upon you and your daughter."

He leaves the room, and you're alone with Joan. She picks at the food, then swivels her chair and the chair the dress is on so that she sits facing it.

"Well, Margaret. We have come a long way, have we not?"

"Maybe there's much farther still to go."

She looks up at you in surprise.

"Do you think I should put on the dress?"

It feels wrong to you. Everything has felt wrong since Joan's life was spared in the wood. However, you can't bring yourself to tell her that. You can't tell her to let go of her life.

"If I had a second chance," you finally say, "I would do everything I could to avoid my fate."

She smiles tenderly.

Freeman Ng

"Would you really? Would you, for example, not become a Christian in the first place? Would you give in to the desires of the Roman?"

You have to smile back.

"I might try."

She laughs. Not the wild laughter of the wood, but one brief letting go of care, as much a sigh as a laugh.

"Very well. I will try, too. It might not be so bad. Tom says it will be like taking holy orders. If that is the case, my mother will be pleased!"

She laboriously strips off her male garb. As you view her body briefly naked, and then covered in the drape of the dress, you realize with a shock that she's no longer the child you once watched sporting in the fields with her brothers. It's not that you haven't been aware of her growing up before your eyes; it's just that what she was growing up into was simply an adult, a human being, neither male nor female, like Bertrand de Poulengy or Dunois or her uncle Durand Laxart. Now, for the first time, you see her as a woman. You count the years – the years! – in your mind, and decide that she must be about nineteen now.

Your age.

She stands before you, arms held out to either side.

"One path or the other," she says. "They both lead to the river."

The soldiers that come for her are two that often guarded her in her cell. They stop short at the entrance to the room and stare at her for a moment, stunned as you were, it may be, by her newly feminine appearance – and a burr of anxiety forms in the pit of your stomach.

"You are to come with us," one of them says.

As she walks out the door between them, they each take hold of one of her bare arms, and the burr in your stomach grows into a cold lump.

They walk her around one corner, and then down the main

passageway of the castle toward the main gate, but just before they reach it, turn down the hall leading to the metal door of the prison section!

"Where are we going?" demands Joan.

"Back to your cell, where else?"

"No!" she cries, wrenching her arms from their grasp. "They said I would be moved to a church prison!"

"We know nothing about that."

She tries to bolt past them, back up the corridor into the main castle, but they catch her. She thrashes and strikes out with her fists, trying to break free.

"Father Manchon!" she cries. "Tom!"

"Get her inside!" growls one of the guards, and together, they drag her in past the metal door and slam it shut.

As the echoes of the shut door fade, Joan falls silent herself. Her eyes take on the searching look they used to have when they scanned the battlements of a city, searching for a weak place to attack, or the night she was captured, as she sought for a way to escape the closing encirclement of enemy horsemen.

They lead her back to her old cell. The guards they pass on the way turn to stare at her. You see one man nudge a companion, a leer on his face like the look the Roman captain directed at you as he shut the door of his bedroom behind him.

"Joan!" you blurt out. "These men. I think there might be trouble! Should I go for help? Will anyone be able to hear me?"

At the door of her cell, she turns to face the guards.

"If you truly knew who I was and Who it is that sent me, you would want to have nothing to do with me."

"You are a self-confessed heretic!"

They shove her into the cell and toss her old male clothes in after her. As soon as they leave, Joan turns to you and whispers, in a voice frantic with fear, "Go!"

"Father Manchon! Father Manchon!"

You race blindly through the featureless corridors and dark

stairwells of the castle.

Stop! you tell yourself. *Stop and* think *how to find him!* But you can't control yourself. Panic drives you on.

Passing through a door, you find yourself at one end of a long corridor, and somehow know that the door at the opposite end is Manchon's. You run toward it and then through it – but no! You're blinded by a white flash of pain, and the next thing you know, you're lying on the floor just inside the slowly opening door.

Guillaume Manchon gets up from where he was kneeling at his bedside.

"Is anybody there? Hello?"

"It's Joan! You have to help her!" you try to tell him, but that crash into the unexpectedly solid door knocked the breath from you. (And why would he be able to hear you, anyway?)

"Help!" you whisper hopelessly. "Help!"

Then you hear it: a faint cry of distress, coming from the other end of the hall.

"My God!" exclaims Manchon, and bolts down the hall. You limp along behind him. He dashes down a flight of stairs and disappears from your sight, but when you reach the bottom yourself, you see the metal door that leads into the prison area just a few feet away. (You must have run round and round the castle in your frantic search and come back near to where you started!) You catch up with him in Joan's cell, where two of the guards stand at attention before him.

"If you try anything like that again," he is telling them, "I promise you, as an officer of this facility, I will seek your dismissal from the army. As a clerk of the court, I will have you arrested and put into prison yourselves. And as a priest, I can assure you that your souls will burn in Hell. Now go!"

They saunter out and he kneels before Joan, who lies curled on the floor in one corner of the cell. Her face is bruised and tear stained, and her dress torn in places.

"Joan!" he whispers. "Are you . . . are you hurt?" She does not reply. "I apologize, on behalf of, of the court, of my government..."

He stands, hands clenched.

"I will speak with the judges. We will fix this. I promise!"

He strides out of the cell and calls over the guards.

"You two are relieved. You will go directly to your quarters and stay there until you hear from your commander. You others: no one is to enter this cell for any reason until I return."

"On whose authority?" one of them asks.

"My own, wretch! But if that is not enough, I will soon be back with the Bishop."

They glance at one another, then reply, "Yes, father."

After one last look back at Joan, Manchon departs.

"Joan?" you venture once you're alone. "Joan!"

She doesn't reply. She doesn't speak or move for the rest of the day, remaining curled in the corner on the hard stone floor. Manchon does not return. The lights go down, and night takes hold of the prison.

You go over and sit down beside her, discovering as you do that you can make physical contact, but she cries out at your touch, tensing her body and cocking a fist.

"Joan!" you cry, throwing up your arms in defense.

For several seconds, neither of you move, and you hear only Joan's labored breathing.

"Margaret!" she whispers

"I'm here Joan. I – I've been here all the time."

The tension in her body dissolves into a flood of tears. She collapses sobbing into your embrace. You don't dare speak, but only hold her. She cries for what seem hours in that changeless place, and you find yourself thinking of your final hours in the body of your earthly life. Did you also cry? Did you pray? Did you rail against the cruelty of those who condemned you?

You can't remember! You can't even bring to your mind the faces of your mother or father, or the streets of your beloved Antioch. The past is as dark as the future: both have been swallowed up in the pitch black of the Now.

"I'm sorry, Joan. I'm so sorry."

It's the darkest part of the night. Morning is probably still some hours away. You're pretty sure Joan has not slept. You're certain she hasn't dreamed. She hasn't made a sound since she stopped crying. Nor have you, until this moment when you can bear the silence and the guilt no longer.

"For what?" she asks absently.

"For failing you! I tried to persuade the judges that you were innocent, but I doubt they heard a word I said. I told you to put on the dress even though I knew it was wrong, and instead of helping you, it's only made things worse. I tried to warn you away from Compiègne, but never told you that I knew for certain you'd be captured if you went there. I was sent to be a guide and help to you, but I've done nothing but harm."

"Ha!"

Her laugh, half a sob and yet still colored by the exuberance of the girl you once saw dancing in the tall grass of a meadow, rings incongruously through the stone passages of the prison.

"It would have made no difference if you had told me that Michael himself commanded me to stay away from Compiègne," she says. "I would not have changed a thing I did! For I had long foreseen this end, even in the days when I slept peacefully in my bed in Domrémy. They fooled me yesterday; I thought I might escape after all. But it did not feel right, and I worried over what might have gone wrong. Now I am back on the path appointed me."

She turns to look into your eyes and takes your hands in hers.

"The one thing I never foresaw, the one surprise God has given me, is that I would not have to walk this path alone."

Later that night, when you feel that daylight must be just leaking into the skies above the castle, Joan slips off the tatters of her dress and begins to re-don the male clothing she wore during her year of military campaigning. She starts off tentatively, picking blankly through the various articles, but soon leaves all hesitation behind. She pulls on the undergarments and leggings; she expertly ties the bindings and snaps the buckles of shirt, vest, breeches, and surcoat. You watch all this in mute horror, for you know what it means: she is assembling her own coffin piece by piece around herself. Nevertheless, as light begins to grow in the rest of the prison and cast its illumination into the cell, your heart leaps in momentary joy, for standing before you once more, clear-eyed and strong and unbound by any chains, is the Maid of Orléans.

"Vive la Pucelle!" you shakily pronounce.

"Vive la compagnie," she corrects.

An hour later, one of the guards looks into the cell, does a double take, and quickly strides off. In less than half an hour, Pierre Cauchon appears with the other judges behind him, but with Guillaume Manchon nowhere to be seen. The others gasp when they see Joan in male attire again, standing calmly against the back wall of her cell with her hands clasped before her, and the dress she wore for one short day crumpled into a pile next to the bars. They stammer in confusion – "What . . . Why . . . Did the Pope . . . Has the prisoner . . ." – but Cauchon does not hesitate.

"Relapse!" he thunders. "You, Joan of Domrémy, have fallen back into the sin from which you turned! This court has no choice now, no choice but to proceed with that judgment which we suspended in holy hope of your true repentance. Tomorrow, as early as may be arranged, you will be brought to the Fire!"

Joan replies calmly, looking from face to face.

"I am truly sorry, not for obeying the commands of God as they came to me through my Voices, but for seeming to disavow them even for a moment yesterday in the wood. If I did so, it was from the fear of death, but I see now that death is preferable to being at the mercy of my enemies the rest of my days. Do what you will. All that I have done has been for God and the Faith."

Cauchon doesn't bother to respond, but departs at once, shouting orders to the guards and court officials. The other judges linger.

Freeman Ng

One of them makes to speak with Joan, but another stops him with a warning gesture. Finally, a third tells his peers, "Come, it is finished," and the group files out of the passageway.

As soon as they and the guards are out of sight, Joan sinks slowly back onto the floor of the cell with a shuddering sigh.

"One more day," she breathes. "One more day to be strong."

You steel yourself for whatever might be required of you in that final day, but all Joan wants to do is converse about the lightest matters you can imagine.

"Remember Marie?" she asks. "Once, when we were eight, she heard that babies came from their mothers' stomachs, and we decided it must be because the mother ate too much! We wondered what kinds of food would make what kinds of babies, and we both got sick that week: Marie from stuffing herself with beef, because she wanted a strong child, and I, because I wanted my child to be pure, from devouring a whole bar of soap!"

Except for the guard who escorts Joan to the latrine in the morning, no one disturbs her or even appears outside the bars of the cell the whole of that day. Somewhere, you know, they're preparing the Fire for her execution, but you try not to think about it. You welcome the idle talk she seems mostly to want.

"My father was a master stonecutter. He oversaw a whole team of men, and worked on many of the grandest temples in Antioch. He was very like yours: a bearer of responsibilities who could be harsh when he thought it for my good. We got along well, until I became a Christian. But – but we made up before the end."

You fall silent as you wonder if your final words with your father (your *final* final words) occurred in truth or only in a dream or vision.

"Did you have any brothers or sisters?"

"What? No. But I had one dear friend named Sennie. *She* had more brothers and sisters than you! I used to wonder what it would be like living with so many people in one small house."

Now it's Joan's turn to pause. The two of you sit side and side against the back wall of the cell, but you don't dare turn to see her expression.

"It is not so bad," she eventually says.

As your talk stretches into the night, sleep begins to overtake you both, but you fight it together, waking each other up with new questions after silences that last too long.

"Um, what about Katie? Did she ever run with you and your brothers in the fields?"

"No, she was not energetic. She preferred solitude and contemplation, I think. I think I hardly knew her…"

You remember (or perhaps begin to dream about) a time you saw Katie dancing alone in a secluded meadow just like her older sister. After a lull, Joan's sleepy voice pulls you part way back.

"Did you prefer to be out playing with other children, or alone thinking?"

"My favorite place, my favorite way to pass the time, was to lie on the roof of my house watching the stars," you murmur, and then you're there.

The mild air of Antioch wafts gently across your bare arms and your face. The stars of night shine down upon you, impossibly distant. Some claim the stars are really angels gathered above the earth in silent witness of its wonders and sorrows. (If so, is Michael among them right now, sitting with his fellows like the judges of Rouen, observing the playing out of his judgments and commands?) Others teach that the stars are whole worlds in their own right, shining in the darkness that separates them. You wonder if each of these worlds is peopled like your own, and if those people also suffer and look to the heavens for comfort. If that's the case, it's not the gaze of angels they will find in those faint lights, but only each other's, separated by gulfs of distance they can never hope to cross.

When dawn arrives, you find yourself rising into the air. You see the roof you were lying on: one small square in the mosaic that is the residential district of Antioch. You see the long colonnaded boulevard that runs straight and true down length of the city. You

Freeman Ng

see the still silent marketplace, the temples and parks.

"Farewell!" you call down to the sleeping populace. "I loved you well! You brought me into this world!"

You continue to rise, seeing more and more of the Earth as you do. Soon, Antioch is but a small patch itself on the surface of a world whose enormity, whose *rotundity*, takes your breath away. You feel like you might perish from your own insignificance alone, that this immense ball of blue and brown and white might simply roll right over you, leaving nothingness in its wake.

To the east and the south, curving away below your line of sight, whole civilizations, many of them as mighty and varied as your own Roman Empire, fill the unknown lands. Millions of people of every aspect labor on mountainsides and islands, in deserts and the darkest jungles, striving for what your own people and Joan's and even the English also seek: a way to live in this world, to carry on from one generation to the next.

You begin to move westward. (Or perhaps the great ball of the world starts turning beneath you.) As the lands roll by, so do the centuries. By the time Antioch fades from your sight, you know in your heart that everyone there that you knew and loved is dead. By the time the city of Rome lies directly below you, it is no longer the capital of the political empire of your time, but the religious seat whose line extends into Joan's. When you reach France, you're certain that you're back in the present. You trace the route you traveled with Joan, from Domrémy to Vaucouleurs, from Chinon to Orléans and then to Rheims. You come to Rouen and look down upon the castle, picturing your body sitting on the stone floor of Joan's cell at this very moment.

As you approach the island nation of the English, you see a wonder curving away beyond it: a Sea so enormous, its opposite shore remains beyond your sight until you've crossed almost half of its span. The nations of France and England together, the entire Roman Empire, could be swallowed up in that sea! On its far shore, you come to the greatest wonder of all. A new world dawns before you: two enormous landmasses on the opposite side of the Earth from the small territories you once considered the whole of the world.

You come to a stop directly over the northern continent.

Below you, bands of hunters creep up on herds of monstrous bearded beasts upon wide plains.

Busy workers excavate living spaces out of the solid rock of a cliff face.

Smoke rises from settlements spread like moss across valley floors and amongst the trees of vast forests.

You descend upon one of these villages, swooping like a low flying bird over the heads of women at work preparing food. Though the food, the tools, and the techniques they use are foreign to you, you can still recognize instantly what they're doing. A small group of men repair one wall of what is clearly the common house, while another man – could he be the village doyen? – discusses some matter of importance with two others who carry longbows like the ones used by the English.

You pass out of the village and into the surrounding woods. Emerging into a small clearing between the village and the sea, you come upon a sight that makes you gasp: a young girl dancing by herself in the tall grass of a meadow!

Around and around she whirls, singing a simple song in a tongue unknown to you. Her dark hair gleams reddish in the sun, and her eyes are a startlingly solid green. The skies above her head recede into depths of blue beyond blue.

"Margaret?"

You wake. You're back in the cell and it's late in the night, but all your weariness is gone. You can see Joan in the darkness more clearly than you ever have before, even in the brightest daylight, and every sound, from her gentlest breath to the movements of the guards in the farthest areas of the prison, comes distinct to your ears.

You feel like you might never sleep again.

"I'm here," you reply.

"They say that when the Roman tried to burn you, the flames would not harm you, so that in the end, he had you beheaded instead. Was that an easier death than the fire would have been?"

It seems your story has grown over time! But how can you tell Joan that God did not in fact preserve you from the fire? You pray to Catherine, the patron saint of those called upon to answer difficult questions, but she doesn't appear before you or whisk you away to Antioch to give you counsel. Joan continues to sit against the wall with her head tilted back and her mouth still half open.

"My death was a blinking of an eye," you finally say. "A nodding off to sleep followed by a swift waking into the Light."

Whether these words came at last from Catherine or arose from your own mind, they arrive too late. Joan doesn't respond to them or give any sign that she even hears them. Instead, her breathing deepens and her clenched hands uncoil.

"How the stars shine!" she murmurs, looking up at the stone ceiling of her windowless cell.

On the morning of May 30th, in the fourteen hundred and thirty first year after the death of her Lord, they came to take Joan of Arc to the Fire.

"Bishop!" she cried to Pierre Cauchon. "I die by your hands!"

"You die," he replied, "because you relapsed and wore men's clothing, which you promised never to do again."

"That would never have happened if you had kept *your* promise and sent me to a church prison to be guarded by women!"

He took a menacing step toward her, but at that moment, Guillaume Manchon entered the cell.

"You were dismissed!" snarled Cauchon.

"From my duties as notary. I am here as a priest."

He bore bread and a silver chalice in his hands.

"You can't do that!" said one of the other judges.

"A heretic cannot be given communion," observed another.

"The law is the law," added a third regretfully.

Cauchon lifted a hand to silence them.

"Give her whatever she wants," he snapped. "You have ten minutes."

He swept out of the cell, followed by his bewildered colleagues. Manchon did not pause to wonder at the bishop's sudden leniency, but began straightway.

"The Lord be with thee."

"And with thy spirit."

"Lift up your heart."

"I lift it to the Lord."

"Let us give thanks to the Lord our God."

"It is meet and right so to do."

Part way through the rite, Cauchon reappeared with the guards. Manchon continued to speak the words of the Eucharist, retreating backward in front of Joan as they walked her through the dank passages of the prison.

"Come unto me, all that travail and be heavily laden, and I will give you rest!"

They recited the general confession of sins together just as the party came to the metal door separating the prison from the rest of the castle, and as they waited for the door to be unlocked, Manchon whispered to Joan, "Forgive me for my part in the deception in the wood. I thought I was saving your life."

She laid one hand upon his bowed head and replied, "All is as God has decreed."

As they came out into the gray streets of Rouen, he began the narrative of the Last Supper.

"On the night whereon he was betrayed, our Lord took bread and broke it, saying, 'Take. Eat. This is my body, which is broken for you.'"

He reached out to place a morsel of bread in her mouth.

"Then he took wine and blessed it and said, 'This is my blood, shed for you and for many for the forgiveness of sins.'"

A roar filled the air. They had arrived at the town square. At its center, a pile of wood rose high off the ground, surrounded by a crowd that cried out for the witch to be burned and Charles to be damned. The judges stood on a balcony overlooking the scene.

"I tried to delay the – proceedings," Manchon whispered to Joan. "But he was too clever for me."

"The sooner done, the sooner free," she replied.

Pierre Cauchon stepped forward to speak.

"We, the court of the Holy Inquisition, judge that you have worn male clothing and fought in the wars in disobedience to the Church and all propriety, and that you have engaged in heresies and magical practices in the aid of a certain Charles, an ignoble and illegitimate pretender to the throne."

"That is a lie!" cried Joan.

"Shut her up!" roared Cauchon.

The guard by her side turned to her but made no move to strike or threaten her, and she saw that it was Tom.

"I am sorry," she told him. "It seems I will never learn patience!"

They turned to face the Bishop again.

"Therefore," resumed Cauchon, "we give you up to the secular authorities, who will execute such judgment upon you as they must. May God have mercy on your soul!"

She was just able to wet her lips from the chalice Manchon offered her before the guards began leading her up the pile of wood to the stake at its top.

"Almighty and ever living God," Manchon called up to her, beginning the final prayer of the mass, the Prayer of Thanksgiving, "we most heartily thank thee, for that thou hast vouchsafed to feed us in these holy Mysteries, with the spiritual food of the most precious body and blood of thy son our savior, and hast assured us of thy favor and goodness toward us, that we be very members incorporate in thy Mystical body, which is the blessed company of all faithful people..."

Joan spoke the words with him as the guards bound her to the stake with loop after loop of a heavy chain. Before they left her, Tom fashioned two sticks of wood into a cross, which he placed into her hands.

The preparations were done. Manchon had reached the end of the rite. He called out the closing words in a voice that broke with grief.

"The Mass is ended! Go – go in Peace."

At that moment, the pyre was lit.

"Jesu!" cries Joan. "Jesu! Jesu!"

It's the only word she has spoken since the flames began climbing around her.

"I'm here, Joan! I'm here!" you shout up at her, but you have no way of knowing whether she hears you, and when you try moving closer, you feel the bite of the fire and have to back gasping away. Guillaume Manchon stands beside you, in much the same torment. He holds up a large golden cross he obtained from a nearby church, straining to keep it always in Joan's sight, leaning in as close to the fire as he dares.

"Ahhhh! Jesu!" screams Joan, and the crowd, which shouted insults and called for her death when she was first brought out to the square, begins to groan and weep in pity.

"Lord have mercy!" they cry, and "What have you done?" to the judges, who stand unmoving in their places.

"Catherine! Michael!" you call aloud. "Why aren't you here? Why aren't you watching?"

Ash flies up from the burning, fluttering high above the crowd. Flakes as big as a child's hand ride the tortured currents of air, flecking the dismal scene with dots of gray and black, but also, increasingly, with flashes of color.

How can this be?

Then you see it's not only ash that fills the sky, but butterflies.

There's a loud clinking of metal, and Joan stands unchained in midst of the fire. The butterflies swirl round and round her, or tumble crazily inward to cling to her white robed shoulders unwithered by the heat. She begins to dance: one step and a turn, two steps and a turn. As she does, she sings the song you heard that first day you found her in the distant meadow of Domrémy, only now, it's no child's voice that sounds the simple melody, but the strong, passionate vibrato of the woman that girl has become:

Orléans, Beaugency,
Notre Dame de Cléry,

Poitiers, Avignon,
Albi, Arles, Rheims, Rouen,

Amiens, Tours, Nancy,
Chartres, Senlis, Troyes, Paris,

Vendôme, Vendôme!

The swirl of butterflies and ash climbs into the sky. You follow its spiraling path beyond the sounds of the fire and the crowd, past the dismal veil of clouds and into a brilliant cloudscape of mountainous whites and grays.

It goes on beyond the sky itself.

The voice of Joan follows it, naming over and over the sacred places of the sovereign kingdom of France, growing in strength as it ascends into the heavens.

When you look down again, she's gone. The crowd, the priests, the soldiers all stand where they were, unchanged in their attitudes – lamenting, triumphant, torn between duty and honor – still looking in to the center of the pyre where only an absence smolders where once, bright flesh burned.

To...

- Learn more about Joan
- Find more writing by Freeman Ng
- Follow Freeman on Facebook/Twitter/Google+ or subscribe to his mailing list

Go to...

www.AuthorFreeman.com

Made in the USA
San Bernardino, CA
17 September 2014